For Pam,

Grin Reaping

Stories

By Rod Carley

A PLEASURE MEETING YOU IN
PICTON TODAY.
BEST ALWAYS,

[signature: Rod Carley]

July 23, 2022

Praise for Grin Reaping

"Many writers are serious. Fewer are funny. If you're lucky, once in a while, you come across that rare writer who makes you laugh and think at the same time, even in the same sentence. Rod Carley pulls it off in *Grin Reaping*, an off-kilter look at death that left me feeling happy, enlightened, and very much alive."

—Terry Fallis, two-time winner of the Stephen Leacock Medal for Humour.

"Imagine if a short story and a peculiar incident had a wisecracking baby possessed of unusual wisdom and a deeply humane sensibility. That almost, *almost* describes Rod Carley's *Grin Reaping*. Line-by-line these episodes are fierce and funny and many of them leave indelible scorch marks on their targets, even while we grow to care about all the characters. The collection is generous, odd and quite wonderful. I hope many people get to meet the unforgettable Rudy Boyle and his associates.

I, for one, will never think about MacGyver the same way again. My view of elevator lifts, dogs, and weddings has also been altered forever. And please, do not get me started on the exceptional tooth-regeneration of the brontosaurus."

—Susan Juby, author of *The Woefield Poultry Collective* and winner of the Stephen Leacock Medal for Humour

"When I say I laughed out loud at *Grin Reaping*, I mean it. Carley writes with a quick wit, keen observational skill, and a sense of playfulness that infuses the language on every page. But to classify this as simply a "funny" book does it a disservice—beneath the surface, this is a book with a truly tender heart. These are stories shot through with a current of grief and loss, and populated with unforgettable characters who, despite their clever jokes and quirky worldviews, are authentic, vulnerable, and wholly human. *Grin Reaping* is a joy to read, and Rod Carley is a writer to watch."

—Amy Jones, author of *We're All in This Together*, shortlisted for the Leacock Medal for Humour

"Carley scribbles in that special space between humour and humiliation, the quaint and the absurd. The stories in *Grin Reaping* are both familial and familiar, cheeky, wistful and human on the best level. His playfulness with language and comedic timing are masterful. Read it and reap.

—Ali Bryan, author of *The Figgs*, shortlisted for the Leacock Medal.

"Rod Carley's previous book, *Kinmount* was nominated for the Stephen Leacock Medal for Humour. He may well win that award for this warmly moving, wildly inventive and wickedly funny collection of tall tales. One of the great compliments you can give a book is to say, "you can't put it down." That doesn't apply to *Grin Reaping*. You will have to put this book down repeatedly because you will be laughing so hard. Indeed, you will laugh out loud on almost every single page. So settle down, buckle up, and prepare yourself."

—Ian Ferguson - Leacock Award Winner, *Village of the Small Houses.*

"If you explore some of Canada's more picturesque literary trails, you might happen upon the spot where Robertson Davies' "The Diary of Samuel Marchbanks" intersects with Stephen Leacock's "Sunshine Sketches of a Little Town" as well as the best Dave and Morley stories from Stuart McLean's "Vinyl Café." That's where you'll find Rod Carley's *Grin Reaping*, a collection of short stories blending whimsy, pathos, melancholy and cheer. You'll find elevators to heaven and talking pets sharing the page with the stark realities of aging, death and dementia. It's an emotionally complex journey, both uplifting and heartbreaking, and it's a literary trip I'm glad to have taken."

—Dr. Randal Graham, author of the *Beforelife* stories.

"*Grin Reaping* is a comic blast of a book. It's so wryly observed with sharply hilarious specifics -- one page in and I found myself booted back to my tiny Canadian hometown with all its rural absurdities. Rod's got a gift for giving dignity to people who'd probably snort-laugh if you ever called them 'dignified'. In these pages, you'll find a definitive power ranking of Timbits decided by teachers enduring a winter work strike. You'll read of friends and family caring for their pets -- be they hermaphrodite border collies or the ghosts of long-dead cats. And you'll learn about a man who constructed a shrine to Muskoka via Hollywood celebrity Kurt Russell. But you'll also realize what a huge heart Rod Carley has, as he lovingly (in a very Rod Carley way) eulogizes family members he's lost by transforming their lives into enduring small town myths."

—Sean Reycraft, screenwriter for *The Witching Hour, Coroner, Slings & Arrows*, and *Degrassi.*

Library and Archives Canada Cataloguing in Publication
Title: Grin reaping : stories / by Rod Carley.
Names: Carley, Rod, 1962- author.
Description: Short stories.
Identifiers: Canadiana (print) 20220207534 | Canadiana (ebook) 20220207542 |
ISBN 9781988989464
  (softcover) | ISBN 9781988989556 (EPUB)
Classification: LCC PS8605.A75457 G75 2022 | DDC C813/.6—dc23

Printed and bound in Canada on 100% recycled paper.
Cover Artwork: Lenika Lopez Pilz and Rod Carley
Author Photo: Ed Regan

Published by:
Latitude 46 Publishing
info@latitude46publishing.com
Latitude46publishing.com

We acknowledge the support of the Ontario Arts Council, Canada Council of the Arts, the Government of Canada and the Ontario Media Development Corporation for their generous support.

Grin Reaping

Stories

By Rod Carley

Also by Rod Carley

Kinmount

A Matter of Will

In memory of John Batchelor

(1961 -2021)

For my brother Greg,

thanks for cutting my half of the lawn so I could read.

family
[fam – *uh* – lee]
noun
A group that dreams, laughs, plays and loves
together, always present, not only in the good
times. Life's most precious gift.
"Family is nailing Jell-O to a tree."

Rudy
[*roo* – dee]
noun
Two and a half twist acrobatic maneuver.
"He swooped over the crowd and performed a Rudy."

Contents

With apologies to Harrison Ford.

FOREWORD

Grin Reaping, let us not beat about the bush, is a book of oddities and quiddities and its narrator, Rudy Boyle, is just the man to deal with them, pinning them to the mat with jests and insights, though sometimes simply left gawping at the world's inexplicable events.

The opening story concerns two people in a church building's lift; the passenger commands the operator, "To Heaven, Now!"

VVVIZZZSPPT!

And the two are never seen again.

Well, it's not exactly a story in the sense we'd usually expect. Neither is it "science fiction"; not "fable" nor "fantasy." Perhaps the stories are better described as "sketches." But even "sketches" doesn't quite capture Rod's invention. "Sketches" usually implies charming recollections of place peopled by "characters," the sort of events and characters that Thurber created so memorably or that the wonderful Joseph Mitchell created in *McSorley's Wonderful Saloon*. Much as there's a Joseph Mitchell world and a Thurber world, there's a Carley Northern Ontario world as viewed by Rudy Boyle.

But...no... "sketches" isn't quite right either; I think I'm forced to call them "pieces." Well, what would you call a story that refers to a dog so clever it did Rudy's mother's taxes? Dogs figure largely in these pieces. Rudy's dog, Salinger, "devours the contents of our cat's litter box like a carton of Timbits." When his ears are pressed together, he "resembles Christopher Plummer." Uncle Irving has a Border Collie that turns out to be a hermaphrodite which in turn causes it to be perpetually incontinent; for fifteen years it wears a diaper.

And then there are Rudy's siblings, his younger sister JoJo and older sister, the uber-sensitive Evie.

There's a splendid texture in Rod's writing which sets him apart from many writers of humour and this loving detail is particularly evident when he writes about childhood. Here is Rudy Boyle recalling the childhood of his younger sister, JoJo.

"Growing up in the early seventies, my life could best be described as *Saving Private Ryan* meets *Lord of the Flies*.

"There were twenty-five boys spilling out of the backyards of ten interconnected new suburban homes. Our neighborhood was a war zone—soft balls, hard balls, footballs, snow balls, orange road hockey balls, skates, hockey sticks, baseball bats, rocks, elbows, fists, firecrackers, pellet guns, and go-carts. Hedges replaced barbed wire and street lights, air raid sirens. Rations consisted of KD and hotdogs. Two girls rounded out the roster—my sisters, JoJo and Evie.

"A horse-loving tomboy, JoJo survived without losing a limb. She could out-climb any boy on the block and was the reigning marble player champion three-years running. Her crock attacks became the stuff of playground legend, causing the boys to, literally, lose their marbles. She scattered her opponent's marbles by unleashing a barrage of well-timed direct hits, her purple Crown Royal bag, courtesy of our father, filled to bursting with the brightly-coloured spoils of victory—aggies, cat's eyes, pretties, red devils, bumblebees, shooters, swirlers, and twirlers. She was twice as deadly at the bowling alley, scattering pins into the air, one strike after another. The other kids' balls missed their targets and wound up in the gutter. Because of her invincibility, JoJo stopped getting invited to birthday parties."

The older sister, Evie, "the tiny alien" was "possessed like something out of a Stephen King novel" and is encouraged in her emotional fragility by crazy Aunt Muriel who taught her nieces and nephews that babies resulted from "moon energy."

Years later, Evie's daughter, Esther, at the age of thirteen, a sort of Northern Ontario version of Greta Thunberg, launches a GoFundMe page to raise money to support edible six-pack rings that sea turtles can ingest without dying.

"I'll know global warming is real," Rudy further asserts, "when hot water comes out of both taps."

Rudy teaches English at the town's community college and is discontented, if not disconsolate at the prospect of teaching yet more classes of "twenty-first century welding students who think a 'preposition' is something to do on a Friday night."

To his sister JoJo, he says, "I've got a Master's Degree in Education and I'm teaching English to welding students. Do you know how depressing that is? I feel like Mozart teaching Chopsticks to four-year-olds."

One of my favourites among these tales—yes! *Tales*, that's much closer to the right descriptive word I've been groping towards—is the tale "Over Easy: No Spring Chicken." JoJo coerces Rudy into attending with her the wedding of "a friend of a friend at the trailer park."

The wedding is to take place in a village notorious for its almost sub-human denizens. Hilary Clinton famously and debatably referred to about a third of the population of the United States as "deplorables"; there is absolutely *no* debate about the wedding throng in East Feral.

The wedding takes place in a derelict community centre which bears a sign NO SHIRT NO SHOES, NO SERVICE. Except the word SERVICE had been crossed out with a Sharpie and replaced with the word PROBLEM.

Rudy observes, "four John Deere caps, two backward baseball caps, eight pairs of cowboy boots, and enough bad suits to put polyester on the endangered species list." JoJo comments that "the groom won his wife's wedding ring by knocking down three milk bottles with a baseball." The imported minister asks for the rings, and Hank, the Best Man, in his cowboy hat, "handed the minister his beer. 'Here, hold this.'"

Rod Carley—do I need to say this?—is a humourist and an inventive improviser on the complexities and comedy of our lives. The tales in *Grin Reaping*, however, are not simply extravagantly funny, not simply a skillfully humorous playing with words; the tales often leave us thoughtful, sometimes uneasy, sometimes touched by something...not sad, exactly...something wistful. The wordplay of the book's title—that cowled figure with the scythe—and Rudy's last line in the book's final story suggest the emotion that underlies these tales: "We laugh because there is nothing we can do about it."

John Metcalf
Ottawa, 2021

PREFACE

When I was nineteen, my thirst for knowledge and my love of books consumed me. J.D. Salinger's fictional Glass family were heroes for me at this age—quirky role models living in their New York City apartment on the Upper East Side. I wanted to be an actor like Zooey, a guru like Seymour, and a writer like Buddy. These of course were not the career paths being pushed by my high school guidance counselor. Unlike the Glass family with its brood of seven children, Salinger only had one elder sister. He wrote his Glass stories to fill that void. I have one younger brother. Both of my parents are gone. As both a critic and creature of the human predicament, I wrote this collection to expand my sense of family, examine the absurdities of life, and cope with the grief of losing loved ones.

Rod Carley
North Bay, ON

Each of my siblings is perfectly normal until we get together. They haven't read these stories, but they did say they hoped the main character died. I told them it was an autobiography.

Rudolph Boyle
Birch Lake, ON

THE LIFT

I don't ride in elevators anymore. I used to. I took the freight elevator to my second floor office each morning at the community college where I teach—out of sheer laziness, navigating the harried custodian and her cleaning cart while trying not to spill my college dark roast.

"Things happen here," she hisses in my ear while wringing her mop. "Good Things Happen Here" was the college motto for years, until recent budget cuts forced the dropping of the first word. "Things Happen Here," the unfortunate result. The slogan is plastered on worn-out billboards across the province.

The Tim Horton's micro-franchise moved out after refusing to spice up their digs. A coat of paint would have done it. The replacement vendor, Java the Hut, hasn't a clue—his burning carafes set off the cafeteria smoke alarms on a near daily basis. His coffee tastes like motor oil. Only the auto body repair program keeps him in business.

But this story is not about the college. It's about Larry and Iolanthe.

Larry, a widower, retired from the railroad a year ago. He rode the last ONR passenger train on a cool September afternoon—no fanfare—like most things in Northern Ontario, here one day, gone the next.

Larry attends Sunday service regularly since his wife Rose's untimely death. The rest of the week he retreats to his basement to tend to his model railroad collection. He pretends he and Rose are travelling to the Rockies in a sleeper car—a holiday cancelled by cancer.

I sit quietly beside Larry in church in a pew at the back. He presses his short chubby frame uncomfortably into the seat cushion. Larry has never been at home in his body—he's more of a squatter.

The congregation discovered Larry is tone-deaf. He is neither a bass nor a baritone, rather, an unfortunate hybrid that has no place in liturgical music, and, when the moment urges him, a voice that causes parishioners to bow their heads in resigned pity before increasing their volume to drown him out. To stand next to Larry is to endure an arpeggio of aural agony. He goes sharp when the hymn asks for a solemn note, and swoops down flat when the tune calls for a more uplifting pitch.

It isn't that Larry has a terrible voice...in musical parlance, he has a bad ear.

I've never been much of church-goer. I had all the excuses for not attending—I didn't have kids, my phone said No Service, I couldn't get the lid off the peanut butter.

One Sunday afternoon in mid-May, Clive, the head of the church Men's Group, pegged Larry to be the lift operator for the month of June. A volunteer was needed to operate the elevator that delivered disabled parishioners from the main foyer on the ground floor at street level to the second-floor sanctuary and, after service, escort them two floors down to the Sunday School Hall in the basement for coffee and sweets. Church and food go hand-in-hand. They always have, ever since Jesus fed five thousand people with two fish and a loaf of bread.

The lift operator opened the church an hour prior to the choir's opening hymn, turned on the lights and the blowers (in winter) and made sure the doors were locked once the service had begun. The surveillance camera monitor, at the back of the sanctuary, took care of the rest. Save for wrestling with the Allen key in the front door, it was not a daunting task.

But there were politics—politics named Clive.

I've never taken a liking to Clive. Clive looks and acts like an assistant manager at a Boston Pizza. He is the kind of guy who is terrified of grief. So, when Clive encounters anyone experiencing loss, he avoids them completely, as if his frigidity will somehow stop him from catching their pain. Clive has to be afraid of something big. It is probably why he goes to church in the first place—to pray for grief to spare him. The poor bastard has it all backwards. Clive is a dyslexic Christian.

Larry arrived for lift duty wearing a conductor's cap. I was stuck filling in as a greeter, having been voluntold by a church lady who issued orders like an Elizabethan privy councillor. Larry scurried up and down stairs turning on lights, colliding into Clive in the foyer.

"No hats in church," said Clive.

"It was my grandfather's," replied Larry.

"And did your grandfather wear his hat in church?" Clive pressed.

"You know damn well he never set foot in here except at Christmas and Easter," Larry fired back, that is, as much as Larry was capable of firing back.

"And your point is?"

"Forget it." Larry stuffed the cap back in his pocket.

His first passenger was a retired minister in his nineties, relying on a walker.

"All aboard!" Larry forced himself to whistle into action. "Where to today?"

"How does Ireland sound?" replied the minister.

"North or South?"

"Wherever the grass is green and the sheep know your name."

"Coming up," said Larry. He carefully escorted the minister into the lift and pressed the release button. The lift lurched upwards, slowly rising above the foyer. Their voices drifted down.

"Enjoying the ride?" Larry asked.

"The last time I was in Galway was for my brother's funeral," replied the minister.

"Tell me about him?" Larry took a genuine interest in his passengers.

"He loved playing cards," said the minister. "He could mend an Aran sweater and win a game of gin rummy without missing a beat."

"My mother can rhyme off a grocery list while changing a flat tire," replied Larry.

A bell chimed, announcing the lift's arrival. Larry opened the door and helped the minister to his accustomed pew. A member of the choir was leading those in the congregation who'd arrived early in a sing-a-long, a church tradition on the first Sunday of the month I avoided like the Old Testament. Since Larry was on duty, he couldn't join them. I'm pretty sure a pair of early worms in a side pew let out a sigh of relief.

He returned to the ground floor, and opened the door awaiting his next customer.

"No need for the small talk," said Clive. "Take them up and come back down."

Larry inspected the empty waiting area.

"No one's here," he said.

"They will be," said Clive. "Take them up and come right back down. No embellishments."

"Maybe they enjoy the personal touch," said Larry.

"And maybe they don't," said Clive, putting an end to their exchange. Clive has the progressiveness of a car going in reverse. I stepped briefly away from the entrance to confront him. "Why don't you give your soul a shake, Clive?"

He wagged his finger at me. "And where will you be sitting for eternity, Rudy Boyle? Smoking or non-smoking?"

I raised my middle finger in a Trudeau pére salute.

Larry sat sadly in a chair by the lift. I knew the look of grief cutting across his face. It is love that has nowhere to go. Larry is my big brother, fifteen years older. We were never close. He left home before I entered kindergarten.

Larry met Rose on a boat cruise when they were both in their mid-twenties. While the rest of their generation was jiving to disco or slashing their jeans to The Clash, Larry and his fiancée were listening to smoky blues on the promenade deck of an old cottage country steamer. Together, they raised two daughters and spent two weeks each summer at a trailer park on the French River. Larry fished for pickerel while Rose painted watercolours of the summer sunset. It was a good life until three years ago when, one morning, Rose woke up feeling tired.

After Rose's funeral, Larry asked me if I'd accompany him to church. I couldn't come up with an excuse. When the pastor found out I was a college English teacher, he asked if I'd be willing to come up with a humorous weekly message to post on the marquee beside the main entrance. Again, I didn't have an excuse. So, every Saturday morning, I got up early and rehung the metal changeable letters. Some of my more popular creations include:

"TWEET OTHERS AS YOU WANT TO BE TWEETED"

"CREMATION IS YOUR LAST CHANCE FOR A SMOKING HOT BODY"

"JESUS HAD TWO DADS AND HE TURNED OUT FINE"

My partner, Neil, liked that last one.

Larry was right about our mother. Up until a few years ago, she *could* make a grocery list without missing a lug nut. She's ninety now, still living on her own, making the best egg salad sandwiches in Northern Ontario. We have two sisters, Evie and JoJo, and another brother, Jonah. Our youngest brother, Nicky, we lost twenty-five years ago in a boating accident. It's the family tragedy none of us has really gotten over.

Jonah is my fraternal twin. He is a dead ringer for a Russian poet, his thick black hair tousled and uncombed, clothes somewhat disheveled, bread crumbs sprinkled throughout his bushy goatee, and possessing dark alluring eyes that made him appealing to women in his younger years. When Jonah and I were growing up, my parents favoured my twin brother. It first hit me when my father asked me to blow up balloons for Jonah's surprise birthday party.

Jonah is married to Sophie, an Ojibwe fancy-dancer he met at the farmer's market, who has a flair for rummage sale hunting, *alchemyzing* she calls it. Sophie works at the service desk of a big box store. Her nametag reads Mrs. White so that none of her customers can get to know her—a way of separating her job from her life. Sophie's humour is wry on the rocks, and as such, marks the heart of her resilience. Sophie budgets carefully: books and DVDs from the public library, grocery flyers compared and clipped, saving here and there for a modest annual vacation to visit family in Northern Quebec.

My brother is on disability. He suffers from a delusional disorder. The incident that triggered it happened years ago but I'm not going to talk about that now. I visit my brother on Friday afternoons with a six-pack of craft beer in hand and we travel our accumulated pasts, sharing the same stories over and over again. Each visit he shows me his renderings for a new Gothic cathedral in Normandy. Jonah could have been a famous architect.

Jonah is friends with a widow named Iolanthe. He is probably her only friend. Iolanthe was the church matriarch for years, singing solos in the choir and maintaining a garden behind the gymnasium. A rickety fire escape still leads down to her perennials. Iolanthe had a reputation for talking back during sermons. The congregation tolerated her, until she made Coronation chicken sandwiches for a luncheon, and a child choked on a bit of eggshell. Last year, her family admitted her to a nursing home, a God-forsaken place where the residents are left abandoned in the hallways. Aging is even more of a curse on a fixed income.

Iolanthe is the embodiment of the colour orange—orange this, orange that. I hate the colour orange because I despise oranges. I detest trying to peel them. The rind gets under my fingernails and creeps me out. I can almost tolerate clementines. At least, they only make an appearance once a year, and their rind tears off in one piece.

On one of our Fridays, about a month ago, Jonah said to me, "Iolanthe really wants to go to church. Can you help me bring her?" My brother doesn't drive and Sophie doesn't own a car.

"What about *her* family?"

"They don't visit her. I'm all she has left."

"But she's so frail, Jonah. One fall and she's done."

"She needs this, Rudy."

And so, I agreed.

The following Sunday, I picked up Jonah an hour before service, and parked in front of the nursing home main entrance while he went in to get her. Fifteen minutes later they appeared, Iolanthe dressed in a bright orange caftan, my brother gently holding her arm. With her dyed orange hair, she resembled a shrunken Lucille

Ball. Iolanthe believed in accessorizing—orange lipstick, orange eye shadow, orange jewelry, and orange fingernails—the whole nine carrots. I'm sure her toenails were painted orange, but they were hidden in her orthopedic orange sneakers. Iolanthe wasn't just a splash of colour, she was a tsunami.

I hopped out and, as Jonah supported her waist, folded her walker and put it in the trunk. Together we struggled to get her into the front seat. Jonah held her shoulders while I picked up her legs and modestly eased her in. Once she was strapped in, Jonah climbed in the backseat. I made small talk.

"Hey, Iolanthe, how's the world treating you today?"

"It's not," she said, without a trace of fragility in her voice. "Every time I leave my room someone sneaks in and steals something. I can't find my purse."

"Are you sure?" I asked. Iolanthe is in the early stages of dementia.

"Of course I'm sure. They take anything that isn't nailed down."

"Well, Jonah and I will look into it," I reassured her, with a glance to my brother in the rear view mirror. His charity wasn't measuring up to reality. "At least it's a beautiful day," I carried on. "Not a cloud in the sky, a perfect day for the beach."

"The perfect day to die," she shot back.

"No better place to die than the beach."

We drove in silence the rest of the way to the church. I tried to catch my brother's eye, but he was rocking in the back seat, staring out the window.

Getting Iolanthe out of the car and over the curb was another struggle. I watched my brother slowly help her inside. They looked like Piglet and Pooh in a *Twilight Zone* episode. I pulled out to find a parking space while Larry delivered the odd-looking pair to the sanctuary under Clive's critical glare.

The topic for the morning sermon was "finding joy amidst suffering."

"A poppy emerges in a field of corpses because it chooses to," my great-grandfather, a World War I veteran, would say, according to my mother, whenever anything went belly up at a family event, which was pretty much every holiday on the calendar. He'd recite, "Find the poppy."

I'm more of an "if life gives you lemons, grab tequila and salt" subscriber.

After the service, Jonah walked Iolanthe through the hall, sitting her down at a table near the snacks, and fetching a cup of steeped tea. A few members of the Ladies' Auxiliary sat down to chat with her.

"See," said Jonah, joining me by the bulletin board, "She needs this." He really is the kindest person. It's why Sophie fell in love with him.

"How are you holding up?" I ask. My brother also suffers from religious paranoia, another by-product of his illness. During moments of extreme stress, he believes he is the personification of evil itself.

"I'm scared and I think I'm burning, but Reverend Will's talk of finding joy really got to me. I feel joy, Rudy, I feel joy."

"That's good, Jonah."

"So, I'm not burning?"

"You're not burning, Jonah."

"Do you love me, Rudy?"

"Of course, I love you, Jonah. You're my twin."

"But if we weren't brothers. Would you still be my friend?

"Yes Jonah."

The following Sunday, Iolanthe was even *orangier* than usual, if such a thing were possible. Even her perfume smelled citrusy. We finished securing her in when, "Could either of you gentlemen pick me up some yarn?"

Jonah's voice piped in from the back seat, "Sure Iolanthe, what for?"

"I'm knitting scarves for my granddaughters for Christmas and some thief stole my yarn."

I'd checked with the nursing home director earlier in the week who assured me that nothing was amiss at the home.

"Orange yarn?" I said, withholding a grin.

"Don't be ridiculous. I'm the only one permitted to wear orange."

"You're an *orang*inal, alright," I laughed and swung out of the parking lot.

"I'll get you some yarn," Jonah whispered, secretly cupping his hand over her right ear. My brother's whisper isn't any quieter than his normal speaking voice. He just spits more.

"I'm getting Iolanthe yarn," he said to my reflection in the rear view mirror.

I knew that after service, Jonah would be asking me for twenty bucks.

"So, it's another beautiful day," I announced, turning right onto Castle Street and heading toward the church. "Anyone want to go on a road trip?"

"Wouldn't that be lovely," sighed Iolanthe, perking up as if I'd plugged her into the USB portal.

"Old Montreal," suggested Jonah. "Lox and bagels on Rue St-Paul." My brother loves Montreal. He studied architecture at McGill but never graduated.

"I spent my first honeymoon in Montreal," Iolanthe began to rhapsodize, resting her wrist on the open passenger window sill. It was a hot day for early June. "Wish I had a cigarette," she frowned.

"Want one of mine?" said Jonah, pulling out a pack of Du Mauriers from his tweed blazer pocket—always the blazer.

"No, Jonah. Iolanthe can't have a cigarette," I said, catching his disappointed gaze in the mirror.

"Damn," she said. She crossed her bony orange arms.

I quickly returned the subject to Montreal. "Tell me about your honeymoon, Iolanthe."

"Oh, it was a grand affair," she sighed, closing her eyes in remembrance. "We avoided all the tacky touristy things."

There'd been three more honeymoons in Iolanthe's difficult life. It was as if she'd stepped out of the pages of a Tennessee Williams play. Local legend has it she gave a heartbreaking community theatre performance as Blanche fifty-some years ago—even won a Dominion Drama Festival award for it, and spray-painted her statuette orange.

"The Basilique Notre-Dame was sumptuous," she continued.

"It felt like the Lord himself was playing the pipe organ."

"Do you know there are seven thousand pipes in that organ?" said Jonah. "It was built in the Gothic Revival style. *And* instead of the usual cliché biblical scenes, all the stained glass windows depict scenes of Montreal's early religious history. I loved sitting in the pews after class, staring up at the deep blue ceiling. It's adorned with thousands of gold stars."

I understood why they were friends—two misfits who fit only when together. I felt oddly left out, despite being my brother's twin.

"Heaven on earth?" I asked.

"No," Iolanthe answered, almost to herself. "Home." Her eyes were elsewhere. "And the Bonsecours Market and its potatoes and pork chops," she grinned, growing younger with each memory.

"Rue Saint-Claude!" Jonah chimed in. "I love the old cobblestones."

"Three nights at the Hotel Place d'Armes." She sounded like a teenager. "I was the most beautiful bride they'd ever seen. The concierge told me that. And I was too. Oh, gentlemen, you should have seen me in those days. I turned more heads than you can imagine."

I had no doubt that Iolanthe was a looker in her day.

By the time we pulled up outside the church, I was craving poutine and one of Jonah's cigarettes.

Something happened during the service. I don't know what exactly, but I'm pretty sure Iolanthe suffered a mini-stroke. At the luncheon, she was more fragile than ever. She fell twice, even with Jonah supporting her and the walker.

"How do you know when Iolanthe's been in church?" Clive said as I passed him to help load the dishwasher in the kitchen.

I said nothing.

"The orange lipstick on her mug." He laughed spitefully. A cold-blooded snake peddling apples had more empathy.

"Why are you here?"

I left the kitchen before he could respond. I wanted to spray him with Agent Orange.

Jonah needed a nurse to help Iolanthe back to her room.

"We can't do this anymore," I said on the drive home.

My brother said nothing, staring at his hands.

"Look, Jonah, it's wonderful that you want to help take Iolanthe to church. But you saw how weak she is. She fell twice, and that's with you holding onto her."

"But this is all she has."

"I know. But if she falls and breaks a hip she's finished. How would you feel if that happened? The situation is beyond our control. Sophie will agree. Iolanthe needs a wheelchair and professional transportation. I'm sorry, Jonah."

I dropped him off, feeling as if I'd caused the golden stars of Notre Dame to collapse on my brother's head.

Mid-week, he phoned.

"Dad's wheelchair," he said brightly.

"What about it?" I responded warily.

"The manor called and said they want us to do something about dad's wheelchair."

Our father is confined to Lakeview Manor in the final stages of Alzheimer's. He won't be using a wheelchair again.

"I visited Iolanthe and she's fine with it," Jonah bubbled, trying to catch his breath. "Can you pick me up and we can go get it?"

"Slow down Jonah." My brother was in one of his manic phases. I checked my schedule on my phone. "I can do it Friday morning at eight. Can you get up that early?"

There was a pause. My brother's nighttime meds knock him out like an elephant tranquilizer.

"Sophie will make sure I'm up and ready."

"Okay, see you then."

"Thanks, Rudy. Love you."

"I love you too."

I drive a used Forerunner so loading our father's wheelchair was not an issue. Seeing our father is. He doesn't recognize us. Jonah plays him Johnny Cash CDs, which appear to momentarily take him some place happy, perhaps a barn dance in his youth or driving on a solitary road trip with the windows down. It's hard on my brother, wishing our father's eyes would look outward instead of inward. I remind him we're doing the best we can in a hopeless situation. At least our father isn't suffering.

The wheelchair delivered, I dropped Jonah off at his studio to sketch while I taught the art of Elizabethan rhetoric to a class of uninterested English students.

The first thing you must do when selecting a rhetorical argument is ask yourself:

1. Are you doing the right thing for the right reason?
2. The wrong thing for the right reason?
3. The wrong thing for the wrong reason?

Macbeth is your classic *c*. I hoped what my brother and I were doing for Iolanthe was *a* not *b*.

"Can we paint the wheelchair orange?" Jonah asked over his second beer.

"I'm not sure, Jonah, if that's a good idea."

"Evie says I can't."

Evie is our older sister. She's a Jungian psychotherapist living in Toronto. "Jung at heart," is her motto.

"When were you talking to, Evie?"

You can never reach our sister.

"I e-mailed her and she e-mailed back almost immediately."

"How is she?"

"I couldn't tell. All she said was, 'Don't paint the wheelchair orange. Love, Evie.'"

"She has a point, Jonah. It is a new wheelchair. It's expensive."

"Iolanthe wants it painted orange."

"Why don't we get some orange material and an orange pillow?"

"I guess..."

"It's still orange, right?"

My brother arranged for a Para-Taxi to pick Iolanthe and him up at the nursing home, an hour before service.

I waited for them at the foyer entrance. The taxi driver, an older man I recognized as a retired prof from our college, wheeled Iolanthe in. The wheelchair reminded me of Cinderella's carriage, one second after midnight. Iolanthe looked awful—gaunt, angry, eyes red from crying. My brother was nowhere to be seen.

"Iolanthe, you look like the Queen of the Fairies," said a greeter cheerfully.

"I'm a useless old woman," Iolanthe snapped back. "Look at this thing." She pounded her fist on the wheelchair arm. "You might as well roll me into the grave and be done with it."

I found my brother sitting on the curb, crying.

"What happened?" I feared *b* was winning.

"It's horrible, Rudy. When I got to her room, she'd forgotten our earlier conversation."

I was afraid of that.

Jonah went on. "I tried to explain to her that the wheelchair was the safest way to get her to church. She begged me to smother her with the pillow."

My brother began to chain-smoke and shake. "I am not a murderer, Rudy."

"No, you are not, Jonah." I sat down beside him, banging my chin on my knees. "Do you remember when there was that big flood in Turkey?"

My brother thought for a moment.

"Last July."

"And you felt you had to build an ark?"

"Yes," he replied sheepishly.

"And round up all the neighbourhood pets?"

"That was pretty dumb."

"What did I do?"

"You explained it was an act of nature, and not God's wrath."

"Iolanthe is the same thing—she's an act of nature. You've done all that you can for her, Jonah, but Iolanthe has dementia. She's not well. *And* she's ready to go. I know it hurts, but it's true. The same way we can't help Dad, or stop Larry from grieving. Can you see that?"

My brother took another moment.

"I can see that."

"Good."

He looked up at me, his eyes squinting in the mid-morning sun.

"So, what happened next?" I said.

"I told her how beautiful she was," he said, between drags. "How I didn't even notice the wheelchair. The driver was helpful. He called her 'The Beauty Queen of the North.'"

Iolanthe depended on the kindness of strangers. It dawned on me that the cab driver had taught sociology at the college. He was the one teacher who accepted late assignments from my students.

"Let's go in." I helped him up.

The foyer was a crowd of well-intentioned confusion, Iolanthe in the centre of it. Larry and the greeters were trying to get her into the lift under Clive's impatient supervision. But she refused, stopping the wheels of her wheelchair from moving forward with her sneakers.

"Just get her in!" Clive shouted, fumbling with the wheelchair brakes. "Push!"

I joined in on the *push*.

"Royal carriage for one," Larry announced, trying to drown out Clive.

"I'll royal carriage you," Clive fired back, releasing the brake mechanism. "Just get her in the lift!"

"Make way for Queen Iolanthe," said the over-enthusiastic greeter, pretending to push.

"All aboard!" shouted Larry, ignoring Clive and defiantly putting on our grandfather's conductor's cap.

That was the moment Clive exploded.

"I warned you!" he bellowed, ripping Larry's name tag off his golf shirt.

"Enough!" I yelled, positioning myself between them.

"I want to go home," cried Jonah and he bolted out the door. "Sophie!"

I'd never experienced a brawl in a church before. Clive shoved me into the coat rack. The hangers clanged together like a discordant wind chime. Before he got to Larry, two parishioners jumped him from behind. Let me just say that Clive's ensuing expletives weren't suitable for a Sunday morning service.

"Get out of the effing way!" Clive screamed, struggling to break free.

By this time, there was a line-up for the lift. The greeter rolled

Iolanthe to the side. The retired minister, a pair of widowed sisters, and an elderly man with an oxygen tank, each boarded the lift. Three trips later and it was Iolanthe's last chance to board. The organ in the sanctuary began to play the opening hymn.

"Please, Iolanthe," I begged, pulling a hanger from around my ear.

"For the love of God, get in!" screamed Clive. "Now!" He broke free and rushed the wheelchair.

Like a mother black bear protecting her cub, Larry stepped in and knocked Clive to the floor. He took control of the handles. "Where can I take you, miss?" There was an odd stillness in his voice.

"WHERE...CAN...LARRY...TAKE...YOU?" shouted the greeter, using hand signals, as if talking to a deaf four-year old.

"Must be the new Sunday School teacher," I grimaced while helping pin Clive against the foyer wall.

"I am not deaf nor am I an idiot," Iolanthe cried. "I want to go to the grave!"

Silence but only for a moment.

The choir's descant poured down the stairs and out of the lift.

"To the grave it is," Larry replied while softly and gently wheeling her into the lift. "Up we go!" he shouted, the perfect imitation of our grandfather.

"To Heaven," Iolanthe commanded. "Now!"

"To Heaven it is."

The door slid shut and up it went.

The narthex lights flickered.

VVVVIZZZZZSPPT!

That's the best way I can describe and transcribe the sound I heard next.

The lift engine cut out.

Silence, save for the muffled voices of the congregation reciting the opening prayer.

Then.

The engine purred back to life.

The lift was coming down.

It came to an easy stop and the door slowly slid open.

There sat an empty wheelchair.
Larry and Iolanthe had vanished.

I have always known our family is different.

"The mental order of the universe is a mystical system," Evie said later, on the phone. "Expect the unexpected."

My sister's explanation is as good as any.

"Iolanthe and Larry went up the lift to God," I explained to Jonah later that afternoon. My brother mulled over my words. A peaceful expression washed over his face—although calling my brother's expression "peaceful" doesn't cut it. An expression—an unearthly smile—that required a new language to understand it, a language not of this world, a language we all want to find in a church or forest, but never do.

It was the kind of expression only a dog, or a very small child, or my brother could hear, if hearing a smile were possible.

"Jonah," I asked. "You okay?"

My brother pulled a cigarette out of his pack on the coffee table and reached in his blazer pocket for his lighter. He flicked it once, watching the flame dance for a few seconds before lighting his Du Maurier. He inhaled thoughtfully, and then blew out a slow, soft circle of smoke and nicotine.

He gave me a nod. "Want to see my new renderings for the Notre Dame altar?"

THE JUNG AND THE RESTLESS

Growing up in the early seventies, my life could best be described as *Saving Private Ryan* meets *Lord of the Flies*.

There were twenty-five boys spilling out of the backyards of ten interconnected new suburban homes. Our neighbourhood was a war zone—soft balls, hard balls, footballs, snowballs, orange road hockey balls, skates, hockey sticks, baseball bats, rocks, elbows, fists, firecrackers, pellet guns, and go-carts. Hedges replaced barbed wire and street lights replaced air raid sirens. Rations consisted of Kraft Dinner and hotdogs. Two girls rounded out the roster, my sisters, JoJo and Evie.

A horse-loving tomboy, JoJo survived without losing a limb. She could out-climb any boy on the block, and was the reigning marble player champion three-years running. Her crock attacks became the stuff of playground legend, causing the boys to, literally, lose their marbles. She scattered her opponents' marbles by unleashing a barrage of well-timed direct hits, her purple Crown Royal bag, courtesy of our father, filled to bursting with the brightly-coloured spoils of victory—aggies, cat's eyes, pretties, red devils, bumblebees, shooters, swirlers, and twirlers. She was twice as deadly at the bowling alley, scattering pins into the air, one strike after another. The other kids' balls missed their targets and wound up in the gutter. Because of her invincibility, JoJo stopped getting invited to birthday parties.

When puberty hit, it came with Richard Dean Anderson— three words that made our thyroids throb, palms sweat, and loins quiver for the first time. JoJo and I were both smitten by MacGyver, although she had more posters on her bedroom wall. Who didn't have a crush on MacGyver? His genius-level intellect, ability to speak French, Italian, Spanish, Russian, German, in addition to American Sign Language and Morse code, superb engineering skills and knowledge of applied physics, military training in bomb disposal techniques, and preference to resolve conflicts non-lethally, stood in stark contrast to the twenty-five boys who pounded me and Jonah into the hedges. His golden-coloured, lightly gelled mullet, parted perfectly down the middle, was a sign that if God did exist, he was a hair stylist. His frosted tips deserved to be on display in an art gallery. MacGyver climbed mountains, parachuted, and hang-glided, despite an acute fear of heights. I got dizzy on the third step of a ladder, and had to close my eyes to climb back down. He could neutralize a terrorist with a toothpick and a paperclip. I could barely fold a piece of foolscap into an airplane, much less make it fly. MacGyver was so awesome his name became a verb. Best thing of all, he entered into a new romantic relationship every episode. I didn't clue into the fact that Big "Mac" was that kind of player. I didn't even know what the word meant. All I saw was hope for my sister and I to be MacGyvered on the couch in the rec room of our parent's basement. We were smitten. I slept with a rubber band under my pillow.

"The guy has a mullet for Christ's sake," Neil said to me on our first date. "How can you like anyone with a mullet?" Neil burst my bubble a few months ago when he told me he saw a recent picture of Richard Dean Anderson online. He's gotten so fat and old, he can't even open the hood of his car. I fed my rubber band to the garbage disposal.

My older sister, Evie, did *not* fit in. Ten adjoining backyards of grass-stained, snot-nosed hair-pulling Neanderthals could drive any girl nuts, but, for Evie, they were unbearable. She caught every illness making the rounds of the playground at recess: colds, the flu, ear infections, and chicken pox; as if being sick was the only way she could safely withdraw from the platoons of hooligan boys.

When Evie was six, her Grade One class held a Halloween party after school. Larry had just turned eighteen, got a job with the railroad, and moved out. Jonah and I were toddlers fighting a particularly nasty flu bug. Our mother, newly pregnant with JoJo, decided to take us to our grandmother's so that we wouldn't infect Evie. Our father had to take Evie to her after-school fright party.

Our mother spent weeks making her a Frida Kahlo costume. Evie changed her mind at the last minute—she wanted to be a black cat. Our father suppressed his frustration with a backyard smoke and MacGyvered up a homemade cat mask using an egg carton, pipe cleaners, and black paint. Evie looked like a pint-sized villain on *Batman*—Frida *Kat*-lo.

Evie stood on the porch, waiting and watching our father attempt to lock the front door.

Sshhhh!

She heard a whisper. It sounded like it was coming from inside the porch rafters.

"Daddy, someone is on the roof."

"Santa Claus doesn't come until Christmas, Monkey," said our father, busy fidgeting with the lock mechanism.

Sshhhh!

"But I hear someone."

"Nothing's there, Evie."

They're leaving.

"They're waiting for us to leave!"

Our father remained patient with her despite being exhausted from six days of on-the-road billboard selling. "You're spooking yourself because you're going to a Halloween party," he explained in awkward dad-speak.

"I'm not scared," Evie swore, stomping her feet. She had the artist's temperament down, even more so as a cat.

Our father retrieved the extension ladder from the garage and climbed up to the eaves troughs. They were stuffed to overflowing with wet leaves. He'd have to clean them out on the weekend, a task he hated. It used to be Larry's job before he moved out. He surveyed the roof. Nothing save for a few loose shingles and a dead tree branch.

"No one's on the roof, Monkey. Maybe you heard a branch fall against the chimney."

"No branch."

He put the ladder away while Evie strained to listen for the voice.

"He went down the chimney," she said, jumping up and down.

"It's Santa Claus!"

"Santa doesn't come until Christmas," sighed our father.

"He's early," said Evie in a panic. "I haven't mailed my letter to the North Pole!"

Our father unlocked the front door and went back inside. Evie watched transfixed as lights in different windows flicked on and off. He returned a moment later.

"No one's there, Monkey," he said.

Evie was confused. "But I heard something."

Our father finally convinced Evie it was just the wind playing tricks on her and they left to join the school festivities already underway. Evie refused to bob for apples, sensing there was something wrong with one of the apples. She put up quite a fuss. Our father masked his embarrassment and cut the apple open. Sure enough there was a worm inside.

They drove home in silence. Our father didn't know what to make of his tiny alien daughter.

When they pulled in the driveway, Evie was first to notice the front door ajar.

"Daddy, look!"

Our father entered the house quickly. We'd been broken into. Drawers were emptied and money stolen, including the contents of Evie's piggy bank. Trash was tossed across the kitchen floor. On the plus side, our father's accordion was missing.

"I told you I heard someone on the roof!" Evie cried, stomping upstairs and locking herself and our family cat, Seymour, in her bedroom.

Around the time Evie was eight, Seymour was hit by a car. Evie was devastated. The night of Seymour's death, as our mother attempted to console her, Evie heard the sound of a bell outside her bedroom window.

"It's Seymour's bell," she said, racing to the window and pulling back the curtains. Nothing but the shimmering glow of the street lamp.

"Honey, the bell is in your imagination," said our mother. "We all miss Seymour."

"No, I heard it. It was Seymour!"

Over the next few nights, Jonah and I heard a scratching sound coming from the back of our bedroom closet. We shared a room until we started high school. When I opened the closet door, the sound stopped, but as soon as I got back in bed, it resumed.

"It's Seymour," said Evie.

Jonah and I were afraid to fall asleep. Our father was forced to rip open the closet wall. He didn't find a ghost cat, but he did encounter an angry red squirrel. Our father turned angrier than the squirrel when it bit him and he had to go to Emergency for a rabies shot. Our mother called Larry who came over and trapped the squirrel in Seymour's travel crate, and boarded up the wall. He released the squirrel beside an old switchman shanty on the outskirts of town. One week later, the red squirrel was back. He sat on top of a telephone pole beside the end of our driveway, waiting for hours. When our father pulled in, the squirrel announced its displeasure, running along the wire that connected the pole to the house, and chattering down insults.

But the strangest tale *and* tail happened six-months later. Evie kept wishing Seymour would somehow find a way to come back to life and return to her. This was long before Tim Burton invented *Frankenweenie*. One night, there came a scratching noise at the front door. This time, we all heard it. My mother cautiously opened the door and the neighbour's cat, who'd never been in our house, ran up the stairs straight to Evie's bedroom. He jumped up on her bed, and curled up, just as Seymour used to. My mother didn't know what to do so she put the cat back outside. Evie ripped open her pillows in protest. Her room resembled a Stratford swan massacre. At breakfast, my mother shared with the rest of us that the cat spent the entire night at the front door mewing. The cat then mysteriously vanished from the neighbourhood.

One morning, shortly after she turned ten, Evie was brushing her teeth in the bathroom sink and looked up at the mirror in the medicine cabinet. "Daddy!' she suddenly began to wail. Every room in our house heard the ruckus. Our father rushed up the stairs, spilling his breakfast coffee in the process and burning his thumb.

"Calm down, Evie! What is it?"

"Something's wrong with Aunt Muriel!"

There was something wrong with Aunt Muriel alright.

"Slow down, Evie," he said. "What's wrong?"

"I was cleaning my teeth and I looked in the mirror. I saw Aunt Muriel. She looked awful!"

Aunt Muriel was our father's crazy sister. If children's literature had a chain-smoking, nocturnal modern-dress version of Mary Poppins, it would be Aunt Muriel. I didn't know one person could own so many scarves and wear them at all at the same time. In my early twenties, I briefly became hooked on the Cult until I discovered that the band's flamboyant lead-singer was Aunt Muriel's doppelganger. Whenever Ian Astbury and his waterfall of white scarves appeared on my television screen, prancing about the stage in the band's "She Sells Sanctuary" music video, I immediately changed the channel.

Aunt Muriel didn't sell sanctuary. She sold eccentricity. She visited psychics and "past lives" specialists on a regular basis while Evie, Jonah, JoJo, and I were growing up, convinced that she had been both a Spanish maid in the French court of King Louis XIV and a medieval witch burned at the stake.

"I had respect, equality, body autonomy, a pack of obedient pack wolves, and pockets in every garment," she told us.

At the age of fifty, she quit smoking while watching an evangelical broadcast on television. She said a crow outside her window told her to switch on her TV and turn to the fifth channel. There were only five channels in the early seventies so it wasn't exactly the stuff of David Copperfield or biblical prophecy. The moderator squeezed his forehead and closed his eyes, as if receiving a transmission from above the ceiling of his million-dollar crystal palace. God's message, on that particular Sunday, apparently concerned a middle-aged woman wearing a lime green pant suit who was addicted to smoking and wanted to quit. The moderator assured the woman she could stop with His help. Aunt Muriel, who happened to be wearing just such a lime green pant suit, trendy at the time, believed the message was specifically for her. She quit on the instant and donated most of the income from her tourist cabin operation in Prince Edward County to the moderator's ministry, dumping her former pagan beliefs in the garbage along with her last pack of Belmont's.

"A miracle," she repeated ad nauseam at family gatherings.

Sadly, the miracle didn't last and Evie's strange vision proved accurate. Years of cigarette smoking invariably caught up with Aunt Muriel. She visited her doctor complaining of bronchitis and died less than a month later of stage-four lung cancer.

But, in her pre-born again days, Aunt Muriel had a lot to say about the full moon. She took us on moonlit picnics whenever our parents went out of town.

"For millions of years, the moon was the only source of light at night," she said while passing out cucumber sandwiches and soft drinks from a picnic hamper. A cigarette balanced on her bottom lip, a long ash dangerously close to falling on our sandwiches. We all stared up at the moon.

"How much is a million?" I asked.

"Lots and lots of birthdays," Aunt Muriel replied. She flicked an unruly ash off her sleeve.

"With cake?" sniffed Evie, waving her napkin to try and reduce the smell of Aunt Muriel's cigarette smoke. Even outdoors, she was sensitive to the odour.

"Of course," Aunt Muriel replied. "Millions of cakes!"

"I want an ice cream cake," said Jonah.

"An ice cream cake it is," Aunt Muriel smiled. Her teeth were yellow.

"With jam?" said JoJo.

"With jam."

We ate our sandwiches and imagined ice cream cake with jam.

Aunt Muriel inhaled deeply, exhaled dramatically, coughed loudly, and continued on with her lesson. "The full moon was the only thing standing between ancient man and being eaten by a wild animal."

"What kind of *aminal*?" asked JoJo, eyes wide as two full moons.

"Why, all sorts, sweetheart. Saber-toothed wolves especially."

I got goosebumps. I'd seen pictures of saber-toothed tigers but never a saber-toothed wolf.

"Wool-elves?" asked JoJo. "Like Santa's?"

"No, these *wool elves* belong to the full moon."

"The *fool moo?*" said JoJo. She had goosebumps too. I imagined a silly cow jumping over the moon.

"Yes, darling, the *fool moo*. Now, do you know why weird things happen on the *fool moo?*"

We shook our heads in a combination of fear and wonderment.

"First," Aunt Muriel began, "the moon goes back further in time than any history book."

"Before the moon landing," said Jonah. He was obsessed with space travel.

"Oh my yes. She is why the earth was able to stabilize so we could exist."

"The moon is a girl?" I asked. I didn't like the sound of that.

"Yes, Rudolph."

"No, he's called the man in the moon," argued Jonah.

"Nonsense. Next you'll be telling me the moon is made of green cheese."

I'd swallowed something called blue cheese on one of Aunt Muriel's salads she served for dinner. I suspected green cheese would taste even worse.

"I like cheese with jam," said JoJo.

"Of course you do," said Aunt Muriel. "I'll make grilled cheese and raspberry jam sandwiches tomorrow. Now, the moon has magical powers. She is why man dreams of outer space."

The moon wasn't the reason I dreamt of outer space. Mr. Spock was.

"I want to go the moon," said Jonah, sneezing from the pepper in his sandwich. Aunt Muriel put pepper on everything. She even put it on ice cream.

"And I'm sure you will, honey," said Aunt Muriel. "Now, the full moon rises when the sun sets."

Every kid knew that.

"Did you know the wolf is the reason for the moon's magical power?" she said, ripping open a large bag of potato chips and passing them to Jonah.

"Really?" Evie said.

"Isn't it because there's no gravity on the moon?" said Jonah skeptically.

Aunt Muriel shook her head. "The moon hunts down the sun and devours him at dusk, allowing her power to come out."

I got goosebumps again.

"The *full moo* eats the sun?" asked JoJo.

"Yes, dear, but only at night. Then she kisses him goodnight at dawn and the sun comes back to life."

"Like a magic prince!" JoJo squealed.

I wouldn't want the moon kissing me if her breath smelled anything like Aunt Muriel's.

"Are there wolves in this park?" asked Evie uneasily, looking around at the darkness.

"Only on the full moon," exhaled Aunt Muriel. A dry, raspy coughing fit followed.

Jonah and I shared a look. Maybe our neighbor, old Mr. Hack, was a wolf. He certainly was hairy enough. Evie stared up at the moon. I thought she was going to howl.

"I don't want a wolf to eat me!" cried JoJo, rubbing her eyes.

"You're all safe with me," said Aunt Muriel, inviting JoJo up on her lap. "Do you want to me to teach you some tricks to protect yourselves on a *fool moo*?"

"Yes, please" sneezed Evie, transfixed.

And so our *fool moo* indoctrination began. Aunt Muriel believed that moonlight shining into our bedrooms would bring bad luck.

"Greet the moon with a polite curtsy," she instructed Evie and JoJo, demonstrating proper form and technique. She looked like Kermit the Frog in drag in her lime green-pant suit. "It will ward off bad luck. You might even be granted a wish."

"I want jam!" said JoJo.

Aunt Muriel told Jonah and I that if we bowed to the new moon, and turned over silver coins in our pockets, we could double the amount of money by the end of the moon's cycle. Jonah and I each received one silver dollar from her on our shared birthday but we never saw our dollars double, but that had nothing to do with the full moon. We'd spent it on candy at the corner store long before sunset.

Apparently, when the *fool moo* pulled the tide, it pulled people as well. I imagined I was a snow globe being shaken by the moon. Evie was especially sensitive, saying it felt like the Pacific Ocean was churning inside her. I asked her if she could spit out a dolphin. Aunt Muriel bought Evie a pair of heavy black army boots to sleep in when the moon was full.

Aunt Muriel warned us that witches and sorcerers could draw down the moon to use its power for their spells. When JoJo couldn't see the moon in the sky she had terrible nightmares, fearing a witch had stolen it.

"Have you ever thought about how when you look at the moon, it's the same moon Shakespeare and Marie Antoinette and Frida Kahlo looked at?" Aunt Muriel said.

"Wow!" said Evie.

"They *all* looked at the moon," replied Aunt Muriel, jabbing the air with her cigarette for emphasis.

"And they're all dead," said Jonah.

"The moon is killing people!" I shouted out.

JoJo started to cry again. I swear she had a water tower in her head.

"That's enough, Rudolph!" Aunt Muriel scolded. "You're scaring your sister."

Aunt Muriel then warned me to never to point at the moon or I would be banned from Heaven for it. I pointed at the moon every chance I got.

Aunt Muriel continued with her lessons anytime our parents were at a billboard convention.

"The full moon can get you pregnant," Aunt Muriel warned us on one such occasion.

"Peg aunt?" asked JoJo.

"Do you have a peg leg like a pirate, Aunt Muriel?" teased

Jonah, brushing a large ash off his sandwich.

"Don't be silly," replied Aunt Muriel, lighting up another cigarette. "Now, you young people have the most energy."

"Jigger!" shouted JoJo.

"No, not Tigger, sweetheart," said Aunt Muriel. "There is a pressure to perform because the time of light is short."

Perform what? I wondered. A sacrifice? My Grade Five teacher said Aztec priests used to rip out your heart and make you watch. I didn't want Aunt Muriel pulling out my heart. "How short?" I asked instead, crossing my arms over my chest.

"When the streetlights go on?" said Jonah.

"Very short," said Aunt Muriel. "There is a tension to make things happen."

"Make what happen?" asked Evie, confused. I had no idea what Aunt Muriel was talking about. JoJo was having fun sticking a cucumber slice on her eye and pretending it was an eyepatch. Jonah returned to looking at the constellations with his toy telescope.

"Stir in a sky full of moon energy," said Aunt Muriel, flicking open the lid of her Zippo lighter. She snapped her fingers and a flame appeared. It looked cool and scary at the same time. "And flash bang it happens."

"Bang!" I shouted.

"*What* happens?" demanded Evie.

"Babies, Evie," said Aunt Muriel, "whining, mewling disgusting babies."

Aunt Muriel was nuts. Babies did not come from a giant lump of rock. They came from the hospital. Our father told me that Aunt Muriel was a spinster and never wanted children which puzzled me because I thought a spinster was a monster trapped in a tornado.

Aunt Muriel also warned us not to sleep in the moonlight, for fear we'd become "moon-struck" and attract werewolves. She told us that werewolves turned their skin inside out to appear human.

I hatched a plan to scare my little sister. I wanted to convince JoJo that old Mr. Hack, our neighbour across the street, was a werewolf. Jonah was oblivious to my prank, preoccupied as he was with charting the night sky and drawing castles. Evie kept to her room in her black army boots.

Mr. Hack had a choppy grey beard, bushy eyebrows, and long hair sprouting out of the neck of his shirts. His wrinkled skin was even hairier than his neck. His limbs trembled and jerked, clinging awkwardly to his slouched, skeleton frame. His face was compact, as if he had been hit by a two-by-four. He looked more like a *were-pug*.

I pointed out to JoJo that Mr. Hack always disappeared on the night of a full moon.

"He creeps around the neighbourhood and stares at us," I said. "There's dirt and leaves on his clothes." Mr. Hack was always going to the park and coming home with leaves stuck to his cardigan.

"He even smells like a wolf," I said. "All the dogs down the street bark at him. They pull on their leashes whenever he comes near them. *They* know he's a werewolf. Have you ever noticed how tired he looks after a full moon? *And* he wakes up in strange places. I saw him sleeping on a bench in the park. You saw him asleep in his flowerbed. Have you looked at his fingernails? They're filthy. They look like claws."

"You're lying," JoJo cried, and ran inside to tell our mother.

"Rudolph Thelonious Boyle! You get inside this instant!" The last time I heard our mother that angry was when I put Seymour in the washing machine. She sat the four of us down at the kitchen table, and glared at me for what seemed a lunar month. I was going to be banished to the moon. And devoured by the sun.

After a long audible sigh, she removed her tortoise-shell glasses with the slow deliberate authority of a judge cancelling recess and spoke.

"Poor old Mr. Hack is a recovering alcoholic and he suffers from *hypotrichosis*."

"What's hippo-trick-a-sis?" asked JoJo.

"Go to the zoo and find out," I muttered. My mother rapped me on the knuckles with a wooden spoon.

"It's a condition that causes people to grow thick hair all over their face and body, honey."

How was I to know?

"Do you know Mr. Hack is a retired dendrologist, Rudolph?" my mother said.

"No." I had never heard of the word. "What's that?"

"He studies plants. That's why he collects leaves."

"Oh."

Mr. Hack was a leaf collector? Boy, did I feel stupid.

"'Oh' is right, young man. Don't you feel foolish now? Filling your sister's head with such nonsense. Poor Mr. Hack is a tired, lonely old man. He deserves our sympathy, not mockery."

I was grounded for two weeks. On the night of the last day of my imprisonment, the full moon was low on the November horizon. Jonah examined it through his telescope. He viewed the moon for a bit, then checked his notes against a lunar atlas, and then looked at it a bit more.

He saw something incredible. There was a crack extending across the moon's surface.

He checked the atlas to see if it was a normal lunar detail that he didn't know about, but there was nothing notated on the atlas. The moon was cracking in half.

He looked through the telescope again. The crack was bigger than before. Not only that, it was branching out in all directions. He called me into the bedroom, bursting with scientific discovery.

"Rudy! Look, the moon is breaking apart!"

I stared at the moon with my naked eye. It had sunk behind a distant tree with bare branches, which was the "crack" apparently branching.

"It's just a tree, Jonah."

It was the day I first realized knowledge ruined many things. But Jonah, being Jonah, chose to cherish the feeling he had before I gave him the logical explanation.

When Evie turned twelve, she started behaving like a child possessed, something out of a Stephen King novel. She either was unusually quiet around the neighbourhood boys or the exact opposite, transforming into Rosemary's baby, and interrupting our Saturday afternoon baseball game with her temper tantrums.

We didn't have rain delays, we had rage delays.

Evie resisted going to bed and, when our mother finally did manage to get her to sleep, she'd wake up screaming in the middle of the night. Our family doctor was baffled. He blamed it on her diet. Evie was anemic and needed more iron, he said. Our father barbecued steaks on the back deck throughout the winter, freezing his fingers nightly, to no avail. Evie didn't stop screaming. A local psychologist looked to our parents as the cause. Was Evie abused physically or emotionally? Were our parents alcoholics? Narcissists? Neglectful?

As a last resort, our mother found an "alternative healer" in Toronto named Karl Jung. No relation to the famous Swiss capital "C" psychoanalyst, Karl sported corduroy bell-bottoms, brightly-coloured velour sweaters, strings of exotic beads, and plastic flowers in his waist-length hair. Hippie healers were all the rage in the seventies. After shining sunlight on Evie from various angles through a variety of crystals and observing her reaction to wind chimes and different incense, Karl determined Evie was a psychic-empath.

"What is that?" asked our mother, perplexed.

"Evie has an inborn temperament. She entered the world with more sensitivity than others. It was there the moment she came out of your womb." He gently patted our mother's stomach.

"Why didn't I see it?" our mother said, politely removing Karl's lingering hand.

"You probably did but didn't know it," replied Karl in a comforting tone "Infants like Evie are more responsive to light, smells, touch, movement, temperature, and sound. She was an empath from the start."

"She did catch more colds than her brothers and sister."

"Your daughter is a psychic feeler and a human sponge," explained Karl. "Just walking down the street can be painful for empaths, because if they're not properly protecting them- selves, they will feel the emotions of everyone they pass. Evie's shyness is actually her trying to ground herself. She withdraws from the world to protect herself. Her angry outbursts are a much-needed outlet for the overwhelming flow of incoming emotion. She can't sleep because she's struggling to stay centred while surrounded by the high energy of the boys in your neighbourhood. In a nutshell, Evie is trying to feel empowered by shutting down unwanted emotional activity."

Our mother took in Karl's words, scribbling notes as he talked. "What about her hearing voices?"

"Nothing more than an overactive psychic imagination. Think of it as a short-circuit in her empathic wiring."

"So, what can we do?" our mother asked. My father was one phone call away from summoning an exorcist. No one wanted another Aunt Muriel on our hands.

"Evie needs to protect herself with white light, and wear certain crystals that match her energy vibrations to stop the emotions of others invading her," said Karl. "Burning frankincense will help. Try putting a wave machine in her bedroom to help her sleep. She needs greenery. Lots of plants and herbs. She'll feel their positive vibes flowing toward her."

"Crystals," my mother repeated, jotting down the words "white" and "plants" in her notebook.

Karl then showed my mother his empath-anchoring techniques, the healer's equivalent of etchings.

"Evie feels overwhelmed," he said, emphatically raising his eyebrows in tandem with the creases on his forehead, "so she needs a point of reference to stay grounded. You and your family have to become the anchor. The first step is to calm your emotions when around her. How can you be an anchor if you're angry or upset? I suggest your family all take up yoga."

This would prove difficult for my father who had little patience for flexibility or downward dogs of any kind. The rest of us had no choice. I fell asleep worshipping the sun.

Karl demonstrated his anchoring techniques. "We start with breathing, Rita. You pretend to be your daughter, and I'll be you. I want you to look into my eyes and point at your own eyes while I gently put my hand on your chest."

Our mother raised an eyebrow.

"We mustn't break eye contact, Rita. Are you ready for the next step?"

"Yes," my mother said, fixing her eyes on his and placing his hands carefully on her chest.

"We're going to take five deep breaths together and count them," he instructed in a hoarse whisper.

"Okay," my mother said, inhaling quickly and holding her breath. His palms felt sweaty through her blouse.

"You can breathe however you want, Rita, through your mouth, your nose, your—" Karl caught himself. "Imagine all of your body breathing."

He accompanied my mother, counting aloud with each exhalation, never taking his eyes off her heaving chest.

"Mom sure breathed funny," Evie shared with me the next day while we helped our father paint the living room walls white.

Eventually, Evie's breathing quieted down her emotional noise. She now had something positive to do whenever she felt uncomfortable. It got so Evie would stop and breathe just about everywhere. It was like having Darth Vader in the family.

Evie sensed when people were hurting. One time, a neighbourhood bully upset me during recess in the middle of a game of marbles. I raced home after school to tell Evie. I crashed through the front door, bounded up the stairs, and found her lighting white candles in her room.

She held out an upraised hand, closed her eyes, and breathed deeply. Before I could catch my breath and utter a word, she whispered, "Cain McKay told you I was a witch."

She always knew what I was thinking. It was all very unsettling. She lit some incense and laid out her plants around me in a large circle. Her room smelled of lemongrass, mint, lavender, and me.

"For protection," she said softly. "Sit."

I felt ridiculous sitting on the floor surrounded by plants—there must have been twenty of them, and all at different heights. Succulents, tall leafy philodendrons, low-level cacti, evergreens, snake plants, fiddle-leaf figs, dancing orchids, and...*herbs*! There was Thorn Magic for grounding, Milky Oat for balance and bathing,

Skullcap for hair loss, Rose for health and healing, Sacred Basil for good vibrations, something called Nervine that relaxed the nervous system, and Dill for dummies like me.

Evie sat across from me, cross-legged on the floor, mirroring me. She closed her eyes, placing her hands inches away from my chest. She scanned me in a grand sweeping motion. I felt like I'd been beamed down to some hippie alien planet on *Star Trek*. I thought I saw something moving in her hair.

"We must both visualize the sun beaming a ray of white light down into our hearts," she whispered.

I tried to visualize the sun pouring into me but all I could picture was Richard Dreyfuss sitting in a shaking hydro truck at a railway crossing. Jonah and I had seen *Close Encounters* the night before.

"I'm taking the white light in my hands and sending it to you," Evie said, aiming her fingertips towards my heart. A caterpillar emerged from behind her ear.

"Feel the light," she repeated.

I felt nothing but a leg cramp.

"Drink it in," she whispered.

I imagined drinking a chocolate milkshake.

She opened her eyes, dizzy and exhausted. Suddenly I felt happy and content. I wanted to hug a fern.

When Evie graduated high school, she went on a serious quest for God. There weren't enough plants and herbs on the planet to help her with that one. She fell in love with her first-year university philosophy professor. He left his wife, got a divorce, and married my sister (who was five years younger than his daughter.) Only our mother attended their wedding, held on the summer solstice, deep in the bug-infested bush of Algonquin Park. Most of the guests were black flies.

On her honeymoon, Evie's husband gave her a Timothy Leary book to read to put her on the path to enlightenment. Soon Evie was taking LSD and travelling astrally.

"Right before my first hit," Evie told me over the phone, "I heard Aunt Muriel's voice in my head saying, 'Remember the *fool moo.*'"

"Did you find any cow bones on the moon?" I said.

"Very funny. I left my body and traveled to another dimension," Evie said.

"*The Twilight Zone?*"

"No, it was Heaven. I saw The Hall of Records, the ancient library that lies under the Great Sphinx of Giza. The sky rolled back to reveal a huge colour TV screen."

"I'm sure glad God doesn't see the world in black and white."

"I'm serious. It showed the Earth, and how each one of us could be seen from Heaven. I saw so many amazing things. Did you know Jesus can body surf?"

That's why I don't do drugs.

"It was LSD, Evie," I said and hung up.

She called me back ten minutes later.

"After you so rudely hung up on me, I heard a knock. I walked to the front door and opened it. And what do you suppose I saw?"

"Aunt Muriel's ghost in a lime green pant-suit?"

"Be serious."

"Okay, okay. What did you see?"

"I looked up at the sky. The sun was shining. Not a cloud in sight. A perfect day. The richest blue I've ever seen. And I asked God if I was really in Heaven to please give me a sign. And, at that moment, on this beautiful sunny day, it cracked thunder and lightning. And I knew. It chilled me to the chakra."

Six months later, Evie gave up everything, left her husband, and moved back home. It took our father two weeks to repaint the walls white.

BACHING UP THE WRONG TREE

My Uncle Irving was different.

As a mouthy kid, I didn't understand him. I thought he was "stupid."

"Have you ever met a stupid person who can play Bach?" my mother said.

I had no idea who Bach was.

"No," I said.

"Memorizing pages of music and moving ten fingers in two directions is not for idiots. Your uncle may have his peculiarities, but stupidity is not one of them. The dedication required to practice leaves him with insufficient time to learn certain life skills," was how my mother delicately put it—life skills like how to boil water or operate a toaster.

Growing up, I rarely saw my uncle. He didn't attend family gatherings and avoided Christmas altogether. I can't really blame him for that; putting my family together in one room was not for the faint of lungs. There weren't enough letters in the alphabet to capture the mayhem and, as the middle sibling, I got more de-escalation training than the police did.

The one time I saw my uncle perform was when my mother dragged Jonah and me to the Symphony when we were ten. It was a strange sight; Uncle Irving perched over a shiny black grand piano with his long black tailcoat, he resembled a nervous cricket. My uncle was as short as his forehead was tall. I figured he needed the extra space to store all those notes.

I jumped up and shouted, "Uncle Irving, over here!"

He shrank at the sound of my voice.

My mother ssshhh'd me and shoved me back down in my seat.

His playing was another matter entirely. I marveled at how his tiny fingers could reach all the keys. It was as if they had magically grown two inches longer. I closed my eyes and imagined it was Bach himself up there on that stage, even though I *still* had no idea who Bach was.

My uncle communicated better with the piano than with people.

"At least he isn't building pipe bombs in his basement or running a child pornography ring," my older brother Larry said. I had no idea what he was talking about.

"Your Uncle Irving had a difficult childhood," my mother reminded me each time we dropped by his tiny bungalow to deliver a casserole. "He suffers from an obsessive-compulsive disorder." It took him ten minutes to unlock his front door. His house was always dark and musty. He kept the curtains closed and the windows sealed. His piano lamp provided the only light in the room—creepy was an understatement. His piano also doubled as a dining room table. He didn't buy groceries. Take-out food containers were meticulously stacked in a living room corner, the cardboard equivalent of the Great Pyramid of Giza.

Uncle Irving was my mother's half-brother, older by fifteen years. In my Grade Ten Social Studies class, we were assigned to research a family member. There was no way I was going to write about Aunt Muriel (I didn't want to revisit her crazy stories of full moons and werewolves). Besides, she was dead so I went with Uncle Irving instead, but he was too nervous to let me interview him. My mother offered to help. On the evening before the assignment was due, I hit the red "Record" button on my father's portable cassette player.

"The day after the Titanic sank," my mother began, "Ira Sandberg, the artist, married my mother. They had a baby boy and named him Irving. Ira loved his son, letting him play with his paints, splatter his canvases, and wreak havoc in his studio."

"What happened?" I couldn't picture my uncle being a splatterer.

"The War happened. Ira was conscripted to fight. The army didn't know what to do with him. A baby-faced artist battling the Germans? But the army was running out of young men and options. He was sent to Yarmouth, Nova Scotia, for basic infantry training. It was there, one night in the autumn of 1917, that a colonel informed him briskly: 'Sandberg! Don't ask me how but Lloyd George has decided they can't win the war without you. You're being flown to London tomorrow morning.'

"Two weeks later, a bewildered Ira reported to the army's historical section in London, where he was drafted into the rarefied ranks of Canadian war artists. He was ordered to link up with Canadian forces in Europe and document on canvas whatever subjects he could find. In a letter to your grandmother, he talked about exploring the French countryside with his driver, Monet."

"Monet?"

"Sergeant Guillaume Monet. He was a young French-Canadian musician. They were looking for subjects to draw. Sadly, all they saw was death and destruction. When Ira returned home at the end of the War, he locked his brushes and pencils in a drawer, tossed the key to the drawer in the lake, and never painted again. With a shell-shocked father and an exhausted mother forced to focus on her husband's trauma, Irving got lost in the shuffle. He was the first to discover his father's body in the cellar. Ira had shot himself through the eye with his service revolver."

It was the first time I heard about a suicide in our family.

"By the time I came along, fifteen years later," my mother continued, "my mother had remarried a childhood friend. Your grandfather was a hard-working, practical man who farmed the land and tried to plant those same seeds in your uncle, but Irving was allergic to just about everything in the barn—straw, horses, pollen, feathers, physical labour, dawn, me."

"What about the piano?" I said.

"The piano lessons were your grandmother's idea. He took to them immediately. Bach became his friend and eventually joined him in his studies at the Royal Conservatory of Music. He remained a loner, rarely socializing and never dating."

My mother began preparing our school lunches while she talked, shouting back over her shoulder whenever she opened the refrigerator.

"When you were growing up, he was scared of you and your brothers and sisters."

My mother was a toastmaster. She buttered the bread before toasting it, so that the butter melted all the way through, soaking into the toast and raisins. It made for a crispier toast on the outside, while soft and fluffy on the inside. Our toaster oven got more of a work out than the big oven. My mother turned the dial to "low" and watched closely through the glass so that the butter didn't scorch or start a fire. She removed a Tupperware container of egg salad from the back of the fridge and plopped a mound of it into a small bowl, adding a squirt of lemon juice and a dash of curry powder. She handed me the tablespoon to lick. Nothing tasted better than egg salad on a spoon, especially when mixed with green onion, mustard and celery.

"Your uncle existed, and that's about it, until the night of his sixty-fifth birthday."

"I was eleven." That part of the story I remembered.

"Just turned. Now, your uncle has never had much of a regular sleep pattern, but that particular night, he woke up unable to catch his breath. Do you remember that time our phone rang in the middle of the night?"

By Grade Five, I knew phone calls at three in the morning were bad news. My father answered, thinking it was the hospital calling to tell him Aunt Muriel had passed on. He'd been keeping vigil at his sister's bedside, and had come home for a quick shower and change of clothes, before returning.

"Your father passed me the phone. It was your uncle. He was in such a state. He was having a panic attack and wanted to know if a dog barking outside his house meant that death was at his door. I assured him the Grim Reaper didn't bark or knock when he made house calls.

"'Maybe God wants you to get a dog,' I told him, half-jokingly."

Ding!

The toaster oven interrupted the strange case of the bark of the Grim Reaper. My mother spread the egg salad, starting from the top of the slice and moving downward in an even layer, nice and thick, just the way I liked it. Never spread side to side—it was her own unique sandwich–making technique. I now know all about strange rituals. Neil hand counts sixty individual beans for his coffee each morning. You don't want to be anywhere near him if he's a bean short.

Something must've gone "ding" in my uncle's head that night, because the next morning my mother and I (it was a Saturday) found ourselves standing beside him, viewing a new batch of puppies at a dog breeding operation south of town.

"Your uncle picked out the runt of the litter."

"Just like him," I said.

"A tiny black-and-white mitten with a quirky white patch circling its right eye. The farmer said the pup's name was Bullseye. Your uncle renamed him Sebastian. Johann sounded too stuffy, he said."

"And Sebastian didn't?"

A border collie was the most impractical breed my uncle could have picked, considering his sedentary lifestyle, but no one had ever accused my uncle of being practical.

"He needed to prepare for Sebastian's homecoming, so I took him to the library and signed out enough 'how to' books to keep him reading and researching well into the night. Eight weeks later, on a surprisingly mild mid-January morning, we picked up Sebastian. According to the manuals, crate-training should have started on Night One, but your uncle couldn't bear the sound of Sebastian's cries. They reminded him of his father's after the War. He opened the crate and Sebastian moved into his bed."

So much for the manuals.

"Sebastian attended rehearsals, curling up under the piano bench. Your uncle claimed that when he played the Goldberg Variations, Sebastian barked in rhythm to the allegro movements. Sebastian started teething. I showed your uncle how to soak a woolen sock in his kitchen sink, stick it in the freezer, and give it to Sebastian to chew on to help ease his gum pain. I noticed the drips on his kitchen floor two weeks in. At first, I thought it was water spilling over from Sebastian's bowl. Under closer inspection, it was dog pee. Fighting back his anxiety, your uncle mopped the kitchen floor.

"You're okay with that, Irv?' I asked him.

"'I don't mind,' he replied stiffly.

"The day Sebastian turned six-months old, we took him in for neutering. He dreaded the operation—your uncle, not Sebastian. After a brief examination, the vet, a kind beefy man with soft features and an open, kind demeanour, sat us down and delivered the news: Sebastian's testicles were missing."

"What?"

"The vet explained that Sebastian didn't have retracted testicles, a common enough problem, he had no testicles. Birth defects. Probably what was causing the bladder problem in the first place. His guess was in-breeding. He asked us where we got him.

"'From a farm,' your uncle mumbled, his fingers involuntarily playing a concerto on his knees. His eyes darted about the examining room. He was paler than a snowbank. I told the vet we bought Sebastian from Maple Creek Kennels in Juniper.

"'I thought so,' he replied. 'They should've been closed down years ago. Disgusting what they do there.'

"He sat down beside Irving. 'Sebastian will never develop a functioning bladder muscle to control his urine,' he explained with a concerned tone. Talking to your uncle was like talking to a bewildered four-year old. 'He'll be a leaky faucet for life, I'm afraid. And it will be a short life. I'm sorry, Mr. Sandberg,' he paused, making eye contact with me, 'but my advice is to put him down and start fresh.'

"Your uncle fled the clinic, clutching Sebastian tightly to his ribs.

"'He's just a little dog,' he said in the parking lot. 'A loving little dog who hasn't done a thing to hurt anyone!'

"'I know,' I said.

"'What has he done to deserve this?'

"'Nothing,' I said.

"'Answer me!' he cried, looking up at the winter sky. It was the first and only time I heard your uncle raise his voice.

"'Let's go home, Irv,' I said. He refused to take the vet's advice so I booked an appointment with the Ontario Veterinary College at Guelph University. The definitive diagnosis arrived a week later. Sebastian was a hermaphrodite."

The one other time I'd come across that word was as a boy reading my *Ripley's Believe It Or Not* comics. Dog-faced women and the world's tallest man paled in comparison to a canine hermaphrodite.

"Sebastian suffered from a rare ovary-testicle hybrid. He had both male and female reproductive organs. As a result, he had an abnormally narrow urethra, and a bladder the size of a birthday balloon. He needed two operations to correct the condition. Neither your uncle nor your father had the five thousand dollars needed to pay for the surgeries."

Five thousand dollars was a lot of money in 1975. Still is.

"I suggested your uncle start a 'Sebastian Fund' and, together, we put mason jars on the counters at local restaurants, motels, and businesses. It forced your uncle to talk to people. Two months later, we'd raised a little over two hundred dollars. Things were looking grim. I was worried your uncle would follow his father's example. The phone call came three weeks later. Intrigued by Sebastian's unusual condition, Sarah Watson, a doctor at the veterinary college, offered your uncle the surgeries free-of-charge—if he would permit her to document the procedures for a new teaching manual she was assembling. So, two weeks later..."

"I went with you." The ride was excruciating—for my uncle, not Sebastian. We had to stop five times.

"One month later, Sebastian came home. It was difficult to repair a weakened bladder muscle. As instructed by Dr. Watson and her medical team, your uncle massaged Sebastian's bladder muscle three times a day. Still, Sebastian dripped.

"'Don't you find this all a little ironic?' I asked him while dropping off a load of clean diapers.

"'How so?' he said.

"'You've been afraid of mess your entire life.'"

I hit the "Stop" button. I knew the rest of the story.

Sebastian soaked through his diapers, forcing my uncle to mop his floors morning, noon, and night. His kitchen reeked of dog urine. Soon, his clothes. Finally, his skin. It got so my uncle couldn't smell the pee, which was fine for him, but not for the rest of us.

My mother checked in on the pair three times a week. She pulled back his musty old curtains and opened the windows. Fresh air circulated for the first time in years. She scrubbed and cleaned. My sister, Evie, filled the house with scented oils. Jonah and I played fetch with Sebastian in the backyard while JoJo tagged along.

My uncle enrolled him in obedience school, but Sebastian got the boot after his second class. He failed to sit and stay. Based on that criteria, I should've failed kindergarten.

The instructor couldn't compete with the ADHD of a crazed border collie. Sebastian grew up undisciplined. He needed fields and sheep—what he got was four small rooms and a rehearsal hall. Consequently, he bit the postal carrier, a jogger, my father, and the first violin. Uncle Irving attempted to walk Sebastian along the waterfront. It was an amusing sight watching him grip Sebastian's leash with both hands and be dragged in and out of traffic. He resembled a water-skier being towed behind a drunk driver.

My uncle, however, didn't give up. He kept quiet and worked at it. And to the surprise of our family, Sebastian matured and settled down. He learned to respond to my uncle's commands. A border collie can understand four hundred-and-fifty words. My welding students at the college don't have a vocabulary that large.

Whenever Uncle Irving performed, Sebastian watched from the wings, his black-and- white markings matching the fifty-odd tuxedos on stage. The first violin forgave him and bought him a bowtie. When the conductor wasn't looking, the percussionist tossed him treats. They became regulars at family events, celebrating holidays and birthdays at my parents' paint-peeling Victorian home. Framed pictures of the pair bedecked the walls of my uncle's living room. At Christmas, their stockings hung together on a brass music stand.

Old age eventually caught up with my uncle. He struggled to keep up with the mopping. My mother hired a housecleaner.

It was a losing battle. Sebastian suffered a stroke in his fifteenth year and soaked his final diaper. My uncle had him cremated, and placed his ashes in an urn on the piano.

The piano, however, remained silent.

The following autumn, while taking out the garbage, my uncle suffered a massive heart attack. A city worker found him lying unconscious at the end of his driveway. Pulmonary heart failure. My mother made the difficult decision to take him off life support. The doctors gave him morphine to keep him comfortable. Our whole family was there. Evie lit candles. I had my father's portable cassette recorder and a Glen Gould recording of Bach's *Brandenburg Concertos* I'd signed out from the library. I inserted the cassette and hit "Play."

My uncle's eyelids fluttered briefly.

Outside the hospital room window, the strings section of "Eleanor Rigby" was playing on a car radio, loud enough to be heard over the Baroque music. I watched out the window. The car stopped at a red light. The strings of the Beatles blended with Bach for an instant.

All the lonely people, where do they all come from. The song disappeared when the light turned green.

A dog began to bark in the parking lot.

Uncle Irving slipped away at the age of eighty-one.

The first violin spoke at the funeral.

Each October, the symphony performs the *Goldberg Variations*. Our family attends. A photograph of Uncle Irving and Sebastian is projected on a screen above the Steinway piano.

I can almost hear barking.

Oh, and I got a C on that paper. My teacher thought I made up the bit about the hermaphrodite.

GOING TO THE DOGS

My younger sister wanted to give birth to a dog, but had two children instead—Jenny and Jerome.

JoJo, has a thing for the letter J. As a kid, she put jam on everything—our mother even took creole cooking classes so she could learn how to make jambalaya.

After Jenny and Jerome graduated college, JoJo and her husband Jimmy bought an RV and parked it at a community trailer park a half-hour south of town. My partner Neil and I go there on weekends before we start our summer holidays. We bring our Jack Russell terrier, Salinger, with us. We bought him from a breeder in Cornish, New Hampshire.

Everyone at the Juniper Berry Trailer Park owns a dog. My sister currently has two jet-black cocker spaniels named Tortilla and Salsa. She wanted to name them Jack and Jill but Jimmy put his foot down.

One Saturday night I realized that there were no dogs taller than eighteen-inches in the trailer park, about the height of two bowling balls. I know this to be fact because I borrowed Jimmy's tape measure. There *is* a German shepherd puppy three sites down, but he smokes cigarettes to stunt his growth.

Jimmy is one of those guys who can build anything, as long as there is something pleasurable waiting on the other side. For instance, his fire pit is a thing of beauty. The rest of the park improvises with old tire rims. Not Jimmy. His fire pit is the industrial equivalent of those little cream-cheese pinwheel sandwiches served at funerals. A ring of stones spirals into another ring and then another. Imbedded in the second ring are solar lights and ventilation shafts. In the middle is the space for the actual fire pit, an ornate steel ring with cutouts of Salsa and Tortilla frolicking to let the air in that maximize the visibility of the glowing logs and cast dog-shaped shadows for ambiance. He's even designed glass holders that attach to the outside ring and sit alongside four push buttons strategically placed at quarterly intervals that release citronella mist to keep the mosquitoes at bay.

Tortilla and Salsa have LED night collars that glow a vibrant red. They look like incandescent miniature hula hoops running about the site. Tortilla and Salsa actually have four collars.

The first is their chain collar from which hang their cactus-shaped ID tags.

The second is a remote-control unit that reacts to the invisible electric fencing that surrounds their trailer site.

The third is an electronic anti-barking device that emits citronella spray should either bark at squirrels, other dogs, or each other.

The fourth is their red-light night collar.

After the evening barbecue we sit around the fire pit, drinking, telling stories, and listening to the music scramble on Jimmy's new tablet. Jimmy and I smoke cigarillos. Trailer park neighbours pass by, walking their eighteen-inch tall dogs.

Tortilla forgets about his second and third collars. Barking and running to greet a friendly cockapoo, he is both sprayed with mist and zapped by the fence. Salsa is more resourceful than her brother. She deliberately barks at the grass to release the citronella to keep the mosquitoes out of her ears.

When I press Salinger's ears together, he resembles Christopher Plummer. At home, he is less sophisticated, devouring the contents of our cat's litter box like a carton of Timbits. Our cat views Salinger as an inferior life form.

Jimmy does not care for cats. They are too independent. Jimmy, a.k.a. Jimmy Thunder, was the morning man on our local radio station for years: "GET READY FOR [followed by a cheesy thunderclap sound effect] THUNDER IN THE MORNING!"

I thought Thunder was his radio name until Jimmy showed me his birth certificate over a cigarillo one Saturday night. There it was, Jimmy Rumble Thunder.

"You could be a character in *Cats*," I told him.

"I was made with a bang and came out with one too," he laughed.

Two winters ago, while lying on the couch with Salsa binge-watching a Netflix series, Jimmy suddenly felt light-headed. Salsa jumped into action. She wiggled her way under his head the moment before he had an epileptic seizure. The doctors said Salsa had probably prevented brain damage. Who knew dogs could detect seizures before they start. My brother-in-law is fine now. He's on anti-seizure medication, retired early, and lives like Jimmy Buffet in Mexico for most of the year.

I like to think that Salinger would curl up under my head if I was about to have a seizure. Our cat definitely would not. The cat recognizes the sound of my voice and can differentiate Neil and me from a stranger, but she chooses to ignore us. I read the other day that all animals will eventually choose to eat you if you're dead long enough and they have no food. Cats are quicker at choosing this option. A forensic study found that cats would generally wait one to two days. Scientists call it post-mortem predation. Our cat would wait an hour. When I fall asleep on the couch, I wake up to her wearing a bib and pouring ketchup on my wrist.

Dogs really do have it over cats. My Uncle Irving had a border collie that re-wired his kitchen and did my mother's taxes. My sister-in-law, Sophie, has a poodle that understands French. Salinger is responsible for digging a series of tunnels under the neighbours' lawns, and helping fellow canines escape from their feline housemates. He has been operating his "underground railroad" since puppyhood, when he first dug up Neil's garden. Our cat, on the other paw, demands a written contract and payment-in-advance before she'll even consider raising a claw to hunt a mouse.

Tortilla resembles a Rastafarian lion, Salsa (who has ridiculously cute white eyebrows), a silent movie actress. And Salinger? What you'd expect a short-haired Jack Russell resembling Christopher Plummer to look like. Salinger speaks with the slightly effeminate mid-Atlantic accent of a college English teacher. His wit picks up after my third beer. Tortilla has the deep bass voice of a retired morning-radio host. Salsa does it all with her eyes. The dogs get going once Leonard Cohen kicks in.

"It's getting so a dog can't even be a dog anymore," Tortilla argues.

"I honestly don't know what to chase anymore," Salinger complains.

"You're both being ridiculous," Salsa speaks up, imitating my sister who is concentrating on scratching Salsa's floppy ears.

"I'm serious," barks Tortilla. "If cats can be dogs and dogs can be cats, what happens to dogs being dogs and cats being cats?"

"Does that mean I get nine lives if I identify as a cat?" says Salinger, his tongue wagging.

"If you start using a litter box, Salsa, I'm outta there," warns Tortilla. He begins to dig a hole.

"No, Tortilla," my sister scolds. Tortilla stops, embarrassed.

"So what if I do identify as a cat? It's my right to choose." Salsa's white eyebrows glow red in the firelight.

"Can I come over and eat out of your litter box?" asks Salinger, perking up. He sniffs my cigarillo smoke.

"You're not serious," growls Tortilla, ignoring Salinger, who is now having a sneezing fit. "Cats already put on the *dog*. What's next? Cat shows? Tell me you're pulling my collar."

"What if I am? It's a new world we're living in. We must have respect for an animal's right to choose," Salsa explains with the conviction of Bob Barker.

"That dachshund two trailers down says it's even worse in France," adds Salinger. He pauses to lick his penis. "They only have feminine or masculine endings. No in-between. I would hate to be a confused poodle."

I think of Uncle Irving's hermaphrodite border collie.

"Dogs and cats *have* to learn to live together," says Salsa, raising a paw in solidarity with her imaginary feline friends. She attempts a meow, but it sounds like she's coughing up a hairball.

"I know how to make a cat sound like a dog," Salinger jumps in.

No takers.

Salinger remains impervious. "Soak it in gasoline and light

a match. *Woof*! Get it?" He laughs himself into a barking spasm, vomiting up grass and cat litter.

"You see what happens when you eat from the litter box," I say to him, bending down to clean up his mess. "We probably won't get invited back now."

Salinger starts to whine and avoids my eyes.

"That's right, buddy. The park owners won't put up with a dog that pukes up cat litter."

Salinger hides under my lawn chair, trying to become invisible. Surprisingly, that is the *one* thing Tortilla's and Salsa's collars can't do.

Tortilla will not let the cat debate go. He is a dog with an identity bone.

"Didn't you see *Ghostbusters*?" he growls back at Salsa. "Bill Murray warns that dogs and cats living together is a bad omen, a sign that the world is coming to an end. Can you imagine what will happen if cats identify as dogs and vice versa? Total Armageddon!" He chases his tail around the fire pit for emphasis.

"You don't have issues with your cousin Crockett being a bird dog?" says Salsa, wrinkling up her nose, beyond frustrated with her brother's narrow-mindedness.

"A bird dog scares up ducks. It isn't a cross between a duck and a dog, you twit," he fires back.

Salinger interrupts. "Do you think there will be a Trans-Canada dog-cat park? *Trans*-Canada! Get it?" he howls.

"WHAT?" snap Tortilla and Salsa in unison, turning their attention to Salinger who retreats under my lawn chair again.

"You're on your own, buddy," I say.

"It's the beginning of the end," declares Tortilla. "Soon, we'll have vegan dog food."

"We already do," says Salsa. "What back yard are you digging in?"

"My point," sputters Tortilla defensively. He shakes his four collars defiantly and renews his attack. "It's going to be illegal to mount a brother to show who's dominant. I'd be worried if I was the Littlest Hobo. We'll all become catnip addicts. Our whole relationship with our humans will change. Think of the awkwardness of everyone trying to relate to you as a cat-dog."

"What about leashes?" Salinger's ADHD is trying at times.

"What about leashes *what*?" growls Tortilla.

"We won't know who to leash or not leash," replies Salinger. He is no match for Tortilla and crawls back under my lawn chair for a third time.

"Enough with the felinophobia," my sister interrupts, gently shooing Salsa off her lap. "We should all be free to be whoever we want to be. Case closed."

"That was a dog's breakfast," says Neil.

"Dogs are the universe's way of apologizing for my relatives," says Jimmy.

Neil doesn't know how to chill at the trailer park. He works as a butler. I know it is an antiquated trade but he likes it. He used to be an English teacher like me.

"I knew I was different when I was four-years old," he says. "I had no confusion whatsoever. I wanted an Easy-Bake Oven for Christmas and a G.I. Joe."

I let out a sigh. "We all know you're more than the sum of your parts, Neil."

"And I've got the gym membership to prove it," he says.

"I got a compliment at the gym yesterday," I say to JoJo. "A guy came up to me and said, 'Your voice reminds me of Barry White.' I thought to myself, That is hot. Deep voice, sexy."

"Then we get outside," says Neil, "and I tell him, 'The guy said Betty White.'"

"Hey, out of the four *Golden Girls*, I think I'd rather be known as the one who cared about animal welfare." I give Salinger a belly rub.

"Want to know what *Reductionism* is?" Jimmy pipes in, gesturing with his cigarillo. He's trying to one-up Neil. "The First Law of Thermodynamics: you can't win. Second Law of Thermodynamics: you can't break even. Third Law of Thermodynamics: you can't stop playing."

"The Three Laws of Teaching," I say.

"So, life isn't worth living?" says Neil rhetorically.

"It wasn't for Larry," JoJo replies glumly.

It's been two weeks since our brother's strange disappearance. Grief is looking both ways before you cross the street and getting hit by an airplane. I look up at the sky. Dusk's pale tint of orange is long past. Night in the country is darker than my mood during our last teachers strike.

Who wants another drink?" JoJo asks, inviting Tortilla up on her lap.

"How about the good stuff," Jimmy grins. "Fifteen-year-old *Ron Los Valientes.*"

"Twist my *rum*ber arm," I say.

Jimmy gets up and weaves his way to his shed to find the "good stuff." My sister stares up at the stars and sighs.

"Why are dogs like a clock?" she asks, stroking Tortilla's ears.

"Why?" Neil enjoys humouring her silly jokes.

"They both have ticks."

The dogs fall asleep around the fire, Salinger nestling down on top of the outer circle of stones. It doesn't look comfortable but he doesn't seem to mind.

"How many stones does it take to make a mattress?" I ask no one in particular, watching him snore.

"How goes the new book?" Neil asks.

My sister is a successful published author, writing a series of young adult fiction novels about a vet tech named Josephine who moonlights as a spy.

"It goes," she says. "I've got Josephine stuck in a Middle East prison. She got nabbed by the military while trying to rescue a pack of street dogs being abused by a black market gambling ring. I'm trying to find a way to break her out."

"*I've* drafted an outline for a young adult novel," Neil says.

"When do *you* get time to write?" JoJo replies. "Aren't you busy folding napkins and polishing silverware for Sir Beverly Big Butt?"

Neil works for the retired president of a mining company, a genial fellow despite being wider than his three-car garage.

"When Mr. Haileybury takes his afternoon nap," he explains, "I take out my notepad and scrawl away."

"I'm impressed," says JoJo.

"It features a transgendered high school drop-out named Ziggy." Neil leans forward. "He's an insomniac. He meets a self-harming vampire named Count Cutter who has a heart of gold and is hell bent on saving the world. Together, Ziggy and Count Cutter embark on a magical quest to find an ancient crystal with the power to reverse climate change, stop pandemics, and render all weapons useless...and Ziggy's mother makes a living selling legal highs to illegal immigrants."

"Very funny," my sister replies drily, realizing Neil is having her on. He does that a lot. She's an easy target. Her face turns serious in the glow of the fire pit. "I'm getting frustrated with the young adult label. Josephine turned twenty-one in my last book. My publisher insists that's where the market is. I have this horrible feeling Josephine will turn forty desperately trying to stay a young adult."

"Like the rest of us," I muse, while examining my hands. "Thank God my liver spots vanish under firelight."

"I don't think I ever was a young adult," Neil observes sullenly, his mood shifting. The "Black Irish" and their band of sorrows have arrived.

"That's because you were already fifty at birth, Holmes," I say, managing a stock British accent. "You were ironing your own diapers a month before your christening."

"I was *not*," Neil protests. He waits a well-rehearsed beat, and then, "It was a *week* before."

The "Black Irish" pull up a lawn chair and begin expostulating. They often do.

"I taught English for twenty years," argues Neil. "I experimented with the classics to excite my students' interest and nudge them that little bit closer to becoming genuinely literate adults. Somehow I managed to do this without ever being aware that there was some quasi-psychological state which I was entirely ignorant of—and which I had somehow managed to skip myself—called young adulthood. Teenage boys will never become literate adults because publishers have decided 'young male adult readers' have an insatiable appetite for dreck!"

Neil knows how to kill a room and a campfire. An awkward silence ensues. Only the crickets continue to harmonize.

"*Un ange passe,*" JoJo whispers. Her voice is quivering. "I wonder if it's Larry."

"Larry was the expert in letting a conversation run dry," I say, goosebumps popping all over my skin.

"I wonder if he caused the silence or was attracted by it?" says JoJo, pinching her arms.

"It's a spiritual chill," says Neil. "Maybe Larry is trying to smooth things over. Let us all know he's okay. Goosebumps are the sign of a message from the departed that needs to be conveyed."

Iolanthe and Larry's ride in the lift has become famous. Even legendary Vegas illusionist David Copperfield showed up for the investigation. I look up at the sky and address the North Star. "Helluva an exit, big brother."

"No one walked over this site," shouts Jimmy from the bar fridge. "Reign in your imaginations." Ever the skeptic, Jimmy won't admit it he's afraid of ghosts. Whenever my sister and I start telling childhood stories about the haunted house across the street, he finds an excuse to call it a night.

"I wonder if Salinger is rolling over in his grave knowing *The Catcher and the Rye* is now classified as young adult fiction," says JoJo.

Salinger wakes up and cocks an ear.

"Not you, buddy," says Jimmy, "the other one."

"The water was as smooth as Glass this afternoon," I say, and we're off.

"People in Glass houses shouldn't throw ashtrays," Neil ripostes.

"Wasn't Lee's vaudeville name *Glass Tiger*?" JoJo returns.

It doesn't matter if the bath of Zooey Glass is half-empty or half-full," I say. "It's -"

"Anyone for another *glass*?" Jimmy interrupts.

A lone loon call echoes off the lake as if by way of a response. It sounds oddly like a distant freight train. We stare into the darkness and listen to its melancholy cry.

"A solitary loon on a quiet lake is Buddhism," Neil recites, breaking the silence.

"A grunge singer killing himself is Nirvana," I say. And we're back.

"Here you are, Jeeves," says Jimmy, making his rounds.

"Jeeves was not a butler," Neil replies. "Technically, he was a valet to Bertie Wooster." He politely declines Jimmy's rum. He always declines. Neil is a wise man.

"Butlers for five hundred!" I announce loudly.

"Shhh! It's past eleven," says my sister. "We're going to wake the dead." I give her a dirty look. "Sorry."

Jimmy drunkenly fumbles with his tablet, and *Thriller* fills the trailer park. He lip-synchs to Vincent Price's campy narration.

JoJo and I attempt to stand up—the trailer park starts to spin as we begin to awkwardly imitate Michael Jackson's zombie dance. Attitude is key. We stand still and glare at Neil for the first few beats. The dogs join in. Then we raise and lower our right shoulders while jerking our heads to the right and back. We shimmy away from the fire pit making a swimming motion with our arms—more of a drowning motion in my case—pelvic thrusts, foot shuffling, hunching, pivoting clockwise, and...falling on the grass in a jumble of undead laughter and barking.

"And jumble starts with J," JoJo squeals in drunken delight.

Midnight, ABBA, and the lawn-wobbling officially commence—the trailer park noise bylaw long forgotten. Two drunken early fifties-somethings and one late forties-something stumbling over divots and trying to remember moves from high school dances they never mastered in the first place.

Whoever said nostalgia's a bitch, was right.

Jimmy has an iron liver. He and the dogs are the first to greet the dawn. They are up with the chorus of mourning doves, sparrows and woodpeckers. Up with the sound of fishermen's boats, their tiny outboard motors a comforting buzz if you aren't comatose with a Mexican rum hangover. Up with more energy than any human being should be allowed at that ungodly hour.

I make my way down the tiny trailer steps three hours later.

I dreamt something out of an old melodrama. A runaway train barreled down the tracks. Ahead, on the tracks, I was tied up and unable to move. Larry sat perched in the cab of the locomotive wearing our grandfather's conductor's cap. The moment before impact, I woke up in a cold sweat. Evie would probably say I was grieving in my sleep.

"Coffee's on," chirps Jimmy. "My radio days," he says, reading my swollen brain.

I pour myself a cup, spill it on my shorts, and join him in the shed.

"I have a surprise for you," he announces with a wide grin. Jimmy reminds me of a dwarf in a Tolkien saga.

He lifts an object off his worktable. It is a small wooden gate with side hinges and a cat door just small enough so that Salinger can't fit through. The litter box dilemma solved.

We sit on his trailer deck, half-listening to Jimmy's old radio station. I still expect to hear his voice. The new announcers pale in comparison to Jimmy Rumble Thunder. The Sunday morning host crackles to life:

"On the Arts scene, the on-again, off-again auditions for the Birch Lake Little Theatre production of *Fiddler on the Roof* are on again. Now, they'd been called off due to a lack of budget. But Doug Lipsey, who is the director of the show this year, said he found a way to go ahead with the production by using sets and costumes from last year's production of *South Pacific*. And according to Doug, this is gonna be the first production ever of *Fiddler on the Roof* set in Polynesia. So Doug says, 'Get on your Hawaiian shirts, and your grass skirts, and your coconuts, and get out there to St. Matthew's United Church at seven-thirty Monday night. We wanna welcome everyone. So, if you know of any Indigenous or any new immigrant actors, have'em come on out and try for a part.'"

"In the chorus," I say to the radio. "Doug Lipsey is an ass."

Neil emerges in his bright orange swimming trunks, the ones I hate, and goes for a dip. JoJo appears in the screen doorway, eyes half-closed, and her blue denim halter-top inside out.

"That's the last time I drink," she mumbles.

She says that every Sunday morning. She then sets about

preparing her "scramble," a mash-up of cheese, bacon, eggs, potatoes, and grease. It is our traditional morning after feed.

An hour later, we're back in town.

I drop Neil off at home to install the cat gate and I pick up Jonah in time for church.

One week later, Doug Lipsey announces the casting of *Fiddler on the Roof*—an Indigenous artist from the local reserve is cast as Tevye and a Syrian elementary teacher as Tzeitel, his eldest daughter. Things are looking up in Birch Lake. And Doug Lipsey is less of an ass.

Three weeks later, my sister texts me the young-adult fiction fall-advance list. The hot ticket is the story of an insomniac, transgendered high school dropout who meets a self-harming vampire with a heart of gold hell bent on saving the world.

Four weeks later, the cat rips the stuffing out of the couch.

BUDDHA AND THE ANT POISON

We don't have wolves at the cottage.

We have coyotes.

However, the coyotes at the cottage do not howl. Well, they do, but for not for long. It's their chorus that ushers in the night, a hunting prologue, the traditional sound we associate with coyotes. But there that association ends. The coyotes at *our* cottage make odd, eerie, high-pitch frequency notes—unearthly wails overlapping, coming from each member of the pack. It is the sound of thirteen Irish grandmothers keening.

I manufactured a coyote stick from a thick tree branch. I place it on my lap when we sit around the candle pit. Forest fires, coupled with no rain and temperatures topping forty degrees Celsius daily, have resulted in a provincial fire ban. We improvise by placing small battery-operated candles in the centre of our fire pit. It is not the same.

Coyote wails are very unnerving at two-thirty in the morning. They are down by the dock. A fresh kill. I check to make sure Salinger is at the foot of the bed. Then, a new sound, as if they're sitting on the porch, having parked themselves in the wicker chairs, sitting up, hind legs crossed, munching on freshly-killed rabbits, and dripping blood all over the deck I just washed this afternoon.

At breakfast, Neil says there is no way the coyotes were on the porch.

"They were two fields over," he says.

"Since when did you become Grizzly Adams?"

"It's the echo of the lake playing tricks on your hearing. There's nothing to absorb the sound waves so the coyotes seem closer."

I hate to admit he is right. The way sound carries on the lake, conversations on the dock across the bay seem to be coming from *our* dock. Neil reminds me to keep my voice down.

"Do you want all of Muskoka to hear you?"

I have a rich baritone that, according to him, can be heard at the marina five miles away.

"Did you see any blood on the porch?"

I resent his patronizing tone. When Neil speaks to me like I'm a child I feel as though my knowledge isn't as "advanced" as his. I want to retaliate and say, "Don't talk to me like I am a child!" But that will just make me look like more of a child. Does it really matter in the grand scheme of things if I'm rarely on time, have a terrible taste in clothes, forget dentist appointments, lose my car keys, or never pick up Salinger's toys? Is God keeping a file? I opt for the mature approach instead, replying, "No," and resort to pouting.

"My point," Neil says and cuts my bacon.

I nod my head in false agreement. I'd pass an infantilization test with flying rainbow colours. I'd probably even get my maturity learner's permit. I told Neil last month that I wanted him to treat me like when we were first dating. He took me out for dinner and a movie, and dropped me off at my mother's. I'm starting to think my purpose in life is to serve as a cautionary tale to others. Unlike Neil, most of my family treat me like a god. They ignore my existence until they need something.

Is climate change leading to more wildfires? Without a drought. Neil's brother, Wing-nut, gave us strict instructions on how to protect the cottage. Neil mows the short green grass and I water it with a sprinkler that refuses to make friends with the garden hose. Evergreen trees become hazardous when their branches hang too close to the ground. Neil prunes the bottom limbs of six nearby pine trees. I rake ground fuels (leaves and pine needles) into piles and clean out the gutters. The roof is the most vulnerable part of the cottage. Neil's family put in a metal roof and double-paned windows last summer. Wing-nut mounted a searchlight on the roof that would give Batman pause.

"Is the cottage safe?" I ask while struggling with a sprinkler head.

"The fire's across the bay," replies Neil, taking the head and connecting it to the hose.

"Can it leap over here?"

"Only if the wind changes direction and it jumps to one of the islands. Or if there's a lightning strike."

"How fast can lightning start a fire?"

"Lightning fast."

Later that morning, we pick up staples at the village Foodmart. Neil checks the evacuation updates. I stop to read a notice from the regional detachment of the Ontario Provincial Police taped to the glass front door: "We have been made aware of multiple coyote sightings within the District of Muskoka. Typically coyotes are nocturnal, but it is not uncommon to see them during the day."

"Great," I sigh aloud.

"Are you coming or going, mister?" says a ten year old boy, standing impatiently behind me.

I open the door to let him pass.

"*Summer* people," he mutters under his breath, mimicking his father and grandfather.

The notice continues: "Merely seeing one is NOT a reason to call 911. However, there are certain behaviours that *are* cause for alarm. Specifically:

Coyotes carrying any product marked 'ACME'.

Coyotes dropping anvils from a hot air balloon.

Coyotes posting signs such as 'detour' or 'free bird seed'.

Coyotes in possession of a giant magnet.

Coyotes in a possession of a catapult.

Coyotes detonating 'TNT.'

Coyotes on roller skates with rockets attached.

Please call 911 immediately if you witness any of the above behaviour."

I am sure the coyotes at our place qualify.

Donny says they are singing. Donny is our handyman, or rather Neil's family's handy-man. We time-share with Neil's brother, occupying the cottage for the last three weeks of August. Wing-nut has all the boat toys. Neil and I don't even have our boat licenses. We remain dry-docked, content to sit and watch the yachts on the lake and guesstimate how much they cost. I'm pretty sure the townies regard us as the biggest losers on the lake.

Donny is a tall and grizzled local in his late fifties who cuts the grass, clears dead trees, and keeps us stocked in firewood. He drinks the summer people's scotch, rolls his own cigarettes, is fond of matching denim, digs graves, and works at the hardware store. He was Kurt Russell's and Goldie Hawn's groundskeeper until they sold their island.

"That Kurt," Donny says to anyone who will listen, "he's the real deal. Down-to-earth as they come. Talked to folks in the store, autographed their garden tools, no muss or fuss."

Donny looked after Kurt's twenty-room cottage year round: raking and burning leaves from Kurt's two-hundred maples during the autumn; shoveling the roof and keeping the pipes from freezing in the winter; re-landscaping the grounds and putting the dock in after the ice melted in the spring; and stocking the cottage for the three weeks in July when Kurt, Goldie, and their celebrity friends actually stayed. Donny was on call twenty-four hours a day during those three weeks.

"Tom's as decent a guy as you'd expect him to be," Donny loves to repeat to his regulars at the hardware store. "And funny! Why, you never seen anything like Forrest Gump doing a cannonball off the dock. Now, Steve isn't a wild and crazy guy at all. He's real quiet and just reads."

Donny's name-dropping is even more annoying after his third scotch. He reminds me of a movie extra boasting about working with "Bobby" De Niro.

The cost of food and booze for down-to-earth Kurt, Goldie and their Hollywood pals was somewhere in the neighbourhood of fifty thousand dollars, give or take a shrimp skewer. We spend five-hundred dollars over our three-week stay. Donny has not been the same since Kurt stopped coming.

When we first arrive at the cottage, I open the screen door and see summer. Neil sees dust. This year we both see ants—tiny nasty *red* ants. They appear to be living under the garden statue of Buddha that Neil placed by the sunporch. Buddha laughs merrily while the ants swarm over his belly. Buddha also laughs at my lame morning attempts at yoga.

Buddha And The Ant Poison | 59

I drive into town to pick up some ant traps. The air is filled with the smell of distant smoke from dawn until dusk. An acrid haze lingers above the horizon line, slowly getting closer. My inhaler works overtime.

Donny is the only person I know who can sleep standing up. He's part horse with the overall appearance of a molting heron.

"You got any ant traps?" I ask.

"Third aisle on the left," Donny neighs, not looking up.

I find the traps and take them to the counter. He complains about the packaging as he rings me through.

"Look at that," he whinnies hoarsely, eyes still closed.

"What?" I ask, not following.

"Look at that ant they got there on the label. Know what that is?"

"A black ant?" I say, not knowing my ant from an uncle.

"That's a John Carpenter ant."

"A what?"

"You don't know who John Carpenter is?" He opens his eyes.

"I know who John Carpenter is, Donny."

"He directed Kurt in his greatest role."

It's a Donny vaudeville routine I endure each time I go to the hardware store.

"You know what role?"

"*The Computer Wore Tennis Shoes?*"

"No, c'mon, get serious."

"*Now You See Him, Now You Don't.*"

"Okay, smart guy, very funny."

"*The Strongest Man in the World.*"

"Ya can't knock Kurt for those three. He was just startin' out. I didn't hear ol' Walt knocking on your door in high school." Donny thinks he's pretty funny. "Kurt's most famous role, c'mon."

"Alright, alright, what role, Donny?"

My summer is rapidly disappearing.

"Snake Plissken!" he exclaims, lighting up like a channel marker. "*Escape from New York.*"

"Right— the eyepatch."

Snake also has a tattoo of a cobra on his six-pack abdomen. So does Donny. Only Donny's looks like what you would imagine a snake tattooed on a skinny man's beer belly to look like. It scares children at the beach.

"Ol' Kurt was killer in New York!"

"What's your point, Donny?"

"Black ants eat wood not the sweet poison in this here trap."

"But we don't have black ants."

"But if you did you'd be in big trouble. You'd need ol' Snake to kill 'em. But not with this poison. There should be a red ant on the label. It's misleading advertising."

I pick up a plastic barbecue scraper beside the cash register and fiddle with it, wishing Donny would shut up.

"Put that down."

"What?"

"It'll melt on the grill." He snatches the scraper from me. "You gotta use a metal one. And only scrape when your barbecue is cold. Hell, even Steve knew that."

I can't see Steve Martin spending much time scraping Kurt's grill.

"Why make a plastic scraper in the first place?" I ask.

"For the Torontonians," he grins.

"I also need some clear plastic bags. I've got to bag some leaves." The dump only takes garbage in clear plastic bags.

Donny shakes his head. "We don't have any." He bends down to toss the plastic scraper into the recycling bin under the counter.

"When will you be getting more in?" I lean over the counter. He peers up at me. "Don't carry them anymore."

"But the dump only accepts clear plastic bags."

"That's right."

"And you don't carry them anymore?"

"Am I not talking to you in English?"

"But you're the only hardware store in town."

Donny hands me the ant poison. "Yup."

There is no escape from my stupid dilemma. I want to strangle Donny with a clear plastic bag.

Driving back to the cottage, I listen to the radio for any updates. When the OPP says, "nine out of ten forest fires are caused by

Buddha And The Ant Poison | 61

humans," all I hear is, "There's a coyote out there who knows how to use matches."

Neil methodically places an ant trap in the same corner in each of the cottage's six rooms. Salinger watches and follows. He places the last trap beside Buddha. I wonder if the mass slaughter of ants is bad karma. I read the fine print on the label. Ant poison kills dogs if the dosage is strong enough. Neil sniffs a trap.

"Smells like peanut butter," he says.

Salinger *loves* peanut butter. Things will become extremely problematic if he eats a trap. The cottage doesn't have Wi-Fi and I am in no mood to drive to the village internet café and enter "my Jack Russell Terrier ate ant poison" in a search engine. Neil spends the rest of the day feeding him an entire jar of Kraft Crunchy. Salinger spends the rest of the day with the runs.

The ants ignore the traps, and the smoky haze across the lake advances. I drive into town to refill my inhaler. It is not until dusk that we get around to thinking about eating. Neil fires up his brother's monster barbecue which is bigger than our garage. I can't figure out why the wing-nut assembled it fifteen feet away from the porch. It makes no sense, just sitting there like a lunar module in the middle of the property (one small shrimp for the grill, one giant grill for mankind). It has a meat-smoking sensory touchscreen that rivals NASA. The device works as a probe thermometer, which sounds disgusting, tabulating real-time data guaranteed to keep Neil occupied for the fourteen hours it takes a pork shoulder to reach maximum "deliciousness," his words not mine. By hour number seven, I'm on the road to pick up Chinese takeout from a town fifty kilometres away. The spring rolls and I pull into the driveway around hour ten. I'm in bed by hour thirteen.

Neil marinates boneless chicken breasts in peanut sauce while I watch a water bomber fly over the lake. I wave at it, hoping it will circle back and water the lawn. Neil carefully makes shallow gashes to increase the surface area of each breast before placing them on the grill. My imprecise dicing skills drive him insane. My poorly cubed carrots give him hives. I bought him a stab-proof apron this past Christmas. He ordered me a Costa Rican tea picked by howler monkeys, who presumably knew a good tealeaf when they saw one.

RRRRUMPA!

The sound of Donny's battered old pick-up truck. Salinger tries to bark but a jar's worth of peanut butter is stuck to the roof of his mouth.

"Hey, ladies, just checking in to see if the ant traps are working?"

"Take a look." I hand Neil the chicken breasts on a thick paper plate. I prefer burning dishes to washing them. The fire ban put an end to my fun. I should recycle the paper plates, but the cottage is out in the boonies. The carbon emissions generated to get to and from the drop-off depot outweigh any recycling benefits. Neil tells me I need to be recycled.

Donny returns a few minutes later.

"Want a drink, Donny?"

"Does a bear shit in the woods?"

We keep a few bottles of cheap scotch on hand for Donny's frequent unannounced drop-ins.

"Boy, that chicken smells some good."

"There's lots," says Neil, ever the gracious butler to everyone except me. He places another breast on the grill. Donny plunks himself down on a lawn chair and rolls a cigarette.

"So?" I enquire, handing him a tumbler of scotch and ice.

"Give 'em time. They're confused," Donny the ant expert explains. "Your cottage reeks of peanut butter. What'd you do? Bathe the dog in it? The ants can't tell where the traps are."

I give Neil a dirty look.

"Did ya hear about the lovesick firefighter," says Donny. "He couldn't get over his old flame." I wish Donny would spontaneously combust. I watch him casually toss his cigarette butt and miss the candle-pit. Nine out of ten, the OPP said. Donny is quickly becoming the Monday in my life.

The sun sets as Neil flips Donny's breast for the umpteenth time. He is a barbecue neurotic since becoming a butler. Last month, he fell in love with Portuguese flakey egg tarts. Flakey egg farts I call them.

At the cottage, night literally falls. Neil refuses to turn on

Wing-nut's searchlight. We have to resort to flashlights to see. I switch on my small LED torch.

"You've flipped that chicken twenty-five times," I whine impatiently. "It's not a tanning bed."

"Five more minutes."

"Are you going for some kind of record?"

"I better wash my hands," Donny announces, downing his third scotch in the space of five minutes and excusing himself.

He exchanges a quick look with Neil.

I gaze up at the stars trying to pick out the constellation of Lupus.

"Almost coyote time," I sigh.

"If ever you are chased by a coyote simply run to the edge of a cliff and stand still."

"Why?"

"The rest of the cliff will fall away." Neil snorts and laughs.

"Very funny." I hate it when he suckers me in.

As I ponder if ACME makes ant traps, I'm interrupted by a different kind of laughter.

"They're back." I leap up and grab Salinger, nervously scanning the darkness.

"It's the sound of the lake playing tricks on you again. They're miles away."

Another laugh echoes off the lake.

"There's another one. They're getting closer."

"Relax. Coyotes are mostly scavengers."

"Mostly?" I repeat the word, stretching out the vowel, testing its authenticity.

More laughter shoots out from behind the porch. I shine my flashlight into the bush.

"I can't see a thing."

"Don't panic." Neil is too calm. He is not registering the gravity of our situation. "I'll get the chicken inside, you cover me," he says. "Just wave your coyote stick and make some noise."

There is no time to argue. I scramble. My coyote stick is lying on the deck. I pick it up and begin jumping up and down, screaming politically incorrect unintelligible gibberish. I feel suitably ridiculous. Salinger just stares.

The laughter in the bush intensifies.

At that moment, Donny walks out howling. Neil joins in.

"Assholes," I say, tossing the coyote stick at them.

AROOOOOOOOOOOO!

The laughter of real coyotes cuts the air. The three of us freeze. I see their eyes glowing blue in the beam of my flashlight.

"Tonight, I'm a vegetarian." I bolt for the cottage, still holding Salinger. Donny, Neil, and the chicken breasts are hot on my heels.

"I thought their eyes were red," I say, once safely locked inside.

"Nope," replies Donny, between mouthfuls. "That's only in horror movies. Now, a rabbit's eyes glow red." He leans in. "You know what has huge, piercing yellow eyes with large black pupils that will send a chill down your spine?"

"A tax auditor." Neil's astute contribution.

"A great horned owl. But the scariest eyes you'll ever see glow green."

"My boss at the college," I say.

"My ex-wife." Donny laughs himself into a nicotine-induced coughing fit. "She left me for an Indian guy. A perfect fit. He worships cows."

I share a quick "can you please make him leave?" look with Neil. I wonder who would want to worship Donny. My best bet is an illiterate, racist misogynistic troll.

"You know what the oldest profession in the world is?" he says.

"Lawn darts," I say. "Isn't that why Snake Plissken wears the eyepatch?"

Donny ignores me. "Grave-digging. Years ago," he whispers, "people were afraid of being buried alive..."

By midnight, I want to bury *him* alive.

The scotch bottle finally empty, he weaves his way home.

It's a family tradition to celebrate Neil's birthday at the cottage. He's a pretty much a health nut except for one thing: coconut cream pie. Specifically, the coconut cream pie made by and served at The Junction, the local family restaurant and breakfast nook.

I like coconut cream pie but I don't order it in restaurants. Decades of being served gelatinous slop that bears little resemblance to the real thing has taught me to know better. To know better, that is, until The Junction. Theirs is an old-fashioned recipe made from scratch and based upon a flour thickened, pudding-like custard pie filling.

JoJo, Jimmy and the cocker spaniels always come for Neil's birthday. A week before the big day, I order the jumbo coconut cream pie with extra coconut sprinkled on top.

Jimmy takes Neil cushion shopping at a cottage store down the highway while JoJo and I slip out to pick up the pie. Fifty dollars later and we leave with a massive cardboard box tied with string.

"Sure you don't want to strap your precious cargo in the backseat?" JoJo says, cautiously pulling out of the parking lot, checking both ways about fifteen times.

"I'm not letting this baby out of my sight," I reply, gripping the string's knot tightly between my fingers and cutting off the circulation. I can feel blisters forming.

"Have you got the candles?" she continues, driving twenty kilometres under the speed limit, hazards flashing.

"Check."

"You've cleared space in the fridge?" She ignores the backlog of cars behind us.

"Double-check."

We wind up the gravel side road that leads to the cottage. Around the bend is Donny's old farmhouse. It has seen better days. Scrap metal and small engine parts litter the front yard.

In the distance, I can see Donny wrestling with a chainsaw and a log. It looks like he's carving it into the shape of Kurt Russell's chin.

He waves.

I wave back.

Then it happens.

The motion of my arm causes the box to slide down my lap towards the glove compartment.

For a brief eternal moment, the box teeters on the edge of my kneecaps, a time delay between what I am witnessing and my brain's capacity to process. Before I can react and reach for it, the pie slips out and falls onto the floor mat in what can best be described as a *Pie Hard* action sequence.

"Nooooooo!" I scream in slow-motion.

Donny looks up, puzzled.

JoJo slams on the brakes. We stare at the floor mat in shock, unable to speak. Coconut shavings are scattered everywhere.

"Oh my God," I cry. "What have I done?"

"How could you drop it?" Her eyes fill with dessert horror.

"I don't know. I waved at Donny and SCHWOOOF!"

The pie is now a custard mound covered in gravel. The aftermath of a bakery suicide bomber. I attempt to scoop the glop back into the box.

"We can get another one," says JoJo, turning the car around and hurrying back to The Junction.

The Junction does not have another pie. The lunch run finished off the last slice.

I am doomed.

"We'll figure something out," my sister says.

We race back to the cottage. We have to beat Jimmy and Neil. A flying stone cracks the windshield.

Once inside, we survey the damage. The pie will not survive triage.

"Pick out the gravel." I frantically extract pebbles from the custard.

"You're not seriously going to serve this."

"We can salvage it."

My sister digs in. "It must be a full moon," she says as she tosses another pebble into the sink. It ricochets like a bullet in a Clint Eastwood movie. We are extras in a Spaghetti Western.

I locate a mixing bowl and ladle.

"Scoop in what's left."

We plop the pie remains into the bowl.

"Stir it."

"You're nuts."

"When life gives you gravel, make a parfait."

JoJo stirs the coconut slop while I tear up the box to destroy the evidence. She is fully complicit in my pie cover-up caper.

I put the bowl in the fridge to chill and we wait. Five minutes later, Jimmy and Neil walk through the door. Jimmy tosses a bag of disposable ventilation masks on the counter.

"We're going to need these," he says grimly. "They've closed off most of the highway twenty minutes south of here."

Neil purchased six outdoor art cushions featuring popular paintings by the Group of Seven. Only in Muskoka can you buy six cushions for the cost of a mortgage payment.

Jimmy puts on one of the masks and fires up the barbecue. The haze is thicker than the smoke rising off the steaks. I can now see an orange glow across the lake.

JoJo plies Neil with alcohol. I proceed to make a series of toasts, starting with Neil's birthday and ending with a shout-out to solar-powered barbecues. The coyotes begin to howl across the lake. I drown them out, "Here's to another notch on the belt of life!"

"You need a new belt," says Jimmy, serving up dinner.

"I need a new waist."

The moment of the big lie arrives. I tell Neil I have a surprise for him—something a little "different" this year. He masks his disappointment. I serve up the coconut cream "parfait."

A few bites later.

"Why is there crust in the parfait?"

"That's what makes The Junction's parfait so unique," I lie. "They actually add bits of crust to create a whole coconut cream pie parfait out-of-body experience." My nose grows longer.

Another few bites.

Neil chomps down on a hard bit: "What's in this parfait? Feels like I just bit into a stone."

"That's nutmeg," JoJo says, jumping to my aid.

"Nutmeg?" says Jimmy. "In coconut cream?"

"Ground nutmeg," she says quickly. "I grated them myself. I must've missed a few."

"I don't taste any nutmeg," Neil grumbles.

"It's a mild nutmeg," I purr. "From local evergreen trees. Recycled Christmas trees."

JoJo gives me a dirty look. God is going to strike me down.

Then, a knock on the door.

I pray it is the Grim Reaper.

"That's got to be Donny," says Neil, removing grit from between his teeth.

"I'll get it." I am grateful for a Donny diversion for the first time in my cottage memory.

A Ministry of Natural Resources and Forestry officer stands patiently on the stoop with a clipboard.

"Good evening, folks," says the Officer, "I'm afraid I have to ask you to evacuate these premises. The MNRF has enacted an emergency management plan this weekend due to poor air quality. We are evacuating everyone in the area as a precaution."

The nutmeg is quickly forgotten and "Escape from Muskoka" commences, minus the misanthropic services of Snake Plissken.

The wind changed direction and the fire did leap to the island in the middle of the lake. Four cabins and a lighthouse were destroyed.

The day after Neil's birthday, the blessed rains of Toto's *Africa* finally washed the land. After three weeks of battling the forest fire from the air and ground, over eight hundred firefighters succeeded in containing it. Not a broken heart in sight.

But the cottage didn't burn down and we returned a week later. In the meantime, the ant traps worked and the cottage spared any further infestations and diarrhea.

A few locals believed Donny started the forest fire when his ATV caught fire after he flipped it in a ravine on the August long weekend. After a brief investigation, the Ministry determined that dry conditions and several lightning strikes were to blame.

Donny erected his Kurt Russell carving at the marina and enjoyed the notoriety of being a social media star for two days.

During the evacuation, I went on a Costco run and bought enough clear plastic garbage bags to last until Neil's eightieth birthday.

Neil got even with me for my coconut cream pie birthday fraud. On the evening of our return, he hid a Bluetooth speaker under the bed, set the timer on his iPhone, and, at three in the morning, a hundred coyotes blasted me out of my wits.

My screams woke up Africa.

Neil didn't stop laughing for eight days.

WHITE TUNA ON MARBLE RYE

Our mom was dying.

It was the Sunday night of the Labour Day weekend. She was ninety-one years old, and she knew she was going to die in the next twenty-four hours. Don't ask me how she knew, but she did. She had complained of back pain during the summer. At our August long weekend family barbecue, we all noticed she'd lost a few pounds, but it didn't cross our minds she might be sick. Mom's weight fluctuated depending on the season.

She decided she wanted to die after Larry's strange disappearance.

"I need to make sure Larry and Rose are okay," she said just last Thursday. She sipped a mug of hot tea prepared from an ancient tea bag. Like our father, she could make a tea bag last a week.

"Isn't that God's job?" I said, pushing a scone around on my plate. It was harder than a World War I trench ration. On further inspection, I discovered the Metro plastic container had expired weeks ago.

"God's got enough on his hands," she replied. Then winked at me. She didn't ask about her husband—there was no point. Our father had become a four-year old child by this time. There was nothing any of us could do for him but wait and watch him slip away one lost memory at a time.

After Larry and Iolanthe vanished in the lift, their bizarre story spread rapidly across the internet. The following day, paranormal investigators, journalists, exorcists, the police, and Randy Quaid invaded the town. Hotel and motel rooms were booked to capacity. The police treated the disappearance as a missing persons case, but ultimately came up empty-handed. The church's notoriety grew like Martian red weed, clogging the airwaves, interrupting Sunday services, and causing widespread theorizing. Attendance increased by the walker-full. Old sick seniors, lonely parishioners, and the dying, wanted to go up the miraculous lift to God. They, however, did *not* vanish. Larry and Iolanthe remained a mystical one-hit wonder. Rumours amongst the elderly in the congregation bandied about in hushed tones, behind closed minds. Perhaps Larry was actually the Grim Reaper, as evidenced by his poor singing voice. Clive, terrified he was next on the list, quit the church and moved to a village outside of Yellowknife.

"A silver lining," I shared with Jonah.

Ironically, six months later, a pack of wolves devoured Clive while he was snowshoeing to church. It became a national news story: Parishioner Literally Wolfed Down.

All my siblings, all of my mother's siblings, all of her grandchildren, and most of my cousins, were in Mom's tiny cramped apartment she shared with her nineteen-year old tabby cat, Franny. Tacky landscapes in cheap frames covered the walls. My mother rescued paintings from Value Village that she felt needed a home.

Mom had three younger brothers: Uncle Clarence, the eldest, who'd worked for the town driving dump trucks in summer, graders and snowplows in winter, and purchasing a new Buick each September. He sold his used car-me-downs to my father. One time, shortly before he retired, Uncle Clarence got caught stealing from his road-worker job.

"When the police arrived at his door, all the signs were there," joked my Uncle Charlie.

Uncle Charlie was my mother's favourite—a good-humoured punster who still runs the small general store in the village of Juniper, just down the road from the trailer park. Sitting in Mom's living room, I told him I spotted a moose on the way to the college earlier that morning.

He replied, "How do you know the moose was on the way to the college?" Uncle Charlie was the Buddha of bad puns. He never missed the opportunity to deliver a corny knock-knock joke.

Uncle Clayton, the most romantic of the bunch, left home early with a thirst for adventure. He built hydro towers across the Canadian Shield until he settled in Hearst.

"Always fight fire with fire," he used to say to us when we were growing up, which explains why he was thrown out of the Hearst Volunteer Fire Department. The three brothers raised large families, even larger bellies, and enjoyed long lives of relative blue-collar discontentment.

We all knew Mom was dying because she said she was. Her doctor wouldn't say.

I volunteered to run and grab dinner for everyone, so I asked Mom what she wanted. I figured she should get dibs on the menu since it was going to be her last meal. But I knew she'd be ambivalent because our mother never demanded anything.

Mom left her family farm in her early twenties and got a job as a receptionist in a small business office in town. She enjoyed her little life of freedom and independence. She had a gathering of girlfriends, drawn from her secretarial pool at work, and they would often go to a barn dance on a Friday night. My mother often wore a fancy magenta dress for the occasion. Patio lanterns hung from the rafters amid the sweet smell of 1950s innocence that longed for a hotter smoke. The dances were packed with community revelers from the ages of twenty to sixty, all there to let off some steam after a grueling work week and get lost in the glow and promise of the summer lanterns and a three-piece combo. In the isolated farmland counties of Northern Ontario, where it was not uncommon to drive thirty miles for groceries, barn dances helped tie people together. They were a dry affair so the men discreetly hid mickeys of rye in their blazer pockets. My mother and her girlfriends sat at a table near the back sipping lemonade, smoking, and checking out the young men, all while waiting for a daring country Romeo to find the nerve to approach and ask for a dance. The men, meanwhile, leaned against the walls in groups of fortified bravado, invariably sneaking out for swigs of liquid courage before beginning the long walk to the girls' tables. This was the simple mating ritual of my mother's generation.

One Friday evening in May of 1952, a tall, devilishly handsome man in his mid-twenties approached my mother's table and politely asked her to "cut the rug" with him. Sporting long sideburns and the greased pompadour fashionable at the time, the scent of

White Tuna On Marble Rye | 73

scotch and nicotine fresh on his breath, he had warm blue eyes that sparkled with mischief. He looked and smelled like trouble. His gentle manner proved otherwise. He two-stepped our mother around the barn floor for hours, making her laugh at his silly jokes and relentless energy. Their dating had begun.

Marty "Mo" Boyle grew up on a farm only a few miles down the road from my mother's homestead, although their paths never crossed until that fateful Friday barn dance. During his teenage years, my father worked as a movie theatre usher and stock boy in the hardware store. By the time he met my mother, he was dreaming of running his own ad agency. Two summers later, they were married. Boyle Media & Marketing and my brother Larry followed soon after. Mom quit her job and set about raising six kids while our father hit the road and sold display advertising for bus shelters and billboards across the North. If our father still had his wits, he could tell the marketing department at the college a thing or two about branding.

From the beginning of their marriage, our mother put everyone else's wants and desires before her own.

"What would you like, Mom?" I asked, expecting an "anything is fine" response.

"A toasted tuna sandwich from The Cozy Kettle," she whispered. "Lettuce and tomato."

"Okay, sure," I said.

"With light mayonnaise, white tuna not dark, on toasted marble rye, not light rye, not dark rye, and no pumpernickel."

"Um, that's pretty specific."

"It's Sunday, Mom," said Evie. "They might not be open."

"So, you'll call."

We did call, but there was no answer at The Cozy Kettle, a restaurant I hadn't heard my mother even mention before. I told her they weren't answering the phone.

"Call again in ten minutes."

Okaaaay.

I stopped myself from saying it aloud. Some things are better left unsaid, which I generally realize right after I've said them.

Bartering over tuna was not how I envisioned my mother's final breaths. I looked to Evie who nodded with deference to Mom. She had her concerned analyst face on, the one that there was no point in arguing with.

When we were finally satisfied that The Cozy Kettle was not doing any business that night, we decided on The White Pine Diner, because allegedly they also made a nice tuna fish sandwich. I took everyone's orders, most of which were grilled cheese sandwiches. I leaned down to be face-to-face with Mom. The muscles in her neck had stopped functioning months ago so she was permanently hunched in a downward position. I had to get down on my knees to see her face.

"I'm going to go get your tuna sandwich now, Mom, okay?"

"Is it on rye?"

"Yes, marble from White Pine."

"I don't think I want a tuna sandwich from there. Did you try The Cozy Kettle again?"

"We tried, there's no answer," said Evie, taking Mom's other hand.

Meanwhile, JoJo went to the kitchen to look for a can of tuna and maybe a petrified loaf of marble rye in the bread basket. Neil followed her to scour the fridge for light mayonnaise. She found two slices of hard, stale marble rye in the basket, and popped them in the toaster. She checked the cupboards. Nothing. She heard a mew and looked down. The last can of tuna was in Franny's bowl, half-eaten, mixed in with her kibble. JoJo considered her options.

"You can't be serious," said Neil, shutting the fridge door, mayonnaise in hand.

"I am never frivolous," responded a female voice.

"What?" said JoJo.

Neil searched for a second. He looked down at his iPhone.

"It's Siri talking back."

"That's creepy. Turn off your phone."

Back in Mom's bedroom, Evie repeated, "There's no answer at The Cozy Kettle."

"Can you get me a tomato, bacon and cheese sandwich then?"

White Tuna On Marble Rye | 75

"Um, okay, uh, that's a different thing," I said. "The White Pine might not have that."

"Okay, just a BLT then."

"Yeah, that's just a *different* different thing, Mom. Listen, I'll do my best. I'll find you something, alright?"

"Okay, whatever, I'll try their tuna sandwich, as long as it's not on light rye."

"Okay, I'm on it."

She grabbed my elbow. Her grip still worked. She looked me right in the eye.

"Do they have a turkey sandwich?"

"I don't know, Mom. I didn't memorize the menu. Do you want a turkey sandwich? Because I can find you one, it's no problem."

"No, I don't want to put you to any trouble. A tuna sandwich is fine."

"Fine."

JoJo and I arrived at The White Pine Diner and, after scraping the front of my Forerunner on their parking barrier, the first thing we noticed was NO TUNA SANDWICHES scrawled on the chalkboard behind the counter. It was a diner for Chrissakes—what kind of diner didn't serve tuna fish sandwiches?

"No tuna?" said JoJo, her voice cracking.

"Owner is allergic," replied the cashier, matter-of-factly.

But they *did* serve an all-day breakfast sandwich with egg, tomato, and cheese.

"Why not go with her second choice, right?" said JoJo, mumbling *please* under her breath.

So, we got Mom that.

Half an hour later, we were chomping away on our sandwiches, an apartment full of happy people, gastronomically at any rate. Everyone that is except Mom.

"This is not a good tuna sandwich," she croaked. Poor choice of words, I admit.

Somebody (me, I guess) forgot to tell her that it was a breakfast sandwich she was eating. Of course, she had eaten almost all of it by then. I leaned in and explained what happened. How I got her what I thought was her second choice.

"Well, it doesn't taste like any tuna I ever had."

"Because it's not tuna, Mom."

Our mother did not die that night.

The next day the same crew and a few close friends assembled in her apartment again.

"Is something burning?" she asked, scrunching up her nose.

"No, Mom, nothing's burning," I said. My mother has smelled something burning since 1958.

It was lunchtime, so once again I offered to organize some food. I asked my mother what she wanted. After all, it might actually be her last meal this time.

"A toasted tuna sandwich from The Cozy Kettle."

This Cozy Kettle thing had become an obsession.

Unanswered calls went out to The Cozy Kettle, several of them. I commissioned Neil to physically go there and knock on the door. He came back with the dreaded news. They were closed for renovations, and unless "renovations" was re-hanging a picture frame, my mother wasn't going to live long enough to see how they spruced the place up.

A congressional subcommittee was quickly formed to find a replacement restaurant and, after much deliberation, Nick's, a Greek restaurant across town, was chosen. No one in our family was actually Greek. I once sent a query regarding our family tree to one of those ancestry websites. Turns out you only need to go back fifteen generations before you find out you are related to everyone.

Nick's served tuna fish sandwiches, so what wasn't to like. I got the orders straightened away amongst my extended family, except for one.

"Mom, no marble rye, do you want it in a pita or on flatbread?" I was still on the phone with the derisive owner.

"A bun" she said.

"You have buns?" I asked into the phone.

"Pita or flatbread," he barked at me as only an Old World Greek restaurant owner could.

White Tuna On Marble Rye | 77

"Mom, they don't have buns. Pita or flatbread?"

"Get it from somewhere else then."

"Mom, everyone's already given their order. We've got twenty-three sandwiches coming. I've been on the phone with this guy for half an hour. If I cancel now, he's going to send over a wooden horse."

I sent Neil to Metro to buy a loaf of marble rye. When the sandwiches arrived, Evie performed the surgery. She gave it a valiant effort, but we lost some tomato and lettuce in the transference. The pickles never stood a chance.

Everyone loved the sandwiches, except one. Yet again, she ate the whole thing.

I leaned in.

"You hated it, didn't you?"

"Let me ask you, who paid for this disaster? Can I at least pay for this disaster?"

A few hours later, I was holding her trembling hand as she asked me what time it was. I was practically prone on the floor looking up into her hunched frame. I checked her Florida-shaped clock on the bedroom wall. "Two-twenty."

She raised a cocky eyebrow. "Almost D-Day."

I smiled back. "Yeah, almost D-day." Then, "Is there anything we can do for you, Mom?"

"You could've brought me a better tuna sandwich."

I swear on my life.

Everyone within earshot cracked up.

A few hours later, she was dead.

Uncle Charlie put a hand on my shoulder.

"Two tuna fish pass by a submarine," he said quietly. "Big Tuna Mommy says, 'Don't be scared little Tuna, these are canned humans.'"

My mother provided me with love as endless as her voicemails. I saved her last message, three days prior to her death, five-minutes long, pleading with me to pay my overdue parking fines before I wound up in prison, and offering me her loose change to do so. I kept the message and listen to it whenever I miss her. I still haven't paid my parking fines—I need to give her *something* to worry about, to keep her around. I find dimes all over the house.

One day, she will stop leaving me change. Then what?

OVER EASY

1. Chicken Scratch

I have the signature of a four-year-old child.

My U's could easily be mistaken for O's, my L's look like E's and my Y's, well, my Y's don't look like anything—at least not anything you could remotely trace back to our modern alphabet.

My handwriting resembles a garden of weeds and it's been that way for as long as I can remember. My fifth grade teacher, Mr. Browning, took me aside one morning. "You know, Rudy Boyle, you'd probably make a great serial killer." Now, you'd think if someone displayed certain personality traits typical of most "great serial killers," it would warrant a call to their parents or the local authorities. As it happens, Mr. Browning wasn't referring to anything related to my personality. At least not directly. I wasn't one of those kids that tore the wings off of grasshoppers or shoved firecrackers downs the throats of bullfrogs. I knew a big kid who did that, and forced me to watch. It was like viewing a Vietnam War newsreel.

No, Mr. Browning was referring to my handwriting and how it slanted drastically to the right. He'd read a report on graphology which apparently showed a glaring similarity among the handwriting of serial killers. Like my own, they all tend to slant rightward to the extreme. I prefer to justify slanting to the right as showing more openness to new experiences—both for life and other people, though not as a cannibal. Sure, my sister, JoJo, has a feisty tongue but that doesn't mean I want to eat it.

"Maybe he meant *cereal* killer," she said. I smacked her with a box of Cheerios.

Classical graphologists are a stuffy lot and find it difficult to countenance poor handwriting of any kind. Apparently, I cross my letter *t* too low on the stem, meaning I have ego- strength issues. As a result, I refuse to sign cheques, my driver's license, or birthday cards.

JoJo wouldn't allow me to be a witness at her wedding because of my illegible scrawl. Last February, Neil and I flew to Mexico to visit her and Jimmy on my winter break. The Customs Officer inspecting my passport suggested I try an X instead.

Neil asks me if I've discovered fire yet.

JoJo describes my handwriting as "looking like a drunk spider dipped in ink and tap dancing." Jonah says my postcards take on new meaning every time he reads them.

I find myself having to apologize for my illegible scrawl. Along the lines of: "Please excuse my handwriting as I wrote this in a moving car."

My low-crossed *t*'s might have made me serious doctor material, except for one tiny insignificant detail: I faint at the sight of blood. I also faint whenever a welding student turns an English assignment in on time. Doctors' sloppy chicken-scratch kills more than seven-thousand people annually. I recently took a prescription for hemorrhoids into my pharmacist. She told me it was impossible to read my doctor's chicken-scratch and asked me what my symptoms were. I discreetly mimed the words "swollen anus" so that the woman behind me couldn't hear.

I read an article in *Vanity Fair* about a chicken admitted to medical school, thanks to its poor handwriting.

My sister, Evie, the Jungian analyst in the family, says that my sloppy signature is a public expression of my true self, that my indecipherable scribble means I don't want others to know what's going on in my head. I don't tell her I have the inner voice of a super villain, that I hatch plots worse than the Joker, threatening to take over Neil's garden and kill all his gnomes.

I asked Evie if signing with a big X would be an improvement. She responded: "An 'X' doesn't mean you're simple, but it does indicate self-destructive tendencies." I deleted her e-mail and lit up a cigarette.

I was one of those kids in the late 60s who had their hand repeatedly whacked by a ruler. Each time I picked up a pencil crayon with my left hand, Mrs. Scissors, my third-grade teacher, whacked me. Hand whacking is an old medieval custom, much like burning witches and sheep buggering. Lefties were in league with the devil. Forcing lefties into using their right hand was known as re-training, or re-teaching in some circles. Re-whacking was closer to the truth. Whacking remained school policy until it was officially banned in 1971. I couldn't wait to rub the news in Mrs. Scissors' face with my left hand, but she died of a heart attack before I had the chance. Her husband found her lying on the left side of their bed, her left hand clutching her chest. History books are filled with self-loathing, secret lefties who punished weaker lefties, thinking they had the upper hand.

Left-handedness is still viewed as a "natural disadvantage" by the Catholic Church. I looked into the Old Testament. Left-handed people appear on three occasions in Judges and Chronicles: the story of Ehud's assassination of the Moabite King, the seven-hundred Benjamites who shot a sling with deadly accuracy, and the two-dozen ambidextrous warriors who came to support David in Hebron. All of these stories of left-handed people, curiously enough, involve members of the same family, the tribe of Benjamin. Maybe Benjamites were genetically disposed to left-handedness at birth, or maybe the trait was encouraged in soldiers to give them a strategic advantage in combat, much like a left-handed baseball pitcher up against right-handed batters who weren't unaccustomed to fighting "lefties." Then again, maybe Biblical writers simply enjoyed a good joke—the name Benjamin means "son of my right hand." It was probably a right-handed disciple, jealous of a left-handed disciple's superior recruitment skills, who started the left-hand whacking craze.

Our brains are cross-wired, meaning the right hemisphere controls the left-handed side of the body. At least, left-handers can boast they're in their right mind.

Years ago, during a visit to my optometrist, she informed that my left eye was dominant. Usually, dominance is on the same side, but I was cross dominant.

"You were meant to be left-handed," she said.

"Tell me about it."

The thing is, now I am hopelessly right-handed with a slant. I wonder how many serial killers were born left-handed? At *least* my handwriting hasn't killed anyone.

2. The Relentlessness of Chickens

Early last summer, Jimmy arrived home after a round of golf to discover JoJo had purchased some chickens—four chaos-fueled feather demons. She was wholly unprepared to raise chickens. Oh, sure, my sister had done loads of intense internet research about what to feed them and how to house them and how to ward off foxes and how to keep the fluffy little cluckers entertained so they didn't peck one another to death. I googled "chicken bloodlust" for a fun (read horrifying) time.

JoJo figured it out. Or, rather, she winged it and cobbled a plan together to at least keep them alive for the summer. Jimmy cobbled a coop together. JoJo and her chickens got to know each other. She gave them new names (Jenny, June, Jasmine, and Jill). JoJo gradually adjusted to her new crack-of-dawn-in-the-middle-of-the-summer-wake-up call and the midnight heart-stopping panic of wondering whether she shut them in for the night. She discovered which one liked hugs (Juliet) and which one thought she was the boss (June) and which one was the escape artist (Jasmine) and which one was just an idiot (Jill).

Then there were the prison breaks. Led mostly by Jasmine (who, like her *Aladdin* namesake, grew weary of her palace confinement), the quartet managed to negotiate their way pretty much around all of Jimmy's attempts at keeping them within their allotted part of the garden and proceeded to destroy his vegetable plot, and peck at the back door for dog treats. In short, they got cocky.

Then there were the chicken droppings, the metaphorical elephant in the chicken coop.

"It's great fertilizer," JoJo explained to me over the phone. She sounded nasally.

"You got a cold?" I said.

"No."

"Are you allergic to your chickens?"

"No?"

"Are you pinching your nose?"

The smell of chicken dung was disgusting and cleaning it was even worse. Chickens can live for *ten years*. I looked up how much crap they can produce in that time: 4,800 pounds! Jimmy had hoped his life would be free from cleaning up feces until he was a grandfather. He didn't count on four grand-chicks.

"The key to keeping the shit from smelling, whether in the coop or run, is to keep it dry," Jimmy shared over a beer one Saturday night. "I cover the poop board—"

"Poop deck?" I interrupted. I had visions of chickens in British naval uniforms.

"It's the floor of the coop. I cover it with sawdust and pine shavings. I scoop the shit off the poop board daily and dump it into a compost pile, which I cover with a tarp." A chicken farmer at their trailer park suggested he add agricultural lime to the shavings. He's planning to switch to sand and some kind of "deep litter method" he's devised.

JoJo had her moments of chicken regret. She grew tired of having clumps of crap stuck to her rubber boots. "Who decided it would be a good idea to take on the responsibility for four extra lives?" June ignored the rhetorical question and pecked my sister's cheek.

But.

JoJo did love the little drumsticks. I'm surprised she didn't homeschool them.

I dropped by last week to pick up some eggs. Chickens are so *weird*. But cute, in a way. They have very fluffy bottoms. They look like they're wearing Victorian bloomers when they run. They get excited about cucumber. They make all sorts of funny little noises and kind of purr when they're happy. Jimmy, who made a firm statement when they first got them that he would help with the upkeep but would not be touching or petting the poultry, was now an unashamed chicken hugger. Juliet turned into a tea cozy when she sat on his lap.

Granted, they're mostly idiots, but they're also curious and persistent and remarkably brave when faced with Salsa and Tortilla, the odd fox, and one unfortunate squirrel who got nipped in the tail and chased up a tree for stealing their feed.

Then there's the magic.

I didn't know chickens were magical. Well, they are.

Every day, around mid-morning, they bustle into the coop and make a little nest and sit there cooing and warbling for a bit and then...Bork! Bork! Bork!

Behold their creation. Every day. Little ovals of magic.

Scramble 'em!

Boil 'em!

Fry 'em!

Poach 'em!

Put 'em in a cake!

Whip 'em into meringues!

Ooh, maybe a quiche!

Mix 'em with mayonnaise and put 'em in a sandwich!

And if your day goes to chicken shit, tomorrow they'll pop out another one. Just like that.

3. No Spring Chicken

WHOOOO-OOO-OOOOOO!

JoJo had arrived. From the loud blast in the driveway, you'd think she'd pulled up in a diesel locomotive. You'd be wrong. It was a lime green Smart Car. Her *Smartie* I call it. I swear she washes it in the dishwasher. Jimmy installed a four-trumpet train-horn kit. It was his idea of a practical safety feature for the microscopic car. He also attached hockey cards to the wheel spokes to make the *Smartie* sound as though it had a bigger engine.

My sister opened the back gate, making her usual old Hollywood entrance, a bottle of chardonnay and two plastic wine glasses precariously hanging from her right fingers. She does that whenever she wants something from me, the value of the vintage in direct proportion to whatever pound of flesh I am obliged to supply.

"I have a favour to ask," she said, coyly removing her black Ray Bans and plopping herself down on one of Neil's brightly-painted Adirondack chairs. Her last favour involved me accompanying her to a new age wind-dancing class. Twenty naked women danced around me in a circle waving bed sheets, chanting the names of their deceased grandmothers.

"Want to go to a wedding with me?" She said it casually. As if asking me to pass her a Kleenex.

"No!" The consonant bounced off my tongue before my mouth could form the vowel sound.

"A friend of a friend at the trailer park is getting married next Saturday." She poured me a second glass and adjusted her chic retro headscarf. She wears it whenever she's driving her *Smartie*. Audrey Hepburn first wore it in her 1963 film *Charade*. My sister bid for it on eBay a year ago and won.

"What about Jimmy?" I said.

"He has his radio station alumni golf tournament."

"Can't you RSVP 'maybe next time'?"

"Nope."

"Where is it?"

"East Feral."

"NO!"

East Feral is a small village in mountain country. It used to have a gas station until the new four-lane highway bypassed it. Now it's a ghost town, except for an old church and a community hall. Stories of inbred children running through the bush were a staple of our childhood. There is no West Feral.

"C'mon, don't be such a chicken. It's field research for my next book."

"An English teacher and his sister are buried alive in a field by some creepy mountain kid with weird eyes."

"Stop being paranoid. Child murderers in East Feral are an

urban legend."

It is amazing how siblings forget your phobias, allergies and cell phone passwords.

"There is no way I'm going to a wedding in East Feral."

"See you in a week," my sister shouted, pulling out of the driveway before I could protest further, her laughter punctuated by the sound of thwacking hockey cards.

A week later, and I was driving her Smartie to the wedding, all because I cross my t too low on the stem.

For a brief fleeting moment, behind the wheel, I felt environmentally responsible. We came around a bend; a cock was resting in the other lane. He was sound asleep, his chest feathers heaving in and out, his comb resting on the asphalt. Was he on the lam? We took a sharp curve and met a large black SUV in the other lane. As we passed each other, JoJo reached over and shouted, "Cock!" by way of a warning. The man driving the SUV in turn yelled back, "Bitch!" and rounded the curve.

RREEEEEEEE! WHAAM!

Screeching brakes and what sounded like an SUV hitting a guardrail.

"If only men would listen," my sister sighed.

I learned that while researching JoJo's chickens. Cocks were great at protecting hens, but too many cocks led to violent fights in the roost. Many cocks were killed once they were identified as male. I envisaged Herod as a chicken farmer, slaughtering chicks, fearing a cock would grow up to become the messiah. Other cocks were turned loose to fend for themselves. For every Rusty that found shelter and success hanging in a book bag on a children's television show, there were thousands more who wound up homeless on the streets. Many went missing—victims of KFC organized crime. The one cock that ended up ruling the roost was one lucky cock indeed. The fellow on the road was not that cock.

"When Audrey Hepburn was running amuck with Gregory Peck in Rome," my sister complained, sliding her sunglasses back up on the bridge of her nose, "*and*, if she spotted a cock on the street, she would've yelled 'cock!' to warn an oncoming scooter."

The word "rooster" didn't enter the English language until the Puritans landed at Plymouth Rock. It originated as a euphemism to avoid the sexual connotation of the original English "cock." Despite concerted Puritanical effort, the phrase, "rooster-a-doodle-do," never caught on.

We arrived in East Feral an hour later. The church was bordering on collapse. It had not been used in months—well, not by any adult humans. I swiped that thought left. The windows were boarded up. A large gaping hole in the roof. Across the dirt road was the community hall. Its weather-beaten old shell a victim of fate and peeling paint, crumbling plaster, damp-soaked walls, rotting joists, and sling-shots.

The parking lot was full. My sister instructed me to park on the gravel shoulder.

"The bride and groom came together," she said, gesturing to an old beater in front of us.

"How do you know?"

"Tobacco spit on both doors."

My sister fancies herself an amateur sleuth, the fallout from writing pet detective fiction for a living. I examined the dark, ugly hardened tobacco stains on the rusty pick-up's passenger door from the safety of the *Smartie's* front seat, although feeling safe inside a Smart Car is not humanly possible.

The tobacco stains were as black as fresh tar. The door looked like a miniature oilrig had exploded down it.

"It depends on what you're chewing and how often you spit," my sister said. "Chewing loose leaf or plug tobacco creates a dark midnight spit. The longer you go in between spits, the darker the spit."

"Since when did you become the big expert on chewing tobacco?"

"Research for the *The Terror of the Tobacco Terrier.*"

The Tobacco Terrier was a big hit among twelve-year old girls. I ducked my head and squeezed myself out of the *Smartie.* I approached the beater and looked through the open passenger window. The interior reeked of tobacco, sweat, sex, and fried food.

"Did they have the seats removed so their kids could fit in?" I said, pinching my nose.

Upon entering the hall, we encountered a sign that read, NO SHIRT NO SHOES, NO SERVICE. Except, the word SERVICE had been crossed out with a Sharpie and replaced with the word PROBLEM.

JoJo signed the Guest Book while I studied the column of signatures. The majority of signatures were right-slanted. I decided to kill time and go on the hunt for serial killers.

Joining the long line-up at the bar, I counted four John Deere caps, two backwards baseball caps, eight pairs of cowboy boots, and enough bad suits to put polyester on the endangered species list. Serving drinks before the ceremony was never a good sign. I leaned in to eavesdrop on the conversation unfolding before me.

"Livestock is a poor choice for a wedding gift," a large man in a cowboy hat was saying to a skinny man in an ill-fitting suit.

"These are good laying hens even if they aren't no spring chickens," replied the skinny man.

"Like Hank's new bride."

"How much older is Carla than Hank?"

"Twenty-five years," the large man whistled. "Hank was the ring-bearer at her first marriage."

"He's going to wind up one hen-pecked rooster." The skinny man clicked his teeth. I thought of the cock on the road. It made me think of the homeless person by the ATM machine downtown who made me think of Jonah who, in turn, made me think of Freud. "Every man eventually marries his mother," Freud wrote. I pictured Oedipus at a dinner party. "Hi, nice to meet you, I'm Oedipus, this is my significant mother." No doubt, she had a Freudian slip under her dress.

"The prenup mentioned chickens," continued the large man in the cowboy hat.

"Sound thinking," said the skinny man in the ill-fitting suit. "At least they're keeping the same in-laws."

As I paid for two white wine spritzers, the bartender gave me a suspicious look. I felt like Jimmy Stewart in the tavern in Pottersville ordering a mulled wine for his guardian angel. I made my way back to my sister and found her listening to the bride-to-be.

"I've been planning this wedding since I was eight," said Carla. She polished off her beer and gushed back to the bar.

"It's her second marriage," said my sister, watching her go. "When Carla was twenty, the groom wasn't even born yet."

"So I've been told." I handed her the second spritzer. "Her bridal veil looks like it's made out of a window screen."

"It's not only cost efficient but also a proven fly deterrent."

I looked up at the lighting fixtures. The shadowy corpses of hundreds of dead flies were visible in the overhead shells. They hadn't been cleaned in years—the same was true for the shells.

Hank, the groom, joined us, a double-rum and Coke in hand, sporting a powder blue leisure suit and matching cummerbund. I counted the dead flies.

"Real spiffy, Hank," said JoJo. "You washed your bowling shirt."

"Cut it out." Hank drooped like a hat brim.

"Hey, Hank, how many chickens would it take to change that lightbulb up there?" I said, pointing to the closest shell above us.

"You're a strange one," said Hank. He slouched off to join the large man in the cowboy hat and the skinny man in the ill-fitting suit at the bar.

"Wait until he opens the skinny guy's wedding present," I said.

Meanwhile, Carla had joined a tiny woman propped up against the entrance wall.

"Who's that?" I said.

"The bride's mother," said JoJo.

A fashionable (by East Feral standards) woman in her mid-seventies, Carla's mother was well on the way to Margaritaville, and dangerously close to pressing her shoulder against the fire alarm.

"Follow me," JoJo whispered, and off she went.

I was preoccupied watching Hank. He was emphatically pointing in my direction then up at an overhead shell while arguing with the skinny man in the ill-fitting suit.

JoJo slunk through the crowd undetected, hiding behind pillars, zigging here, zagging there, freezing whenever Carla looked over in her vicinity. The D.J. should have put on a Henry Mancini record. My sister, by the age of eleven, was the undisputed champion of "Red Light, Green Light" four years straight. She stopped within hearing distance of Carla and motioned for me to join her.

"You drew your eyebrows too high," hissed Carla's mother. She had the reedy voice of a weed-whacker.

Carla looked surprised.

The minister arrived, a small badger of a man with darting, nervous eyes and an unsteady gait.

"How would you feel presiding over a wedding where the groom won his wife's wedding ring by knocking down three milk bottles with a baseball?" said JoJo.

"Impressive."

We watched as the minister attempted to speak to Carla and Hank. He looked as if he was about to cry.

None of the guests could figure out which side of the room to sit on. They were all members of both Hank's and Carla's families. The skinny man in the ill-fitting suit solved the problem by separating them based on whether they drove a Ford or a Chevy. My sister and I sat at the back.

The minister took his place at the front of the room. Hank and the large man in the cowboy hat stood beside him.

"Last call for drinks before the ol' ball and chain goes on!" the bartender shouted. The assembly rushed the bar. It reminded me of a cattle drive, even though I've never seen a cattle drive, except for in the movies, or at an all-you-can-eat Sunday Chinese food buffet.

The "Wedding March" crackled over the sound system.

The minister asked Hank for the rings.

The large man in the cowboy hat handed the minister his beer. "Here, hold this."

Hank and Carla exchanged rings. The minister quickly concluded the nuptials and bid a hasty retreat.

There was no dinner, rather Carla's sister and her kids served up snack trays with Vienna sausages, coleslaw, nachos, and potato chips. A Dairy Queen ice cream wedding cake in the shape of a tractor was rolled out in a wheelbarrow decorated with daisies. The table centrepieces consisted of ashtrays and emergency candles.

I continued on my manhunt for serial killers.

"What's the difference between the red and green coleslaw?" I overheard the skinny man ask the large man while hovering over the snack table.

"They're both red except for the green one."

During the snacks, guests went up to a microphone to share stories.

Carla's father, a retired livestock vet, stood up to read the opening toast, which he had scribbled on the back of a paper serviette. He held it in his left hand. Several times during his speech he halted, overcome with what I assumed was a moment of deep emotion. But after a particularly long pause, he announced, "I'm sorry. I can't seem to make out what I've written down." Looking out into the crowd, he asked, "Is there a pharmacist in the house?" He was a man after my own scrawl.

JoJo and I slipped out to the parking lot to share an emergency smoke.

"I found out Hank's brother invited his new online girlfriend to the wedding." JoJo loves a juicy bowl of steaming gossip almost as much as I do. "She said yes, if he'd pay to fly her here. So he wires her the money, shows up today, and she's a no-show."

"She cat-fished him." A Russian online bride scam took a lonely colleague at the college for five thousand bucks.

"Not even a phone call," said my sister.

There was a commotion at the hall entrance. A woman burst in screaming. "You cow-tipping useless piece of deadbeat shit!" She grabbed the wedding cake and chucked the melting tractor at the newlyweds.

"It's Hank's ex-fiancée," my sister whispered.

And that's when the skinny man's wedding gift broke free from their cages. Two police officers arrived just as the chickens attacked. JoJo and I managed to escape with only a few minor pecks and scratches.

"I told you it'd be weird." I said as we drove around the infamous cock bend. The guardrail was smashed to bits. No sign of Gregory Peck.

A rooster's legacy, like weddings in East Feral, was a mug's game.

KOOKABURRA SITS IN THE OLD BURNT TREE

You never know what you'll think about on a winter morning jog.

One Saturday in early January, I was out huffing and puffing, and found unwanted thoughts of the apocalypse popping into my head. Nothing too heavy, just the destruction of the earth and every living thing on it. Specifically, I was thinking about climate change, *the* hot topic, the global calamity that's threatening to raise temperatures and sea levels, increase the intensity of storms, droughts, forest fires, potentially destroy civilization, and make Northern Ontario winters bearable.

I want to do something about climate change, but as I ran, lumbering along to nowhere in particular, imagining how I would survive in an apocalyptic wasteland on a stockpile of Spam and Nutella, I knew that the pictures on social media of polar bears trapped on melting ice aren't working.

Most people don't even realize how bad climate change is going to get. They know glaciers are melting. They know weather can be weird. But they don't get it. They haven't spent time paying attention to climate research. My niece, Esther, spends that time. She can tell us all a thing or twelve-thousand about it. Esther is the only child of my sister, Evie, and her husband, Roger. Esther wants to be reincarnated as a renewable energy resource to combat climate-change. Last Christmas, she asked her parents for a climate refugee. Moreover, she just launched a GoFundMe page to raise funds to support edible six-pack rings that sea turtles can ingest without dying. Did I mention my niece is only thirteen-years old?

According to Esther, the global warming outlook is much worse than originally predicted. Which is pretty bad when they originally predicted it would destroy the planet.

Prompted by my concern for my niece's future, I decided to

read some legitimate climate research. Two nights later, I lay awake imagining the world turning into a wasteland. I walked down the street with Viggo Mortensen, pushing a shopping cart. In another nightmare, I sported a Mohawk, wearing leather, and fighting Mel Gibson for gasoline.

What I do know is we can't let the Earth disintegrate into some real-life version of *Waterworld*. Water covers everything and Kevin Costner is a half-fish who never once picks up a baseball. I sat through it twice in the nineties. I had to make sure it was *that* bad. I'd rather not relive that terrible apocalyptic mess of a movie for a third time.

The IT guy at the college thinks technology will protect us from the environmental crisis.

"Imagine the not too distant future," he says, 'anti-hurricane missiles' and 'ice cap rebuilding' apps." Just last month A&W announced its new "Beyond, Beyond, Beyond Meat Burger," the off-off-off Broadway equivalent of eating a shred of lettuce.

The soothsayers of ancient Rome have become today's climate scientists. But society has reached a saturation point for gloomy and threatening science-centered discussions. The real question for those concerned about climate-change should be how to make it as interesting as Leonardo DiCaprio's dating life. If it weren't for an iceberg sinking the Titanic, we wouldn't have the movie that launched Leo into stardom. It is little wonder he's so passionate about climate change, he owes his entire career to an iceberg.

Climate change will not be easy to solve. This isn't people picking up after their pets. Tackling climate change requires a concerted effort, bigger than winning World War II, bigger than the moon landing, bigger than the four-story mural of Greta Thunberg in San Francisco painted by a group of her teenage fans.

My niece, Esther, loves Greta. She has pictures of Greta plastered on her bedroom walls. She wears her hair in identical braids. If she could, Esther would change her surname to Thunberg. She's even taking Swedish lessons.

Esther is frustrated by my seeming lack of basic knowledge. She gave me a science lesson last weekend when Neil and I were in the city to celebrate my sister Evie's fifty-fifth birthday. I haven't visited an ashram before, but Evie's home sure smells like what I imagine one to smell like. Healing oils drip on lamp bulbs, sacred herb incense smokes in every room, and there's enough smoldering frankincense to give Buddha an asthma attack. Evie goes to yoga class five days a week. She plans vegan meals a month in advance. I eat cake over the sink so I don't get crumbs in my bed.

Evie's home has all-white interiors—"breathing rooms" she calls them. Her Scandinavian overstatement is no understatement. Only the planters and plant-stands add a splash of colour. My sister rearranges the furniture daily in order to refresh the energy of the house. Everything in its proper place, no clutter, except for Evie's second husband, Roger. A game of acid-induced Pictionary ended my sister's first marriage. She drew a feather and her husband thought it was a leaf. It cost him the game and their marriage. Roger is a harried over-worked estate lawyer with a bad haircut, and a penchant for death, particularly life insurance policies. He's actually addicted to them. It's the fear of the unknown future written down and made known.

"Where there's a will, there's five hundred relatives," he jokes wearily.

Roger does most of the cooking, out of fear of getting accidental food poisoning from Evie. I feel for Roger, trying to satisfy my sister's ever-changing diets and his daughter's ever-shifting interests. Last year Esther wanted to be a Buddhist (reincarnation was making a comeback), the year before, a wizardry student at Hogwarts (he had to track down a dragon's scale for her for Christmas.)

Roger has been suffering from chronic existential dread since the 70s. On the outside he looks relatively normal, but on the inside he's trapped on the Titanic. He blames his illness on globalization.

"When you see how other people are living in horrible places like Syria, but you're still pissed off that the barista forgot to add ginger to your ginger latte, eventually the cognitive dissonance gets to you," he said over a latte at *Starbucks* last Christmas. "It's like... you know your latte is meaningless in the face of a limitless global supply of suffering, but you're still mad." He stared into his artfully branded coffee cup for a while, and I couldn't help but wonder if the frothy beverage was staring back at him.

If anxiety were a superpower, Roger would be so powerful he'd make Superman look like Aquaman. When I was eight-years old, I used to wet the bed. I lay awake at night wondering if there were bathrooms in Atlantis, or did Aquaman just swim around pissing freely. Later, I thought my father was secretly Aquaman, until I realized he just liked taking us to Red Lobster. With the likely probability that we'll all wind up underwater, Aquaman could very well solve the problem, except for the fact that he's a comic book character and bound by no actual laws of reason, physics, or reality.

The stress finally got to Roger and he bought himself an emotional-support turkey. Mr. Gobble, as named by Esther, is a Royal Palm, a breed not known for its tastiness but one that could easily make the cover of *People's* sexiest-poultry issue. His plumage is primarily white, but many of his feathers are accented with a tip of jet black, giving him a Frida Kahlo vibe.

Usually, the only turkey you see on a commercial airliner is the kind that's sandwiched between two slices of bread. Roger and Mr. Gobble made headlines when they boarded an Air Canada flight together last autumn. Domestic turkeys can *only* fly on jets. Otherwise, they're flightless. I learned that watching the Thanksgiving episode of *WKRP in Cincinnati*.

Roger pushed Mr. Gobble through Pearson International Airport in a wheelchair.

"You're taking this bird on board with you?" the flight attendant asked, unable to mask her surprise.

"Yes, I am," Roger replied with a frozen smile. He handed the young woman two boarding passes. Mr. Gobble flapped his wings in distress, dispersing a good amount of down into the air, and let loose a series of loud, rapid gurgling sounds, not unlike the electronic beeps that Roger's hybrid car makes when he's too close to the curb.

"Did you talk to the airline?" the attendant asked.

"Yes," Roger lied.

"Does your turkey have all his shots?"

Kookaburra Sits In The Old Burnt Tree | 97

"Yes." Robert proceeded to show her a list of Mr. Gobble's immunizations. "And he has a five-star Thanksgiving life insurance policy. Do you need to see that?" The attendant shook her head, wishing she'd stayed in college.

"How much does he weigh?" asked the man in line behind Roger, no doubt envisioning Mr. Gobble on a plate with a side of cranberry sauce. Passengers gathered in the aisle, taking selfies with Mr. Gobble until he snapped.

"Ooolulllu!"

"Easy boy," Roger whispered to calm the turkey down. "He's my therapy animal," he explained to the other flight attendant. His smile hardened. "Do you want to see the letter from my therapist?"

The flight attendant quickly ushered Roger and Mr. Gobble down the aisle.

"Is that a real turkey?" a woman asked as they passed by her.

Soon the jet was taxiing down the runway. Mr. Gobble sat in the window seat nervously tucking and untucking his wings, eyes fixed on the air traffic control tower.

"Easy buddy," said Roger, sliding in beside his turkey, anxiously crossing and uncrossing his legs.

"What kind of emotional support do you get from him?" asked the aisle-seat passenger.

Mr. Gobble gobbled loudly.

"OOOLULLLU!"

"It sounds like your emotional-support animal could use an emotional-support animal," the passenger snorted.

Depending on his mood, a turkey's head and neck will either turn red, white, or blue if overly excited, or a combination of the three, if really upset. Mr. Gobble's head turned purple.

"He doesn't look so good," said the passenger. He motioned to a flight attendant. Mr. Gobble started to shake his head and bang it against the glass. "Is he having a seizure?" the passenger asked.

The flight crew determined Mr. Gobble was "too stressed" to fly so Roger and his emotional-support turkey were forced to disembark the plane. Roger and Mr. Gobble were the subject of social media jokes and memes for months.

Esther gets along fine with Mr. Gobble. She reassures him he'll never wind up on a platter. That turkey has scored. It doesn't even wear a diaper indoors.

Roger prepares a birthday dinner of seaweed and mint per Evie's request.

Esther illustrates for me why melting sea ice doesn't cause sea levels to rise, but melting land ice does. It's a lesson most elementary school kids learn with a glass of water and some ice cubes. After the addition of the cubes, the water level rises and then spills over the brim of the glass.

She wipes the kitchen counter top dry with a towel. My face lights up.

"Wait a minute! Global warming, giant towels. Problem solved."

"*Var allvarlig, Farbror Rudy.*"

The Swedish language is curiously clipped. It gives off a lovely melodic quality when a Swede is speaking it. Esther sounds more like a German toddler with a fake Baltic lilt, cute yet annoying, like an animated cartoon character.

"The excess water just flows down the edge of the Earth. Did you know the flat earth society has members around the globe?"

"*Det ar inte roligt.* Climate denial isn't funny, Uncle Rudy. Look at the horrible brush fires wiping out vegetation all over the world."

"They're just plants."

Esther can't take a joke.

"I can see carbon dioxide in the air," Esther says, which I know is impossible.

"Carbon dioxide is a colourless and odourless gas."

"I see what other people can't see. I see how it flows out of chimneys and how it changes the atmosphere to a landfill."

I say nothing.

"Imperial Oil is the largest crude oil producer in Alberta." Esther adopts an even more defensive tone than her usual defensive tone. I only know Imperial Oil for its gas station, Esso. And its NHL hockey player stamps. As a kid, I collected them all. Every time our father filled up at an Esso he'd come home with a booklet with six stickers in it. I kept mine in a special Esso wallet. They were the only hockey card produced that showed Gerry Cheever wearing his famous mask. Esther needed a similar muzzle.

"Imperial Oil is headquartered in Calgary," she argues. "Exxon Mobil is headquartered in Texas. The Calgary-Texas conspiracy. Exxon contributes twenty-million dollars annually to the Alberta economy which is why lobbyists are against climate change legislation. The government's inaction increases Exxon's share price. Exxon then uses that money to influence politicians."

I can barely count to ten on my fingers.

"Esther is at the top of her Grade Seven class," Evie beams, her eyes becoming animated. "She can be anything she wants to be."

"You're so weird, Evie," Esther snorts. "Why should I worry about university or having a job? We're in the middle of a major extinction event. Do you really think I need a degree if the Earth is dying in twelve years?"

"She's got a point," Roger says, rolling one eye. "Think I'll call it quits with the practice, cash in my RRSPs, and make solar-powered barges for polar bears."

"Don't patronize me, Roger," Esther says, drawing her eyebrows close together. I hate it when kids address their parents by their first names. Becoming a parent is a beautiful and rewarding experience— it's almost as good as not becoming one.

"But, you have to admit, Esther," I reason, coming to my brother-in-law's defense, "what comes most naturally to environmentalists is doom and gloom."

To illustrate my point, I reference the systematically stacked books on the coffee table in the living room: *Learning to Die in the Anthropocene: Reflections on the End of a Civilization*, *Requiem for a Species: Why We Resist the Truth about Climate Change*, *Storms of my Grandchildren: The Truth about the Coming Climate Catastrophe and Our Last Chance to Save Humanity*.

Those were the lighter titles.

Esther plows on. At times, she has the personality of a Tonka toy. "At age twenty-three Oprah was fired from her first reporting job," she says bluntly. "At age thirty, Harrison Ford was still a carpenter."

"How do you know who Harrison Ford is, Esther?" asks Neil. "You weren't even born yet."

"Don't be ridiculous," she replies. "He's a climate crusader. He's the International Vice Chair for the Global Climate Action Summit."

"He's a hypocrite, Esther," Neil says. "His private plane collection alone includes two gas-guzzling corporate jets. Not to mention nine motorcycles and six gas-powered cars. His whole lifestyle depends on fossil fuel energy, yet he goes on about his commitment to fighting climate change. He's all one big *Indiana Jones and the Fossil Fuel Lie*."

"Okay, Boomer." Esther turns to me. "What they all have in common is that *they* had time to find success because climate change wasn't an issue for their generation. Although it should've been. Me? Probably no time."

"Okay," I say, playing devil's advocate, "suppose we can do something about global warming now, but what if we find out in fifty-years that the researchers made a mistake and that climate change doesn't exist?"

"Then we will have improved air quality in all major cities, gotten rid of noisy and smelly cars, cleaned up toxic rivers, and destroyed dictatorships funded on money from oil for no reason." Esther arches her back the way our cat does when she wants her litter changed. "But *you* people want to walk rather than drive towards a solution."

"But isn't walking preferable to driving?" Point for Neil. I swallow a laugh.

"Do you know why they call us Generation Z, Uncle Rudy?"

"Because you're more absurd and nihilistic than Albert Camus?"

"*Because* we'll be the last ones left if we do nothing about climate change."

"I don't know how to solve climate change," I shrug. "Other than convincing Christian Conservatives that the rising temperatures turn people gay."

I know how to get Republicans to care about climate change," says Neil. "Blame it on the poor."

"I'll know global warming is real when hot water comes out of both taps," I say, trying to lighten the mood, "and, when I go outside, my shadow stays inside."

Banging her fist on the table, Esther pulls out a list from the back pocket of her fashionably-ripped grey designer jeans, retailing for two hundred and fifty dollars at Diesel. She slides her chair back and stands up in contempt. "I've cancelled our trip to Belize."

Evie chokes on a piece of seaweed dirt.

"The jet fuel for the return trip will cause more damage to the atmosphere than driving our car ten minutes a day for a year."

"You cancelled our trip?"

"Yes, Evie."

"When?"

"You really should change your security code."

"You hacked into my tablet?"

"Your cancellation insurance covered it."

I close my eyes and pray for Mr. Scott to beam me up.

"*And* I donated all your Air Miles to Dingo Aid."

I catch Neil's eye. He shakes his head—now is not the time for a Meryl Streep joke.

Esther turns to confront her father. "And you should get rid of your car, Roger."

"It's a Prius," he sputters.

"We don't need a car in Toronto. We have public transit. Ride your bike."

"In the freezing cold," Roger scoffs.

"All you need is a pair of fat tires."

"I'm not cycling in the snow."

"Five million kangaroos died in Australia and you won't cycle in the snow."

"No, I will not." Roger puts his eco-friendly sock down, as much as he is capable of putting his sock down. He accidentally brushes against Mr. Gobble who is sleeping under the table. The turkey wakes up with a startled cry.

"OOOLULLLU!"

"Do you know how many koalas have been burnt alive?"

Maybe next year Esther will want to ride horses, or listen to Selena Gomez.

"I didn't start the fires," Roger says, his chin trembling.

"Billy Joel did," I say. Neil kicks me under the table.

"No, you didn't Roger, you *all* did."

"But isn't the cause of the wildfires arson?" asks Neil, coming to the defense of all reasonable men over the age of fifty.

"The government deliberately flung Australia into the global disinformation spotlight," argues Esther.

"I've given five thousand dollars to Australian Relief." Evie steps up to the plate. "*And* I sent you to that global warming summer youth conference for your birthday. On an electric train."

"And I appreciate that, Evie, but it's not enough."

"It's not enough?" My sister starts to cry. Her birthday is officially forgotten.

"Nowhere near," says Esther. "That's what Greta says."

"Greta this. Greta that," Roger exclaims. "Everything for the Greta good." He is rapidly becoming his own environmental disaster in the making.

Mr. Gobble is shaking. His head and neck turn a bright purple.

Esther climbs up on her chair. "Greta is making a difference to climate change!"

"Sure she is," Roger fires back. He is redder than the reflection in a firefighter's visor. "Every time she comes on TV, one million people switch it off. I didn't rob you of your future. I'm not the villain here. I donate to Greenpeace. I got rid of all our plastic bags. I've replaced our lights with LED bulbs. I installed a Smart thermostat. I planted a cedar hedge. We compost!"

"We still live in a white privilege household that's double the size of what we need. Our carbon footprint is disgusting."

"So, I suppose you'll be putting our house on the market," Roger says with a dark facetious shrug.

I want to tell Roger to quit while he's behind.

"Don't be ridiculous," Esther laughs. "It's Evie's birthday."

Kookaburra Sits In The Old Burnt Tree | 103

A general sigh of relief around the table. Mr. Gobble quiets down.

"Good," my sister sighs, regaining her composure.

"At least that's something," says Roger, getting up and clearing the dinner plates.

Esther sits back down and we eat dessert in silence. A vegan chocolate cake as dry as a Yahtzee cup.

"I'm selling it tomorrow."

Ba-bang!

"You put our house on the market?" says Evie.

"You are not selling this house, young lady," says Roger "If you're so concerned about your carbon footprint, you can sleep in the garage."

"Roger, please stop," says Evie, flashing a brittle smile.

"No, I will not stop." Roger's lips pinch together. "Esther, for all I care, you can sail to Australia on a carbon-neutral raft and sleep with a smoking kookaburra."

Esther triumphantly holds up her iPhone. "Twitter's going to love this." She doesn't miss a trick that kid. Publicly shaming your father. I don't think that's in the Greta playbook.

"I will not be black-mailed by a thirteen-year old zealot," says Roger. "Even if she is my daughter. Your internet privileges are cancelled."

Esther pockets her phone, reaches into her other untorn pocket, and reveals a slip of paper. She hands it to her mother. "Here's the receipt."

Evie nervously clears her throat. "For what?"

"I ordered solar panels and a windmill for the backyard."

"Did the wild fires melt your brain?" Roger clasps his knuckles so tight they turn white.

"Hush, Roger." says Evie, turning to Esther. "We don't have a backyard, honey. We have a plot. This is the Annex. No one has a back yard."

"You will once you tear the garage down."

"No car, no need for a garage. Makes sense to me," I say drily, refilling my wine glass.

"Don't you start," snaps Roger. He looks at Evie. "Your daughter is out of her mind."

My sister doesn't respond. She attempts to hum her mantra, and frantically begins lighting incense about the living room.

"Your eco-fascism has gone far enough, young lady." Roger is cracking like a melting iceberg.

"You ever hear the sound of a mother wombat screaming, *Roger*?"

"Go to your room!"

"EEEEAAAAAAKKK!"

Esther lets out a high-pitched scream. Not Swedish, more like a raunchy turtle.

"EEEEAAAAAAKKK!"

I wonder what a mother wombat would make of it.

"EEEEAAAAAAKKK!"

I text my audiologist instead.

"OOOLULLLU!"

Mr. Gobble joins in.

"EEEEAAAAAAKKK!"

Esther faces off against the turkey.

"OOOLULLLU!"

Mr. Gobble is convulsing on the floor.

"EEEEAAAAAAKKK!"

"OOOLULLLU!"

"EEEEAAAAAAKKK!"

"OOOLULLLU!"

Who knew rock bottom had a basement.

"EEEEAAAAAAKKK!"

"OOOLULLLU!"

"EEEEEE—" Esther stops mid-wail. Then. "What do pedophiles and climate change deniers have in common?"

SCREECH!

No one says a word. We are each digesting the word *pedophile* coming out of a thirteen-year old's mouth.

"They both enjoy fucking the next generation."

Esther storms out of the room. I have to say, as exit lines go, it's right up there.

"Language," shouts Evie, impotently from the living room.

"That's enough, young lady," Roger yells, spilling his coffee, and wiping out most of North America on his Planet Earth place mat.

I'll be searching for Dryland with Kevin Costner.

BOTOX AND THE BRONTOSAURUS

I wish I had the teeth of a brontosaurus.

The brontosaurus did not chew her food. Her chisel-like teeth swallowed plants whole. My dentist reminds me to chew my food before swallowing. I also grind my teeth. According to dental paleontologists, so did the brontosaurus. It is a subconscious action—the jaw clenches and the upper and lower arches of the teeth rub against each other.

I was not aware that I ground my teeth until my partner, Neil, woke me up in the middle of the night. At first, he thought the harsh gnashing sounds were Salinger's snores. Or a raccoon in the attic. Perhaps a guerilla army of crickets under the bed.

Stress and anxiety are the usual causes of grinding. I admit I have been depressed since my mother's death—I miss her long and winding voicemails. Moreover, I have a lot on my plate at home. Neil has become obsessed with his ancestry and recently discovered that he and I are seventh cousins, dating back to the Elizabethan aristocracy. He was a Lord and I was a Jester. Some things never change. Psychologically, I find it hard to have sex with a cousin unless I play the banjo, have one tooth, and live in East Feral.

At the college, I'm fighting a losing battle against the collapse of the English language. It isn't my students' inability to properly use a comma that sends me into a punctuation coma, it's their apathy.

Three solid reasons for eleven rounds of nocturnal teeth grinding. I feel guilty when I compare my plight to that of the brontosaurus. She had to worry about predators with twelve- inch sharp teeth and the possible extinction of her species. Come to think of it, so did I.

The following week I took my first sick day in years and went to my dentist to get a mold made for a mouthguard. The brontosaurus did not have a mouthguard; she didn't need one because she replaced her teeth very rapidly, going through thousands in her lifetime. The average brontosaurus replaced a tooth every thirty-five days. The process was continuous; as the worn crowns were shed, other new pristine teeth took their place and the root of the tooth was absorbed. Grinding problem solved.

Evolution is not kind to teeth. Any brontosaurus genetics I might have inherited disappeared generations ago. Otherwise, I could've made a fortune in tooth fairy stock and retired at the age of forty.

Evie emails me unsolicited helpful quotes. Apparently, Carl Jung was the first to theorize that too much of the dinosaur distorts the civilized man and, conversely, too much civilization makes sick dinosaurs. He actually said "animal" not "dinosaur," and was referring to the shadow-side of human nature—which makes a lot more sense when you think about it—but my sister prefers to mix her species. Evie firmly believes that civilized people in the western world are uncivilized and grindingly sick. I cannot disagree. It is more than just the fall of the English language. "It is sexting, selfies, and TikTok," her last e-mail read. "Global narcissism is destroying us."

My dentist resembles the Bohemian novelist, Franz Kafka, big rubbery ears and all. He wears a necklace under his green dental scrubs made out of human teeth he's pulled. I worry I'll be sitting in his reclining chair someday and a giant cockroach will enter the room and rip out a tooth. Maybe the cause of my teeth grinding is a fear of my dentist.

The last time I was at Dr. Kafka's office for a filling, he was in the middle of telling me how important it is to floss when his dentures fell out of his mouth, and hit me on the head. Dr. Kafka does not exactly inspire confidence. Lying in his examining chair, I imagine him metamorphosing into his true insect self. Whenever the hygienist opens the door, I expect him to run and hide under the rinsing sink.

"It's not brain surgery, unless I slip," he jokes cryptically in that thick German accent of his, picking away at the crown on my back bottom molar before preparing the mold.

CRACK!

A small piece of the crown breaks off. "Not good, Mr. Boyle, you're going to need a new crown."

Crowns are expensive. Moreover, they aren't covered by my college benefits package.

"Can't you just do a tiara instead?" I say, able to speak because Dr. Kafka has momentarily removed his scaler from my molar.

He ignores my quip and sticks his latex glove further in my mouth. It is a raspberry-flavoured glove designed for children. Under normal circumstances, I like raspberry—pie, jam, tarts, basically anything. But an artificially flavoured latex substitute being rammed down my throat is another story.

"Can you guess the taste?" he says. He sounds like an overly enthusiastic third-grade teacher who just got a new issue of *MAD* magazine, translated into German.

Dr. Kafka always asks me questions when his hands are somewhere in my mouth. When I answer in gibberish, he laughs, "What's wrong, dentist got your tongue?" He puts his ear to my mouth and acts surprised. "I can hear the ocean!" he guffaws. My dentist is a frustrated stand-up comedian.

"You have a lot of decay, Mr. Boyle," he says removing the glove. "Are you flossing regularly?"

"Every day," I lie.

I have not flossed since the day of my last teeth cleaning four months ago. I strive to floss daily but fall short of my lofty goal, not because I am lazy or can't manage the proper technique, but because my bottom teeth are crooked. I shred dental floss the way Moby Dick shredded whalers. Growing up, my father was too cheap to pay for braces. There is a big difference between frugal and cheap. My dad was cheap. He used the same coffee grounds for a week. His dentist's nose resembled a mashed-in eggplant. He moonlighted as an amateur boxer and took one too many blows to the head. He convinced my father that, if he pulled the correct tooth, the rest of my teeth would naturally fall to the right, lining up in formation—the dental equivalent of a Rockettes kick-line. Crowding problem solved at half the price. He pulled the tooth and the remainder of my bottom teeth fell to the *left*, leaving them more crooked and crowded than they were before. The inside of my mouth, to this day, resembles a nineteenth-century tenement apartment. It is like having twenty-five Irish immigrants living in my gums. I am still afraid of stupid people.

My zealous dental hygienist is a super flosser. "Hug the neck of the tooth," she screams while ramming her elbows inside my mouth. She gets so far below my gum line I think she's going to discover oil.

"I brush my teeth all the time," I tell Dr. Kafka, sounding like one of my students explaining how they studied for days but still managed to not answer a single test question.

"What end of the toothbrush are you using?" he deadpans.

Dr. Kafka makes me feel like I am the missing link of dental care. I don't have tartar; I have fossilized stone. You could construct a brontosaurus skeleton out of my plaque.

I am his captive audience of one, subject to his dentist babble whenever the dental hygienist steps out of the room: "Your molar is like bad sex," he whispers hoarsely in my ear, "If it hurts, pull it out."

He creeps me out. I leave in a hurry without having the mold taken or snagging a complementary toothbrush, making up an excuse about being late to proctor an exam.

"Did you order one hundred green tennis balls from Amazon?" Neil says, as I walk through the front door, a half-hour later.

"No." My teeth start to grind and it is not even noon yet.

Salinger pretends to read the newspaper. I have to remember to change the password on my tablet. Last month he hacked into my Instagram account.

I plunk myself down on the sofa. "I'm through with Dr. Cockroach."

"Keep your friends close, and your 'enamels' closer," Neil replies.

"Very funny." I am not in the mood for more dental humour.

"You should try Botox," Neil says nonchalantly.

"What?" My grinding comes to an abrupt stop.

"I looked into it while you were visiting the Cabinet of Dr. Caligari," he says smoothly.

"I don't need my lines and wrinkles removed." Well, I do actually. "I need my teeth to stop grinding."

"Botox blocks the nerve signals to specific muscles. The injections inhibit the muscle movement in your jaw." He sounds like one of those fake physicians in commercials. All that's missing is a white lab coat.

I put on my teaching voice. "You do know Botox comes from the word 'botulous?'"

"And your point is?" he responds briskly, scrolling on his phone.

"You know where botulism comes from?"

"Rotten sausage. And you're being a silly one."

"It's the poison found in bad meat. It can paralyze you."

"You're overreacting."

"It can kill you."

"That's only in rare cases. If you use too high a dose. Botox is no more dangerous than laser eye surgery or flying to Mexico."

"Which is why I wear glasses, take a sleeping pill, and book an aisle seat next to a safety exit."

Neil shrugs. "You hate Dr. Cockroach, right?"

"Yes." He's backing me into a corner—of a sofa cushion. "So?"

"Botox will relax your jaw muscles while you sleep so you stop grinding your teeth," he says. "The injection is effective for six months. A fifteen-minute procedure and it doesn't affect chewing, talking, or eating. Piece of cake."

"When did you become the big Botox expert?" It hits me. "*You* are using it." Before he can protest, it's my turn to back him into a sofa cushion. "You're getting Botox injections."

Then it *really* hits me—Neil has barely moved his mouth in months.

"No wonder you never age."

"I was going to tell him," he confesses to Salinger who looks away and licks his penis.

"You're not Dorian Gray, you're Boris Botox."

"I didn't intend to keep it a secret."

"What, that you've been injecting your forehead and cheeks with poisoned sausage?" And I wonder why I have trust issues. "Just when were you planning on telling me?"

"I knew this is how you'd react."

"How else would a sane person react? Have you ever watched a sausage go bad?"

"It's not a big deal, Rudy"

"Not a big deal? You've been lying to me, Neil."

"Don't get your speedo in a twist. Just because I didn't tell you doesn't mean I was lying."

"Equivocator!"

"Will you calm down?"

"You're worse than Macbeth."

"You'll grind your teeth to dust."

"How long has this been going on?"

He spills the Botox beans. "I've been going to a specialist for a year."

"A year? No wonder you look like Simon Cowell. How much does this little fountain of youth of yours cost?"

"Four hundred and fifty dollars." He pauses, avoiding my eye. "Every four months."

"And now you want to turn me into Courtney Cox?" I manage a smirk.

"I *want* to save your teeth so you're not wearing dentures before you're sixty."

My grandmother always took good care of her teeth—she kept them by her bedside in a glass of water.

I read up on the history of Botox on the internet. First found in some rotten blood sausages back in 1820, the maniac who discovered it went on to inject himself with varying amounts of the poisonous organism to see what it would do. He found that it caused paralysis, which could prove deadly. He was the first posthumous recipient of a Darwin Award. Sixty years later, someone brought a bad ham to a post-funeral dinner party in Belgium and six guests died as a result. Another mad scientist caught wind, did some research, and eventually all of the different strains of botulism were sussed out and named.

From there, governments tried to figure out a way to use it as a weapon. During World War II, some evil geniuses devised a scheme to have prostitutes sneak botulism capsules into the cocktails of high-ranking Japanese military personnel, but the plan never materialized. The prostitutes gave them syphilis instead.

Then, in the late 1970s, a post-hippie scientist lights up a joint and says to his lab assistant, "Hey, remember that paralysis stuff from a hundred years ago? Let's chill on the warmongering for a second and see if we can do anything kind-hearted and revolutionary with this?"

Then he did.

The first major medical use of bad sausage toxin took hold in the early 1980s. It was tested as a treatment for cross-eyes. Botox, the toxin's new clinical name, relaxed specific muscles which controlled movement in the eye, reducing the misalignment. An accidental side effect occurred: frown lines and forehead wrinkles disappeared. Faster than Jennifer Grey could say facial paralysis, the American Food and Drug Administration approved Botox for cosmetic use. Canada's lines and wrinkles followed suit. Lawyers and politicians turned to Botox to stop their facial expressions from giving away their lies in court and government.

The closest I've ever come to a skin care regimen is lowering the bulb wattage in the bathroom vanity light. My real hesitation with Botox comes from not wanting to look weird: waxed, stony, or eerily airbrushed. Unlike myself.

A week later I make a phone call to book an appointment with Neil's specialist for an anti-grinding Botox treatment. His plastic surgeon, a confident handsome man in his early forties, injects my jaw muscles. He speaks quietly, "Want me to fix those crow's feet while I'm at it?"

I'm having a low self-esteem day; the creases in my forehead are getting deeper, my wrinkles are breeding, so...

Evie said I fell under the spell of the Halo Effect: I equated the doctor's good looks with actual goodness. I did that enough times in my youth to disastrous effect, so you'd think I would have known better by now. Apparently not. "You aren't going to turn me into a Kardashian?" I respond with a halo-loving grin.

"I'll be using this new 'Tom Cruise' Botox," he grins, filling a needle. "Top Gun."

"I'll pass." The last thing I want is to look like a plastic scientology freak. "How about just a few hits of the same stuff you use on Neil?"

"The 'Bradley Cooper' it is. I can also inject some into your scrotum to stop your testicles from perspiring."

I can't tell if he is joking with me, so I pass. I am too embarrassed to admit my balls sweat like two baseballs in a shower.

He pokes me twice between my brows, three times above them, and six times around my crow's feet. Some of the shots hurt, some I do not feel at all. He boasts of a light steady hand and subtle technique. He turns my forehead into concrete. It feels heavy and numb, like my mouth after a filling.

Botox takes up to a week to become fully effective. At first, I don't notice any difference. However, slowly I see my face begin to change. I stare in the mirror; my wrinkles are barely visible. By the following Friday my forehead is preternaturally smooth. I look like Lord Voldemort.

Unbeknownst to me, Neil's doctor also gave me a brow lift that left me with embarrassingly-winged eyebrows, a bizarre hybrid of Maleficent and Jack Nicholson.

I try to blink.

Nothing.

I try to open my mouth.

Nothing.

My smile has gone terribly wrong. It drops in the centre, giving me a strange, slightly sinister curve. My left eyelid starts to droop. The asymmetry is slight, but to me, it is glaring. I look like a Picasso painting come to life.

I take to staring at my shoes.

It gets worse. A few days later, my left eye closes shut. I can't open it no matter how much I concentrate while looking in the mirror. I take to wearing an eyepatch, telling colleagues and students that I've had surgery on a sty. I phone Neil's doctor. He does not return my calls. I send him dozens of photos of my face, all of which look the same. I am trapped in my own skin.

My expressions are essentially crippled. I am a different person; a woefully dispassionate man whose smile I do not recognize. I can't show outward disgust even if I want to. At best, I appear "nice" and "vacant," two descriptors I despise and actively shun. At worst, I look like a mannequin.

I receive a terse email from Evie. "There's evidence that not being able to express empathy through mimicry and mirroring inhibits the ability to *feel* empathy. Good luck, Narcissus."

Neil and Salinger react to my frozen face by laughing so hard, they collapse on the living room retro-shag rug.

"Thanks," I try to say. "Thanks a lot."

"No, I feel bad for you." Neil gasps between laughing spasms, clutching his stomach and wiping away tears. "I do, I really do."

Salinger cannot stop laughing. His bark scares off ten mail carriers, forty neighbourhood dogs and cats, five newspaper girls, twenty-three cyclists, and two Mormons.

Unlike with Neil, I can't explain to the guy working the Tim Horton's drive-thru, or my colleagues and students, why my face doesn't move the way it used to. The paralysis is only supposed to last for three months at which point I'll begin to slowly get control of my muscles.

But what if the paralysis doesn't go away?

It'd be just like me to be the one paralytic irreversible Botox injection statistic.

Forget booking an aisle seat, I'll have to travel in the cargo hold.

Trapped in my own face gives me a new perspective on the popularity of Botox. I start watching reality shows starring middle-aged women, and I am shocked to see that they accuse each other of being phony, of shedding crocodile tears, of iciness, and cunning.

I now want to defend these women. It is not that they're actively *choosing* to hoodwink television audiences; they are themselves being duped and imprisoned in the pursuit of everlasting youth and beauty. A frozen face is not a beautiful face. No wonder they have to scream hysterically and flip tables to get their feelings across.

Botox is to actors what steroids are to athletes, a performance-enhancing lie. Even animals are getting Botox. Saudi Arabia's annual camel beauty contest disqualified twelve camels after a vet got caught injecting them with Botox to make their pouts look more alluring.

For six weeks, my eye remains closed.

I visit Dr. Kafka for a grinding check-up. As I lay foolishly back in his chair, he instructs me to open wide.

I can barely open my mouth.

"When I was growing up plastic surgery was a taboo subject for men," he smirks. "Today if you mention Botox no one raises an eyebrow."

I should have ordered a mouthguard with a cyanide capsule.

Eventually, I tell friends and colleagues about my stint as a pirate. As I suspected, they are completely mystified. Why did I get a toxin injected into my face to begin with?

"Two paths merged in the woods," I explain, "I took the psychopath."

Something changed in me after I recovered. As I looked at the multitude of frozen faces on TV, I began to see the beauty of the natural ones. Botox is a tool of oppression, no less sinister and insidious for the fact that its users willingly self-administer. My silly six-week trauma has helped me settle into the idea of my mortality. When I die, I don't want to donate my face to Tupperware.

The brontosaurus didn't have to worry about Botox injections and eyepatches. However, unlike the brontosaurus, I *did* eventually stop grinding my teeth—fear of aging, the culprit all along. Getting older is a reality, and I have decided to embrace myself like a recycled teenager, despite being able to pinch an inch on my forehead. After all, age is only a state of chewing and eating slower. My face remains injection and sausage free.

Neil stopped his injections too.
He still has no wrinkles, the lucky bastard.

STRIKE ZONE

The strike was on.

We gathered downtown in the parking lot in front of the college's main doors. Ours is the smaller of the two college campuses, what Quebec was to France in the early seventeenth-century, a stable. In its heyday, the campus was a tannery. During Northern Ontario's industrial age of steam and horses, it gave off a putrid odour that stunk up the waterfront for blocks. Salted hides were folded into bundles the size of a Hudson's Bay Company steamer trunk to cure before being dumped into a row of massive vats—one vat to take the hair off, one vat to cure, and one vat to dye. The hides, soft, hairless, and grey, were then spun in a revolving drum containing grease until the leather was impregnated. After waterproofing, each hide was then stretched out on a table and pounded with a heavy hammer. You had to have the strength of Thor to work in a tannery. I learned all this from Dill Pickle, a wiry old custodian at our campus. That's his name, he showed me his college ID. I must admit Dill does smell a bit vinegary. His squint reminds me of Popeye.

I was complaining to Dill last week about the amount of grease left on the bread of the cafeteria's grilled cheese and bacon sandwiches. The sandwiches aren't merely coated in grease, they're positively soaked in it. I have watched a sandwich drip like a faucet. It takes three paper towels to absorb the grease. All because I'm too lazy to pack a lunch.

"Grease!" Dill's retort was not so much a laugh as a squawk. "They shot all the grease outta this place when my grandfather worked here. Oh, then there was grease flying! He banged down on a hide until it was smooth. Arms on him like a telephone pole. There was a big furnace where the cafeteria is now and they put the hides on the upper floor to dry."

I imagined cow hides hanging from the ceiling tiles upstairs. I'd like to hang a few students from those tiles.

"Oh, it was a smelly place," said Dill. "One time a farmer brought in a cowhide to sell, slipped on the greasy floor, and fell into one of the vats. He stunk like a rat after my grandfather pulled him out. Now, my grandfather was an impeccable dresser when he wasn't pounding hides. Seeing the fellow's sorry state, he escorted him down the main street to the haberdashery and staked him to a new suit of clothes. Most tannery workers adjusted to the slippery footing. My grandfather trailed his feet, just skidded them."

I've slipped on the cafeteria floor many times, usually right after Dill's finished mopping and I've failed to see his yellow warning signs. I need to work on my "trailing" skills. Maybe I'll start with skidding my tires in the parking lot.

"Then there was the problem of all the unwanted hair. I don't have that problem," Dill chortled. Dill is bald. As bald as, well, as bald as a dill pickle. "The hair was heavier than the water so it stuck to the bottom of the vats and had to be drained. Now, where the tannery disposed of it and the vat fluids isn't on record, but my grandfather told me that cow hair paves the bottom of the lake."

The lake fronts the tannery. The tannery stopped operating in 1946, shortly after the war ended. Soldiers no longer needed leather insoles to keep their boots dry and the dashing RAF pilots who posed for photos in their manly leather bomber jackets, hung them up for good. Local environmentalists—all three of them—have protested for years about the danger posed by the leaching of toxic and cancer-causing chemicals coming from the old cement tanning tanks underneath the college. Faculty rumour has it that the college bought the tannery for a song. In terms of real estate crimes against humanity, it ranked only slightly lower than gangs laundering billions of dollars in real estate and inflating housing prices. You can still smell the faint odour of leather dye and cow manure in the college cafeteria, a reminder of the tannery's gory days. Dipstick Diane, the automotive repair technician, claims the smell is the shit being rammed down our throats by management.

Fittingly, the campus now houses several trade programs as

well as hairstyling, cosmetology, and...English. Teaching English at the college *is* rocket science. Let me caution you. This isn't English as taught at university, the English of Shakespeare and Hemingway, no, this is English by way of Dr. Seuss and the *Dick and Jane* primers.

Dick and Jane arrived on the scene the same time the tannery closed down. Once a beloved teaching tool *Dick and Jane* was later denounced by child psychologists as dull, counter- productive, and even misogynistic—perfect for a class of twenty-first century welding students who think a "preposition" is something to do on a Friday night.

In a desperate attempt to help my young charges relate, I've remodeled the characters; Dick is now a welder and Jane an electrician, Baby Sally is a plumber and Spot, the well-behaved dog, a tool-and-die maker. "Before we weld, we look and see, we join and link, and we braze and fuse, such fun with Dick and Jane," and so forth.

Each edition of *Dick and Jane* contains three hundred words, perfect for my students who have a working vocabulary of ten words. I worry that Dick and Jane might be too much for them.

I am an English department of one. My office is a converted custodian's closet—I have to rinse out a bucket each morning before I start my computer. My primary function as a college English teacher is to make sure the welding students graduate and are able to write a job application letter. Proper spelling is encouraged but ignored, punctuation optional at best, grammar entirely unnecessary.

I spend my classes teaching my students the relationship between letters and sounds ("M" makes an "mmmmm" noise like in the word "mmmmmmmechanic"). So my revised *Dick and Jane* goes something like this: "Look, Spot. Oh, look, look Spot. Look and see. Oh, see. Dick cut his finger off with a mmmmmmachetee." With enough repetition my students learn (at least in theory) to "sight read" a given word and, hopefully, add three new words a day to their initial ten-word vocabulary.

Some eighty-five million first graders plowed through the *Dick and Jane* books between 1946 and 1970. By contrast, my students plow snow with a grader and can barely count to 85. The pictures are helpful. The original illustrator regularly consulted a *Sears* catalogue so she could fit the family with "modern" clothes and cars. I encourage my students to add graffiti at will. For instance, Dick now has a plumber's butt crack when he bends over. In my classes, Dick washes dishes and Jane cuts the lawn. Better yet, I have both mother and father do things together, like fixing a car, rewiring a garage, or fighting off a zombie apocalypse.

Dr. Seuss bragged about how he helped to kill off *Dick and Jane.* He wrote the *Cat in the Hat* in answer to his publisher's challenge to create a story a first-grader couldn't put down. My students love Dr. Seuss—one nail, two nail, short nail, long nail.

We voted ninety percent in favour of striking.

It was a warm, sunny mid-October morning and we were all in good spirits. The picket signs were pristine, freshly-stapled to wooden stakes and ready to go into battle against the education-sucking vampires of the provincial government.

"PUT STUDENTS FIRST!"

"SAME WORK, SAME PAY."

"NO CUTS TO EDUCATION."

"IF YU KEPE KUTTIN EDUCATION, MORE SIGNS WIL LOK LIKE DIS."

I held up a blank sign.

"What does that mean?" demanded Harry, the welding teacher, a pint-sized teamster in blue coveralls. Harry was loud even when he whispered, so loud that Joe Pesci wanted his voice back.

"It's a chart representing the teaching experience of most people making decisions about education," I replied.

"What the fuck? No one's gonna get that," Harry shot back. He handed me his Sharpie.

I wanted to suggest to Harry that he should audit my class, but I scrawled, "TEACHERS FIRST OR STUDENTS WILL BE

LAST," instead. My bad handwriting was even worse in large block letters, glaring in sharp black relief against the white bristle board.

"Teach Her Fists or Studs Will Blast?" Harry attempted to read my sign aloud. "What the fuck does that mean?

"Skip it," I said, embarrassed and annoyed. I grabbed another sign from the pile of extras.

There were fifteen of us walking the picket line at the tannery campus. We followed each other blindly, like a chain gang, repeating a large endless loop that lasted for hours, breaking rank to use the portalet (set up overnight by one of the plumbing profs), or grab a handful of Timbits and a coffee refill from the snack table. I preferred the glazed sour cream Timbit. So, as I discovered, did Harry. Tensions were mounting, and it was only Hour Two on Day One.

Essentially our job as responsible picketers was to slow down the vehicles of support staff coming to work and delivery trucks, hand out pamphlets, and spend as much time as possible gossiping at the snack table.

Big Moose Graham was our strike captain. Big Moose headed up the Electricians Program. His hands and personality were the size of an Easter ham. He was tall, broad, and blocked out the sun. He set up the snack table and barricades, doled out our strike pay, and, most importantly, brought the fifty-pack of Timbits and coffee each morning. In short, Big Moose Graham was our hero.

The amount of strike pay you received depended on the individual strength of your local union chapter. Our union chapter was on the low end of the power pecking order. A four-year old child could beat our local union in an arm-wrestling competition, which, in money talk, meant my weekly take home pay was cut down to one hundred dollars a week for the foreseeable future. If I didn't walk the line, I didn't get paid *and* was fined by the union to the tune of one hundred dollars. The math sucked. At least I still had Thanksgiving leftovers in the fridge, although I'd already eaten enough turkey sandwiches to grow a snood.

Hygiene was not Harry's friend. He reeked of stale sweat and was unaware of his immediate surroundings—so much so that whenever he backed into a blackboard, he'd step away leaving a sweaty outline of his back on the board. At least, that's what his welding students told me.

Besides Harry and Big Moose Graham, the usual suspects rounding and pounding our slice of campus pavement were:

1. Bit-Part Bart, a pin-sized, bow-legged, battery-kicking Johnny Cash who ran the Automotive Repair Program
2. Sliver-man Slim, the Coordinator of the Carpentry Program, tall and lean, with wood shavings that fell from his unruly mop of grey hair like an epileptic snow globe
3. Foghorn McPhee, the silent instructor of the Tool-and-Dye Program, whose mild manner made the meek of the New Testament look like a binge of college students on spring break
4. Randy Andy, the long-suffering, perfectly-coiffed Plumbing Technician, plying his trade and physique under the steam of Hot Water Hank, a quick-tempered, leaky faucet of a man, and the curmudgeonly Coordinator of the Plumbing Program
5. Sid the Serious, our Union Steward, and the stalwart messenger for Toronto's Darryl "Two-Ton" Delaney, president of OPSEU, the province's college teachers' union. Sid sniffed out management mismanagement like a pit bull on Red Bull
6. Gabby and Gord, the no-nonsense hair-styling team, a Northern Ontario Thelma and Louis with scissors, who silenced Harry and his dirty blow-dryer jokes on Day One
7. Cassandra the Cuticle Queen, the rainbow-coloured, nail-chewing cosmologist who could have been a hand model had she not had her pinky finger bitten off by a snapping turtle on a hiking trip. After that, she never really came out of her shell
8. Last of all, there was me: Rudy "Tuesday." Harry hung the moniker on me on my first morning reporting for duty. The nickname stuck like a dead pigeon around my neck.

Dipstick Diane was smart—she went to work for her brother in his auto body shop, making a hundred bucks an hour for jacking a car up.

Together, we were a reluctant band of misfits in our own Dirty Dozen college-teacher Spaghetti Northern, standing up against the evil ranching practices and prostitution of management. We were not demanding free-grazing or an inflated wage increase. We were fighting for job security and intellectual freedom (a contradiction in terms, in my case.) On a positive note, not being in the classroom meant Dick and Jane could go on a long holiday.

Program coordinators were burnt out from dealing with a lack of funding, deliberate administration miscommunication, facilities long in need of a face lift, a government that didn't value the opinions of its teachers and students, and cafeteria salads more expensive than a flight to Mexico—all were on the table and the provincial Education Minister refused to pull up a chair.

I am a creature of routine and try *not* to change with every new day. I feared this was all about to change so I decided to create a "Book of Days" to document life on the picket line. I'd be honouring the tradition of my ancient Roman ancestors. I don't have any Roman ancestors, but the thought of keeping a daily journal in the spirit of Ovid's epic poem *Fasti,* appealed to the English classicist in me. Keeping a book of hours was also popular in the Middle Ages, the early forerunner of our modern-day calendar. During plague outbreaks, the pages remained blank. I wondered what would happen during a strike.

RUDY BOYLE'S BOOK OF STRIKE DAYS; OR A FUNNY THING HAPPENED ON THE WAY TO THE SNACK TABLE

DAY 1
We were a good-spirited lot. The weather was warm and our dispositions sunny. Gabby and Gord brought their dogs to join the line. We joked and laughed. We were in serious denial.

Quip of the Day: "When I die, I want college management to lower me into my grave so they can let me down one last time." – Big Moose Graham

Number of Timbits eaten: 12 sour cream glazed, 11 honey crullers, 10 chocolate snowballs, 9 honey dips, 8 apple fritters, 7 raspberry-filled, 6 old fashioned glaze, 5 golden napkins

Distance Walked: 3.5 km

Number of Walking Steps: 5,250

Number of minutes spent gossiping at snack table: 25

Number of minutes spent hiding in portalet: 15

Total Weight Gain: ½ pound

Weather: Sunny and Mild. Clouds shaped like chickens.

DAY 5

I've started moonlighting as a server at a Mexican restaurant. I ruined a family's graduation dinner two nights ago.

"Hi folks," I said. "My name is Neil, and I'll be taking care of you tonight."

The customer replied, "Hi Neil, our daughter graduated from York University today with an English Degree."

He was some proud. His daughter blushed.

"Oh my goodness," I said, "that is fantastic! I actually have a Master's Degree in English Literature from York. Can I get you folks started with some chips and salsa?"

DAY 10

Timbits are a striking teacher's best friend, the same way a pack of cigarettes was for soldiers during World War II.

"Twenty little buddies that don't talk back," grinned Sliver-man Slim, licking icing sugar off his fingers for the fifth time that morning while still managing to walk, text, smoke, and wield a picket sign.

Things were at a standstill between OPSEU and the College

Employer Council. The Council said meeting the union's demands would add more than $250 million in costs each year. Everyone was forgetting the fact that half-a-million students were not in school and tuitions were not being refunded. Students always get the short end of the stick. The vocabulary of my fifteen welding students was about to be reduced to that of *Quest for Fire*.

Sid the Serious reported to the line that Darryl "Two-Ton" Delaney had issued a media statement: "It's unclear when the strike might be resolved."

Hemingway was more verbose. The Dirty Dozen now referred to "Two-Ton" Delaney as Captain Obvious.

"Both sides say there are no talks scheduled," Sid added cryptically, zipping up his windbreaker. The weather was turning nasty, and November was just around the corner. I felt like I was part of the doomed crew of the *Edmund Fitzgerald*.

Big Moose Graham started bringing in three fifty-packs each morning. We have transformed from a devoted band of educators into a ravenous pack of sugar junkies. I ranked Timbits while hiding in the portalet, starting with the least popular.

12. Old-Fashion Plain. The most boring of the bunch. Tastes like stale bread.

11. Old-Fashioned Sugar. Not even a coating of white sugar can hide the boredom.

10. Chocolate Snowball. Chocolate Timbit covered in icing sugar—messy and tastes like a shrug.

9. Chocolate Glazed. The instinctive choice but the most disappointing choice. Not at all chocolatety. Dry as hay dipped in chocolate.

8. Old-Fashioned Glazed. Number One of the "old-fashioned" triptych. Sweet and to the point—unlike the College Employer Council.

7. Honey Dip. The fence sitter. A yeasty ball of honey that does not disappoint but doesn't thrill either. The OPSEU Timbit.

6. Birthday Cake. The trendiest Timbit. The colours of a rainbow, sprinkles, funfetti—sweet and popular, like my sister JoJo was in high school.

5. Raspberry-filled. A fruit-flavoured powder bomb. Big hit with kids and striking college teachers.

4. Apple Fritter. Apple and cinnamon-flecked Timbit covered in a sugary glaze. An all-round favourite. The Betty White of Timbits.

3. Honey Cruller. Light an airy with melt-in-your-mouth fluffiness. One bite and even the portalet smells airy.

2. Venetian Cream. Miniature Boston cream novelty doughnut. Rare and tastes like a Timbit in dessert form. Gabby and Gord had dibs on this one.

1. Sour Cream Glazed. The best of the bunch. Good for morning, mid-afternoon, or nighttime snacking. A delightful sweet twang. The ultimate go to Timbit.

Harry challenged me to a public duel tomorrow at dawn. "There's only room for one sour cream glazed Timbit-eater on my watch, Tuesday," he said. I felt like a character in a Chekhov pastry play.

DAY 15

I stole Harry's sharpie. It felt good watching him snap, and then snap his picket sign in half over his knee. He spent the rest of the day limping and cursing. While hiding in the portalet, I managed to scribble down a few words of wisdom on the back of a soggy Tim Horton's napkin. I taped it to the inside of the door with Harry's duct tape:

1. A student will remain in bed unless acted upon by a large enough panic. It is Newton's lesser-known Fourth Law of Motion.

2. Comic sans is never an acceptable font. Inspired by comic book lettering, it isn't meant to be taken seriously, unless you're an eight-year old writing a poem about unicorns.

3. A coward lives to eat another Timbit, even if it isn't sour glazed.

DAY 20
For the rain it raineth every day.

We arrived for picket duty dreading the hours ahead, tired from the anxiety and wet clothes we wore home the night before, with the exception of warm and dry Randy Andy. I hated him. The mercury dropped steadily, the trees were bare, and we were sneezing on each other. Cold season had arrived. Big Moose Graham ordered us to walk ten-feet apart and to stop coughing.

"Sneeze into your elbows," he barked after each rotation.

Teacher contract negotiations never failed to turn into a province-wide scandal. One of my colleagues lost it and threw a Timbit at a reporter today. Thank God, it was an old fashioned plain.

We were taking strike action with students in mind. I tell my students to choose a major they love and they'll never work a day in their life, because their field won't be hiring. When I ask my students if they have any questions, there is always one welding student who responds, "Can you repeat the part of the stuff where you said all about the things?" His name is Chuck. I was impressed that he managed to cobble *fifteen* words together.

"You're wasting $15,000 on a college education you could get for $1.50 in late fees at the public library," I replied. Chuck's mind says college graduate but my mind says isolated goat herder in Wales.

"I dream of my dog. I wonder if he dreams about me?" asks Dilbert, another student as thick as a Timbit.

"I meant questions about the assignment."

Here is an example of an essay I received from Dilbert: BUCKLE YOUR SEAT BELT, MOTHERFUCKER, BECAUSE IN FIVE SHORT PAGES I'M GOING TO LEARN U A THING THAT I ONLY LEARNED MYSELF ABOUT TWO HOURS AGO, SO SIT DOWN, SHUT UP, AND ENJOY THE EXPERIENCE OF MY 4 A.M. RED BULL-INDUCED SELF-HATRED-FUELLED WRITING BUFFET.

He got an A for that.

I give out an annual Bermuda Triangle Award to the student whose homework has gone missing the most. True. I keep a garbage can beneath the chalkboard. Above it in block letters: LATE ASSIGNMENTS. False. There is no such thing as a due date in our current education system.

The last thing I said to a welding student before the strike started was, "No, Chuck, I can't round your 49.8 to a 90."

Now, that is what I call a legacy.

On the last day of classes, I assigned homework for my students to do during the strike. I used a PowerPoint slide. The assignment filled the screen. Please do one of the following by the end of the strike:

1. Learn another language.
2. Master Kung Fu.
3. End world hunger.
4. Find your nemesis, earn their trust, and then vanquish them (preferably with magic).
5. In the shower, use conditioner first then shampoo just to see what happens (I'm curious).

DAY 25

Job security and retirement package—the five words that make my colleagues hold onto teaching jobs that make them stressed and miserable. I never got into teaching for the money. If I can make a difference in just one student's life, well...that will be a pretty poor average.

Unlike high school, college teachers aren't allowed to communicate with a student's parents. I imagine if we did have parent/teacher interviews, they would go something like this:

"How's my son doing?" asks a welding student's mom.

"I have never seen this man in my life."

The College Employer Council asked the union to suspend the strike for now and allow classes to resume. The union, however, refused and stated its members were standing strong on the picket lines—the phrase "standing strong" synonymous with "shivering bleak." Sid the Serious reported that collective bargaining would not resume until next week.

Things worsened. Big Moose Graham grimly reported that Timbit rationing would begin after the weekend break. The news did not go over well. Gabby got down to work in the portalet. She hastily put together new picket signs and handed them out.

"WE WANT OUR TIMBITS AND EAT THEM TOO"

"WE'RE OLD ENOUGH TO CHOOSE."

"SAY NO TO CUTS, YES TO TIMBITS"

Cassandra the Cuticle Queen broke a nail and went home. We were now the Lackluster Eleven.

DAY 30

You know you live in Northern Ontario when you get a blizzard in the middle of November. Big Moose Graham arrived by dog sled team. He unloaded *one* fifty-pack.

A collective gasp of horror ensued.

Robert Service was about to get ambushed by medieval history.

Harry aimed and fired the first snowball. Big Moose Graham took it in the chest. Hot Water Hank fired next. A rising curveball.

SMACK!

A direct hit to the head. A volley of snowballs and picket signs filled the sky. They soared over the parking lot, reminiscent of the Battle of Agincourt. Big Moose Graham went down hard. A delirious pile-on followed. Just as we were about to cremate him alive, Gabby noticed Gord was missing. We drew coffee stir sticks and sent out a search party. Gabby was the first to find him, naked and half-mad, belting out Anne Murray ballads while making snow angels in the back parking lot. It is a strange thing done when our wits decide to run.

Big Moose Graham sent him home on the back of Randy Andy's snowmobile. Both failed to report for duty the next morning. And each subsequent morning. Snack table gossip had it they ran off and opened a hair and plumbing salon in Costa Rica. Hot Water Hank was some pissed. That left the nine of us.

The Nihilistic Nine soldiered on, trudging through the new-fallen snow, each stepping heavily in the foot imprint of the lone picketer ahead of them—lemmings frozen to the picketing core. Our rotation output declined rapidly. An undercover news reporter, hiding in a city works snow plow, snagged a picture of us. The caption in the local newspaper likened us to a band of survivors after an airline crash on a remote mountain top. The same question was on everyone's mind: when will we eat Big Moose Graham?

"Mush!" he shouted, snapping his whip in the air. Big Moose Graham's "whip" was fashioned out of a radiator hose and black electrical tape.

We mushed on.

Despite the weather, students lent support to a rally outside the province's education ministry building in Toronto. The students, as is always the case, were caught in the crossfire. A shivering teenager, in clothes better suited for a summer day at the beach, was interviewed by a CBC journalist.

"The length of the strike is nerve-wracking," she said. She got that right. I was impressed she used eight words.

DAY 35

Foghorn McPhee has disappeared. I fear we have lost another one.

"Ahoy!"

The scream came from Harry.

There he was, standing on the snack table, trying to brace himself against the raging wind, all the while pointing a bright red index finger into the blizzard. I followed the direction of his finger to the back parking lot. Far off in the distance I could make out a dark speck battling the elements. The speck was carrying something—something large. I prayed it was a thousand sour cream glazed Timbits. As he came closer, I made out what appeared to be a large cylinder slung over his right shoulder.

Foghorn McPhee emerged into view, his eyebrows and beard covered in ice, carrying a large metal garbage can, its broken chain dangling from the rim. He collapsed on the snow in front of us. Gabby and I rushed to his rescue. Big Moose Graham filled the garbage can with broken picket signs and empty Timbit boxes. Sliver-man Slim pulled out his Zippo, leaned in, and—WHOOSH!

Slim's eyebrows were gone.

We took turns warming our hands over the fire.

Foghorn McPhee was our new hero.

DAY 40

One rotation.

Two rotations.

Fifty rotations.

Two-hundred-and-fifty rotations.

Three-thousand rotations.

We were the frostbitten Walking Debt.

At five p.m., faculty from both campuses gathered at the legion hall for a union meeting that included free pizza and Timbits. All of my male colleagues now sported beards, resembling a softer and paunchier version of the crew of the Franklin expedition.

Sid the Serious cleared his throat and rose to speak. "Nobody wants to be on strike. I thank each and every one of you for doing your part in this nasty weather. The college is offering a one-point-five percent increase over four years. We are asking for a two percent increase over three years. We are at a standstill."

"Splitting hairs!" I yelled from the back of the hall after stuffing my pockets with sour cream glazed Timbits. No, I didn't. I said nothing. I was busy sponging the grease off a slice of pizza with a paper towel.

"And there is no agreement on academic freedom," Sid continued. He was trying to be in his element. "The union feels it is absolutely the core—it is the crux—around our issues of quality education in the system. Management cannot have the authority to make the day-to-day decisions in our classrooms. When you look at the language of their offer that is exactly what they want."

"Isn't it always?" Big Moose Graham shouted. A chorus of solidarity followed.

"Management is saying to the press that we're the problem," Sid shouted back, no match for the volume of Big Moose Graham.

"A leopard doesn't change its stripes!" yelled Harry. Oh Harry.

"Their offer is *off*!" Sid threw his slice of pizza up in the air. The rabble rabbled. The slice fell back and hit him on the head. Michael Collins had nothing to worry about.

"You spray insects with *Off*," roared Big Moose Graham. He could derail a freight train. "We should give management a blast!"

Laughter filled the hall.

"*They're* the stumbling block!" Sid sputtered. Pepperoni slices were stuck in his side part. "The offer on the table does not work. They are tossing us the crumbs of Timbits."

My ears perked up.

"We will not end this strike until our demands are met."

I survived the previous college strike fifteen years ago. The chances of the union's demands winning the day were slim. Either the union would cave once our members were forced to start eating their pets, or the provincial government would bring in back-to-work legislation. Nevertheless, the rhetoric sounded good. Especially on a full stomach.

Quip of the Day: "D does not stand for Diploma." – Foghorn McPhee, local union hero

Number of slices of pizza eaten at union meeting: 5

Number of sour cream glazed Timbits stuffed in pockets of parka at union meeting: 27

Number of minutes spent hiding in portalet: 0 (due to line-ups for the portalet, all male faculty are now required to urinate in the lake behind the campus until further notice)

Toxin Increase in Birch Lake: 6.5%

Total Weight Gain: 24 pounds

Number of broken picket signs burnt in garbage can: 37 (Big Moose Graham sharpied "STUDENTS FIRST" on his face)

Number of times Harry dropped the F-bomb: 257
Weather: Heavy snow and freezing rain. Fifth layer of clothing
required + waterproof boots +
balaclava + one pair of thermo-chip heated glove liners + snowshoes.
I'm thinking of changing
my name to Frobisher.

DAY 45
Today we lost our benefits.
    Scabs are coming in.
    The union snack fund is gone.
    We burned our last picket sign.
    Morale collapsed.
    I cancelled Christmas.

DAY 50

Timbit withdrawal—day five.
Weather: The Seven Plagues. First Bowl: locusts and loathsome
sores

DAY 51
Timbit withdrawal—day six.
Weather: Second Bowl: the seas turn to blood

DAY 53
Timbit withdrawal—day seven.
Weather: Third Bowl: frogs fall from the sky

DAY 54
I need to write a will.

Weather: Fourth Bowl: sun causes major heatwave to scorch the planet with fire

DAY 55
Thick darkness covers the Earth

DAY 56
The strike is over.

The government legislated us back to work.

"This terrible chapter is over," the Education Minister read from a prepared script on a CBC current affairs show. I don't think he'd recognize a chapter in a book if he saw one, much less be able to read it. The colleges welcomed the government's back-to-work legislation, saying all efforts at the bargaining table had been exhausted and that the semester would be extended.

"No college student has ever lost a semester," the President of the College Employer Council stated in a press release. "We need only two days to restart classes."

You could almost smell the cigar smoke.

Forty-eight hours to condense eight weeks of curriculum down to two weeks.

In forty-eight hours, Mozart wrote a six-piece canon titled *Leck mic him Arsch*, literally Lick my Arse.

Over two sleepless nights, I reconfigured eight weeks of "English-as-a-second-language-for-Welding" down to two weeks. Dick and Jane were in a panic. Dr. Seuss had to get his cat back. I didn't even have time for a vowel movement.

On Tuesday morning, late as usual, the welding students slouched into class and took their seats at the back. I cleared my throat and asked how they were doing. Chuck, the student with the high-flying D, raised his hand.

"Yes, Chuck?" I said, my body tensing, preparing for impact.

"Bueno, Profesor Boyle," he yawned. "Fumé mucha hierba, jugué mortal kombat y solté un cobertizo."

I have a rudimentary understanding of the Spanish language. To the best of my translating ability, Chuck smoked weed, played video games, and did something to a "cobertizo." I was accustomed to him communicating via a series of short or long grunts.

"I didn't know you spoke Spanish, Mr. Graves."

"I didn't," he said. "I learned it over the strike."

"You learned to speak the entire Spanish language over fifty-six days?"

"Sí."

I was flabbergasted. "And what's 'solté un cobertizo' mean?"

"I arc-welded a metal shed," Chuck replied. "Es la bomba total."

Another student raised his hand.

"Yes, Dilbert," I said. Had Dilbert memorized the Bible?

"I did like you said, Professor Boyle. I tried using conditioner before shampoo."

It was good to be back.

THE LAND OF THE LIZARD-PEOPLE

Enjoying a family reunion is the ultimate improbability.

Specifically, the annual summer gathering starring all of Neil's hapless relatives. He needs to appreciate the effort I put in to not being a serial killer. I want to strangle the lot of them. I drink coffee first thing in the morning to help *them* live longer. The Price family is into strange cults, all of them—with the exception of Neil. I can almost handle the tenets of sacred geometry, and the notion that our eyeballs are shaped like mystical fish bladders, but the weirdness that Neil's family believes in drives me bananas. They're mad enough to make a druid start a forest fire. Can one family all be deprived of oxygen at birth? I worry that Neil is genetically predisposed to their galloping insanity and I'll wake up one morning to find him sacrificing Salinger to his garden gnomes. I'd like to lock them in a room for eternity—relatives and gnomes.

Neil's younger sister, Violet, is a botanist, having spent the last thirty years studying tree architecture—poetic botany, she calls it. She chooses tropical plants much like herself: strange, odd looking, and stinky. Trees that walk, vines that dance, orchids that kill, a palm with a leaf the size of a catering tent, floating seaweed with an inflatable bladder, a flower that smells like rotting flesh, and other weird French-kissing plants. Neil says she sees poetry in the unusual habits of rare plants in the same way a person who loves literature is fascinated by the cadence of poetry versus the narrative of a novel. To my way of thinking, she's the original crazy cat lady. She is also a member of a horticultural cult known as the Church of All Plants, based on a 1962 counterculture science fiction novel, *Stranger from a Green Land,* about a human raised by trees in a tropical rain forest who comes back to society and challenges the status quo view of sex, religion, and lawn care. Violet dresses like an aging flower child, waves a willow wand, and talks to trees. She married a birch tree named Herb after successfully petitioning to have the tree granted the same legal rights as a human. When I told her I didn't have a green thumb, she said it was because my roots didn't go deep enough. "You're barking up the wrong tree," I said and peed on her husband.

Neil's Uncle Ned is a Pythagorean, meaning exactly what the name implies. He worships the geometry of Pythagoras. The ancient Greek mathematician, besides loving triangles, also believed in reincarnation. When Uncle Ned was a teenager he witnessed a man beating a dog, and called for the beating to stop, not because beating a dog in itself was a cruel act, but because he recognized in the yelps of the dog the voice of that of his deceased grandfather. Uncle Ned is also addicted to hallucinogenic mushrooms. He believes that Salinger is the reincarnation of the famous dead author. At last year's family fiasco, I told him Salinger is currently writing a sequel called *The Fetcher in the Rye*.

"Be serious, Rudolph," he exclaimed and stormed off in three different directions.

Neil's parents are obsessed with the Heaven's Gate cult— not the embarrassingly awful movie responsible for destroying the Western, killing independent film making, and forcing Kris Kristofferson to never leave his day job again, but a bizarre religious cult based on the Book of Revelation. Neil's parents believe the Earth is doomed to be "recycled' and the only way to survive is to escape from the Earth itself. For the past twenty-five years, Neil's father has been building a spaceship in his barn using old tires, refrigerators, tin foil, and recycled cans. He steals the recyclables out of his neighbour's blue boxes.

"How many tuna cans will it take to get to Mars?" I asked him last summer.

"Ask Ned," he replied, missing the joke. "He's the math expert. Last I saw him was measuring some twigs branching out of Herb."

But it is Neil's big brother—and I mean big—who is the cherry on the top of the nut-bar sundae. Wing-nut is obsessed with lizard-people (his real name is Walter Price but I call him Wing-nut in front of his back). The idea of shape-shifting lizards taking human forms in a plot to rule the world dates back to the early 80s, coming from the disturbed mind of David Ick, a certifiable nut-bar who first rose to fame playing British football. After receiving one too many balls to the head he quit professional sports, becoming a spokesperson for the Green Party of England and Wales. His mad speeches made communists look tame by comparison. On a cold day in January while Operation Desert Storm bombed the crap out of Kuwait, Icky, as I prefer to call him, was busy hugging a cluster of trees in Kew Gardens. A bolt of lightning must have struck him in the head because, from that moment on, he's dedicated his life to warning mankind that the earth is secretly controlled by alien lizard-people.

In Canada, Wing-nut carries the alien-lizard conspiracy torch. Neil has one of Wing-nut's old Green Party election signs hanging in the garage as a souvenir. It reads THE PRICE IS RIGHT. Beneath the text is the image of an iguana in a business suit within a red circle with a diagonal slash through it.

"Lizard-people are cold-blooded humanoid reptilians who have the power to shape-shift into human form," Wing-nut explains to me for the umpteenth time at this year's reunion.

Encroaching on other conspiracy theorists' territory, Wing-nut claims that lizards are behind secret societies like the Freemasons, the Illuminati, and the cast of *Friends*. He's convinced that lizard-people filled Canadian television programming in the 1970s: Al Waxman on the *King of Kensington*, Bruno Gerussi and Robert Clothier on *The Beachcombers*, *The Friendly Giant*, *Mr. Dressup*, and anyone ever connected to *Front Page Challenge*.

"They made us dumb by getting us hooked on Canadian TV," he says.

I do not know anyone who ever got hooked on Canadian television programming.

Wing-nut says there are more lizard-people living amongst us than we are aware. "Keep in mind that this isn't counting all the people who, in their heart of hearts, believe that lizard-people exist but are nervous they will be found out if they publicly disclose their beliefs," he whispers to me while inhaling a slice of Neil's homemade

rhubarb pie. "It's more dangerous than the communist witch hunt."
If alien-lizards pose such a threat to global security, funny how a
modern day Joe McCarthy hasn't risen from the ashes to launch
a full alien-lizard senate investigation. I asked Wing-nut that. He
replied, "It's obvious. McCarthy was secretly a lizard-person." He
can't hear me scream inside my head.

"How do I know if someone is a lizard-person?" I ask.
Humouring Wing-nut is the only way to avoid the rest of Neil's
family. I tried playing sick last year and was inundated by foul-
tasting birch tea remedies, missives stating I was a peasant during
the Black Plague in a previous life, and repeated warnings to recycle
and pack my things.

"There are numerous ways to spot lizard-people in a crowd,"
Wing-nut hisses, moistly flicking his tongue.

"How?" I say, already knowing the answer.

"Green, hazel or blue eyes that can change colour like a
chameleon," he says. "Keen eyesight and hearing, red hair or reddish
hair, unexplained scars on the body, low blood pressure, psychic
abilities, a sense of not belonging to the human race, and a capability
to disrupt electrical appliances—they're all signs."

The toaster rarely works when Neil is in the kitchen. But's that
because he forgets to plug it in.

"The Prime Minister is a lizard-person," Wing-nut grunts.

"Doesn't he have dark brown hair?" I say. "How can *he* be a
lizard-person?"

"He dyes his hair."

"Trudeau's secretly a red head?"

"You betcha. According to his doctors, he brags about his low
blood pressure. He doesn't wear glasses or a hearing aid. Three
days after he took office, there was a spike in UFO sightings in
his home province of Quebec. That guy on the CBC who has
that science show claims that Trudeau told him he'd seen a UFO,
and communicated with it telepathically. His aides say he has an
uncanny ability to assassinate flies with an elastic band from the
doorway of the Prime Minister's office. His father knew a guy who
ran Area 51. Castro was involved *and* Barbara Streisand. That's

about as reptilian as you can get."

"Ah, well, that just about says it all, doesn't it?" I'm ready to head back to the motel.

Wing-nut leans in, holding his fork up like a trident. "What makes lizard-people lizard people is something that you can't see," he whispers. I wish a summer breeze was leaning in. Wing-nut reeks.

I nod in understanding, pretending to connect with my inner Buddha. "Ah, so it's about the soul inhabiting the body, not the physical body alone," I say languidly. I got in touch with my inner-self last month. Then I unfriended him on Facebook and shamed him on social media. I hold my hands out to the side, palms up. "The inner-self of the lizard-person."

"Yes!" he shouts, spitting rhubarb in my face. "Now you've got it!"

"So, what do lizard-people want?" I ask, scanning the backyard for Neil. Family members are dispersing. Uncle Ned is still drawing triangles on the driveway.

"World domination and cheaper Tim Horton's coffee." Wing-nut's mouth, throat, and chest begin to vibrate. I think of William Shatner battling a Gorn on *Star Trek*.

Aside from his paranoiac brain, I ask Wingnut where lizard-people come from. I can see Neil collecting his Tupperware through the kitchen window.

"The Fourth Dimension. The constellation of Draco," says Wing-nut, attempting to wrap his arms around himself. He gets about as far as his elbows.

Draco is the constellation that is allegedly shaped like a dragon or, if you go with its Latin name *Draconem*, means "huge serpent." It's the eighth largest constellation. On a clear summer night we can see Draco at the cottage.

"Reptoids from Draco are very tall and have retractable wings." Wingnut demonstrates. He resembles an obese rhubarb-dripping pterodactyl. He fixes his gaze on me. "Though there are some theories that reptoids come from other systems like Sirius and Orion too."

"And they send messages on Sirius radio?"

"Yes! You're finally getting it." He is overjoyed at my progress. "Sirius radio is their broadcast system for secret messaging and brain-washing. Basically, they're all aliens too."

Lizard-people have been visiting Earth since the day the Serpent first showed up in Genesis. "A reptoid in disguise," Wingnut assures me. They have been breeding with humans, which has resulted in more lizard-people, and more humans with the potential to be lizard-people.

Most lizard-people are usually A-listers. The list of alleged lizard-people celebrities includes Celine Dion, Wayne Gretzky, Anne of Green Gables, Ben Mulroney, Chris's Pratt, Pine, Hadfield, and Hemsworth, and Justin Bieber among others. I did watch a Justin Bieber video accidentally at the gym in which his eyes seemed to shift and turn like a reptile. Chris Hadfield is the most promising candidate—an astronaut singing David Bowie's *Ziggy Stardust* in outer space has certain lizard-alien potential. Plus, he was born in Sarnia, a chemical city choking on refineries and smog, the perfect incubation site for science fiction lizard disasters. Ironically, Hitler was not a lizard-person. He just thought the Jews were.

"Could I secretly be a lizard-person?" I ask, all mock wonderment.

"Possibly, Rudolph." Wing-nut's eyebrows draw together. "Do you like the taste of flies?"

I stroke my goatee, deep in thought. "Deer, black, or shad?" I ask as if awaiting the answer to a cancer diagnosis.

"Only you know the truth," he replies gravely, backing away, and leaving in a hurry.

I guess there are worse things I could be than a humanoid lizard with plans for world domination. Neil's nephew is definitely not a lizard-person. Last week, he called the police because his fake ID didn't arrive.

A week later, I read an article in *The New Yorker* about ancient lizard limb muscles found in a human fetus. Babies in the womb have extra lizard-like muscles in their hands that they lose before they are born. Probably the oldest, albeit fleeting, remnants of evolution seen in humans yet, some Harvard biologists say. The biologists date them as 250 million years old—a relic from when reptiles transitioned to mammals and Betty White first got into acting.

"Humans have lost the lizard muscles because we don't need them," explained the Harvard biologist leading the study. "So, there is no danger of us becoming super-human."

This isn't Wing-nut talking; these are serious, lab coat-wearing scientists paid to hunch over a microscope. So while there hasn't been a humanoid lizard born yet or transformed by a serum like the Lizard in *The Amazing Spider-Man*, the human uterus is showing signs of some really creepy reptile ancestors. Might Wing-nut actually be on to something? Could I have the remnants of a dinosaur's thumb? It all sounds like the hitchhiker's guide to evolution.

I go deeper down the rabbit-lizard hole.

Researchers from a Sleep Team in the Nevada desert recently confirmed that lizards exhibit two sleep states similar to humans. Bearded dragons, in a hidden research lab near Area 51, experienced both slow-wave sleep and REM sleep patterns.

I begin counting lizards in my sleep. I have a paranoid thought: what if a lizard-alien on a faraway planet is counting me? My life is turning into a Philip K. Dick short story.

Up until this point, when I think of reptiles, the image that comes to mind is a garter snake slithering through the grass at the cottage or the little lizards that climb the walls at my sister's rental *casa* in Mexico.

"Can lizards really feel or display emotions?" I asked Salinger's vet during my last visit.

"Lizards do demonstrate basic emotions, fear and aggression for instance," she replied while injecting him with his rabies shot, "but they also indicate pleasure when offered food."

"So does my cat, but she's just ensuring her needs are met. When I fall asleep on the couch, I wake up and she's wearing a bib and pouring ketchup on my wrist."

Salinger's vet gave me her look of are you telling that same stupid joke again.

'C'mon, lizards expressing love?" I said with polite opposition.

"I don't know if it is love," she explained, all science, "but lizards appear to like some people more than others. They also show the most emotions of reptiles, appearing to show pleasure when being stroked."

Lizards do get a bad rap in movies, comics, and TV. From Godzilla to the alien reptiles of *V* to that tyrannosaurus chasing Jeff Goldblum in *Jurassic Park*, they're portrayed as scary, sneaky, and unknowable—much like the administration at the college.

I go even deeper down the lizard hole—I've become a paranoid miner looking for evidence of the fake moon landing in Sudbury.

Most lizards have movable eyelids, unlike snakes, although some cannot blink, and have to lick their eyeballs instead, which is preferable to watching Salinger lick his penis. Some lizards even have eyes that shoot blood to frighten predators. I bet Chris Hadfield can shoot blood out of *his* eyes. He survived a spacewalk after his left eye suddenly slammed shut. Supposedly, a big ball of oily anti-fog solution, meant to keep his astronaut visor clear, built up over his eye because, without gravity, his tears had nowhere to go. The ball got so big it spread like a waterfall over the bridge of his nose into his other eye. He was completely blind outside his spaceship. Nevertheless, he warded off primal terror, lived to sing the tale, and finished the mission. Also, Chris Hadfield seems like a really nice guy, so it only makes sense that he's a giant lizard underneath.

Lizards smell with their tongues, shed their skin in large flakes, and can regrow their tails if attacked. Lizards can walk on water and can reproduce by themselves. I never understood how or why chameleons changed colour until recently. I thought it was just about camouflage—it's not. Switching hues reflects emotion, according to a back issue of *National Geographic* I read in my doctor's waiting room while waiting to have a skin tag removed. Skin tags are not a characteristic of lizard-people. Changing colors sends different messages to other chameleons—a form of lizard texting and sexting; a "baby, you make me hot-blooded" sort of thing.

✧

Ranging from the crashing waves of the Pacific Ocean to the tranquil turquoise seas of the Caribbean, Mexico has more than enough beaches to keep Canadian expats, who aren't afraid of drug cartels, happy.

"What you see in the news is Mainland Mexico," Jimmy explained to me a few years back. "We are far away from the rest of the country."

JoJo and Jimmy rent a small rundown two-bedroom beachfront *casa* in Cerritos, south of Baja Sur, miles away from Cancun. It's a rugged spit of land flanked by the Pacific and the equally wild Sea of Cortez. The little surfer town isn't entirely off the radar, but it has a ram- shackle, low-key vibe that suits Jimmy's bohemian hippie fantasy life. Development has remained relatively tame and the beach is blissfully free of high rises. There are only a couple of large hotels so it isn't overrun by tourists, and most of the town consists of a mix of local fishermen (the *pescadores locales*) and surfers. Fresh fish and seafood are available in thatch-shaped spots called *enramadas*, which line the beach. Still, there are enough tattoo shops, yoga classes, and fresh juice vendors to keep JoJo happy. The ocean is safe for swimming, but the big breaks mean that most people come armed with a board, with the exception of Neil and I, who come armed with books and sunscreen. The town is also home to a massive population of sea turtles which nest on its shores in season. They wait until the full moon to come ashore to lay their eggs. The higher tide takes them further onto the shore, where it's better for them to make their nests. The reef offshore is protected so the sea life makes for amazing snorkeling possibilities for Neil. Best of all, it is a natural barrier to sharks. For me, other than the sun and the sea, it's all about cold beer and margaritas, cheap eats, and sunsets on the beach.

The nearest airport to Cerritos is La Paz International Airport. It is only a five-hour direct flight from Toronto, and customs is a breeze.

I am going to run with the new identity given to me by Juan, the La Paz customs and immigration officer who, after checking my passport signature, dubbed me "Mr. X."

The terrible jokes about my handwriting by immigration officials around the globe has gotten stale. I have heard all their questions:

"Has it always been this bad?"

"How did you manage in school?"

"*Eres disléxico?*"

The real winner doesn't come from the mouth of an immigration officer but from a loud Texan behind us in line: "My writing looked like that when I was two," he bellows, pointing at my passport so that everyone in the airport can see.

"At least I can write," I fire back. No I don't. I want to though.

"Handwriting el malo es un sign of inteligencia superior," I manage to say in broken Spanish to a second mustachioed officer.

"*Al menos puedes leerlo,*" he says and waves us through to find our luggage.

"C'mon, Professor X," Neil smirks. "Shave your head and you're set."

Professor X does have possibilities. I could be the creator of the X-Men. All I need is a wheelchair, a conservative blue suit and the voice of Patrick Stewart. I am, however, lacking in the telepathic powers and scientific genius departments.

Professor Xavier dreams of peaceful coexistence between mutants and humanity; for me it will have to be humans and lizard-people. Maybe I can open a school for higher learning to help me reach out to young lizard-people and help mold them into responsible lizard-people who only use their powers for the benefit of all mankind.

"You're addicted to that thing," I say to Neil as we wait by the baggage carousel. He's preoccupied with checking his phone.

"What are you talking about?" he replies. "I'm messaging Jimmy to say we've landed safely."

Neil is in love with his phone, although he won't admit it. The longer I spend on my phone, the more I think I could be doing something more useful, as if I would otherwise be reading a Russian novel.

✧

JoJo and Jimmy pick us up out front in a bright orange Jeep rental. It is a two-hour drive to Cerritos due to road construction on the worst four-lane highway in Mexico. Jimmy has the top down. The dry wind blows into the backseat causing my ears to ring. I suffer from crooked inner ear canals which leads to a wicked wax build-up. I have them syringed before I fly. I make a candle for my niece from the wax each Christmas. Syringing, chewing gum, and wearing ear plugs for takeoff and landing prevent my eardrums from exploding.

The rough desert terrain stretches out in all directions interrupted by patches of dramatic jungle scenery and white-sand beaches. Jimmy pulls over and the three of them take a quick dip in a *cenote*, a freshwater swimming hole created by a sinkhole in the limestone bedrock. For the first time I notice he's sporting a new sea turtle tattoo on his right bicep.

"What about crocodiles?" I ask, nervously scanning the surface while they laugh, dive, bob, float, splash, and otherwise enjoy each other.

"This is a busy tourist route," Jimmy yells back. "Mexican crocodiles stay away from it."

"They're listed as a 'Least Concern' species," JoJo shouts.

I am not convinced. That was the view Democrats had of Trump in 2015.

Back in the Jeep, we pass by a Mayan ruin. I feel a deep reverence for the local culture and history, although their calendar begs a rethink. The Mayan calendar resembles an Oreo cookie. The Oreo calendar tells us not to worry and just dip ourselves in milk.

"As close to paradise as you'll find," says Jimmy breezily, looking over his shoulder at me. "The best kept secret in Me-hi-co." He turns onto the winding dirt road that leads down to their tiny rental casa. "Wind chill of thirty-three degrees Celsius today," he announces with a mirthful laugh.

As much as Jimmy likes to imagine he's roughing it, JoJo makes sure they indulge themselves. They have a housekeeper, which they don't have in Canada. The casa is spotless. We throw our stuff down on the floor in the guest room and I quickly change into my trunks for an ocean dip.

"Best keep your things off the floor," advises Jimmy, passing by the open doorway. "Scorpions sometimes crawl into things. They're not big enough to kill you but they still pack a sting. Make sure you check your flip-flops in the morning."

Wearing flip-flops in bed is a done deal.

The sun in Mexico is brutal, and I am a perfect storm for developing skin cancer—a triptych of fair skin, a constellation of moles on my back, and the wheezing ozone layer. I lather on waterproof sunscreen and SPF protection first thing in the morning. I spend most of the day slippery to the touch, applying and reapplying the messy sunscreen. I learned the hard way last year not to be fooled by overhead clouds and cool breezes. My skin got so tight *I* was in danger of becoming a lizard-person. Neil is naturally dark-skinned so he is more protected. The bastard.

Jimmy has cleared a path for those who visit, becoming the Expat King of Cerritos. He took Spanish lessons at the local school last year, but quit shortly thereafter when it interfered with his beer-drinking schedule. He speaks Spanish in the present tense only.

"I'm living in the moment. Mindfulness, amigos. Not living in the past or future," he rationalizes as he cracks open a beer at nine in the morning.

Yesterday's hangover is today's first beer.

"It's less expensive to live down here," he grins. Jimmy has been trying to convince Neil and I to retire to Cerritos for the past three years.

"Fruits and vegetables are cheap, cheap, cheap" adds JoJo.

"You sound like a parakeet," I say, wiping sunscreen off my glasses.

The pair of them love to cook and entertain. JoJo reads and writes her books, takes yoga classes, and continues with her Spanish lessons. Salsa and Tortilla, the cocker spaniels, are shaved to cool them down. Their paws bring to mind Edwardian spats.

"I love to grill," Jimmy announces at least three times a day. He sounds like Tony the Tiger. "For everyone."

Note to self, meeting my brother-in-law's expat friends will soon be on the agenda.

The first grilling happens that night.

Expats love fiestas. The guest list includes a core of now-permanent residents and four snowbirds for whom the Cerritos beach is their part-time winter haven. Cerritos is a welcoming community, where you make friends easily whether you want to or not.

One of the expats, Al, is a former New York firefighter who took an early retirement package after 9/11. Al is used to the heat. His claim-to-fame is that an actor in the movie *Reservoir Dogs* served with him in Manhattan's Little Italy during the early eighties.

"That's right, Mr. Pink used to pull people out of burning buildings for a living," Al broadcasts loudly over drinks. Al says everything loudly—he is a walking fire alarm.

After 9/11, the oddball character actor returned to his firefighting platoon and worked twelve-hour shifts alongside Al, digging and sifting through the rubble from the World Trade Center looking for survivors.

"It's hard to visualize," I say, "Steve Buscemi on a firefighter calendar. He looks like a cross between Don Knotts and a bottle opener."

Can Steve Buscemi be a lizard-person? He is such an obvious choice I rule him out immediately.

"Just so I'm clear," says Al, flexing a bicep. "Steve may look like a bug-eyed cigarette but he's a total bad ass." Al can say that because he has the rugged good looks of Steve McQueen in *The Towering Inferno*. He is one of those annoying guys who can change a tire blindfolded, without a jack.

Al's wife, Brenda, is a former fire department badge bunny. She listened to scanners, chased sirens, made loaves and loaves of banana bread and brought them to firehouses, and watched Al from the sidelines, showing up at the blazes he was fighting dressed in her best man-bait attire.

"The early eighties were the War Years," Al says, dropping his voice an octave. He speaks of the eighties as if the Vietnam War had come to the streets of New York City. He reminds me of that older F.B.I. agent in *Die Hard*, the one with the bad skin.

"Because of the recession," Al elaborates, "people were burning down empty buildings for insurance money. Landlords abandoned buildings because they couldn't afford to keep tenants there. It was nuts. We'd get a call, go to a building, come back and get another call."

Brenda eventually tracked Al down, showing up at his local "bar for badges" and made her move. Things moved from hot to inferno very quickly.

"John Mellencamp should've written that song about us, not Jack and Diane," she says without moving her mouth.

"Our fire was hotter than any backdraft," Al winks. He imitates a siren. I swear a pelican stopped fishing to listen. Fanning the flames further, I learned they had their first tryst in Al's station pumper.

"Just like William Baldwin and Jennifer Jason Leigh," giggles Brenda with the laughter of a fifteen-year old. All very unsettling coming from a fifty-five year old sunbaked trophy wife. Now an aging beach bunny hooked on Botox, Brenda opts for olive oil instead of sunscreen.

The other expat couple introduce themselves as Christopher and Elizabeth Van Prattle, a pair of retired Dutch international IT consultants turned Mexican real estate developers. They are fit, casually but fashionably well-dressed, and exude a kind of ease that only rich people can. In another life they could have been Wimbledon tennis doubles champions. They are JoJo and Jimmy's landlords.

"We pay only two-hundred dollars in tax on our condo," Elizabeth shares, nursing her second margarita. "Instead of paying eight thousand in property taxes, we travel."

"You guys should look into it, Neil," Christopher joins in. "Real estate deals are everywhere. And the farther from the beach you go, the better deals you can find. It's still a reasonable walk or quick bike ride. Head farther west, into the local Mexican neighbourhoods, and you pay even less. I've got a two-bedroom bungalow next to the beach listed at $199,000." He glances over his shoulder. "A few blocks inland from the water, but still a pleasant walk, is a two-bedroom unit for $109,000. Now if you want real luxury, I can find that for you too. We're building a condo compound on the beach with resort amenities. Daily house cleaning service, the works. Available for $399,000—and it comes furnished. American dollars of course."

Of course. Christopher and Elizabeth are the kind of people I hate in my real world.

Two of the snowbirds are from Michigan. They both dye their hair black, that fake black that smacks of cheap Halloween fright wigs from Value Village.

"They look like they bleach their faces," I whisper to Neil.

He's short, she's tall. I can't remember their real names. No one can.

"How come men get called hot silver foxes when they age and women just get hot flashes?" says the tall spouse.

"Men naturally age better," says Al, catching his reflection in his glass.

"Men only look distinguished with grey hair if they already looked distinguished before," replies the tall spouse, curtly. "Take George Clooney. Not Woody Allen."

Or the short spouse. He could be cast as a hobbit with a black mullet.

"Grey hair is aging naturally?" he asks rhetorically. "I've had a hip replacement, open heart surgery and chemo. If I aged naturally, I'd be dead."

Personally, I think a house looks best with some snow on the roof. The other snowbirds are Ricky and Sally who rent a bungalow beside Jimmy and JoJo. They also share the pool and outdoor common area. Ricky is an East Londoner that no one can understand. There is a lot of nodding in agreement whenever Ricky is speaking.

"Yewe Knadians are tewe palite," Ricky spits. "If this plass err packed wit' me mates, they'd be ping pong tiddly an' garden hosin' and peas and carroting inna bushes, thay wood. And Posh and Beckin' wit' the local Birds."

It is a job for Alan Turing trying to decipher Ricky's Cockney accent. Ricky laughs himself into a spasmodic fit and almost swallows his cigar—one of those big Freudian stogies, the smoking, sexting kind. By day, Ricky lounges and bakes by the pool, blasting classic pub tunes and modern hip-hop on his iPad—imagine Sydney Greenstreet in a speedo. Ricky is into TikTok. He tapes himself dancing and posts the alarming videos on Facebook. It can put you off tacos for life.

Sally, Ricky's wife, is the spitting image of Michael Palin during his Monty Python drag days. Sally rarely remembers how she got home from the bar the night before.

The sun sets at 6:40 p.m., a whimsical tiger-tail swirl of colour. JoJo lights an assortment of candles and tiki torches, setting the mood while keeping the bugs away. Jimmy pours us all a Mexican red wine and serves up his feast, consisting of Mexican barbecued chicken marinated in achiote paste and a healthy salad with romaine lettuce, black beans, cherry tomatoes, avocado, queso fresco, and cilantro in an avocado-yogurt dressing.

After dinner, the rum and tequila come out. I am going to spend the next seven days of my vacation self-quarantined in bed with a Mexican hangover.

To quarantine or not to quarantine is the topic of post-dinner conversation.

"Did y'ear about tha crewz hip?" says Ricky, lighting up another fat stogie.

We all nod until Al finally says "What are you talking about, mate?"

"Crewz hip," repeats Ricky.

"Crew zip?" says Al.

"Crewz hip!" repeats Ricky again, waving his cigar for emphasis. "Crewz hip!"

"Cruise ship?" asks JoJo. She is a contestant on *Wheel of Fortune for Dummies.*

"Tha crewz hip off tha roast, aye."

Christopher steps in with the diplomacy of a U.N. translator. "There's a Norwegian cruise ship stranded in the Caribbean Sea off the coast of Cancun."

"Isn't there a flu bug on board or thomething?" thays Brenda, thlurring her words, well on her way to a fifth margarita grand thlam.

"Something like that," says Elizabeth. I detect a slight trace of condescension. "Twenty crew members and passengers are sick. The captain wants to dock in Cancun so they can disembark."

You will never catch me on a six-storey cruise ship. There is something about a mass-market luxury cruise that's unbearably sad. A giant mall and buffet table housed in a giant sardine can floating on water with no land in sight. It is not my idea of a relaxing vacation. Your capacities for choice, error, regret, and despair? All are removed. Plus, I don't want to see seasick passengers dressed in cheap formal dinner wear. Jimmy says you are too high up to hear the ship's big engines. I am sure I would be the exception, developing an unnerving spinal throb, losing my balance and falling overboard.

"Mexican authorities are trying to decide whether to let the Captain land or not," explains Christopher. "The WHO is weighing in."

"Who?" Brenda thays thloppily.

"Exactly," says Christopher.

"Who?" repeats Brenda, stamping her bare feet in the sand. Small children and faded beach bunnies have a lot in common.

"Of course, that's their job," says Christopher with a quick conspiratorial wink to the rest of us.

"Whose job?" says Brenda. It hasn't dawned on her yet that she's the only one not in on the joke.

"Precisely," says Christopher.

"C'mon, stop it! What is the name of the organization?"

"Not what...WHO," says Jimmy, joining in, his old radio days timing still on point.

"That'th what I'm trying to find out!" Brenda screams, knocking her glass over in the proceth. Salsa and Tortilla race to the accident site.

"World Health Organization," says Elizabeth drily. "They arrive at a decision tomorrow."

"All because of a Norwegian flu?" asks JoJo. Young adult fiction writers and current events rarely go together.

"It's not the flu. It's something else," says Neil. "A virus of some sort."

"Anyone want a Corona?" says Jimmy, weaving his way to the outdoor bar fridge.

"Sure," shouts Al. "Leave them out there. Give them supplies and let them refuel, but don't let them land. They can go back to Norway and let the Norwegians deal with it. If Cancun gets sick, we'll all get sick."

"You're being paranoid, Al," says Jimmy. "Not everything is a disaster waiting to happen." He takes a long swig of his Corona.

"Once a firefighter always a firefighter," says Al. "The WHO should quarantine the entire ship."

"Is Roger Daltrey on board?" It's Sally perking up, "That's my generation," and she passes out.

"Tomorrow is another day," says Jimmy.

"Leth go thkinny dipping," Brenda pipes up. She stands up, starts to spin, and gets caught up in her halter top. "Fuck!"

Ricky begins stripping off his shorts.

The sound of an ATV pulling up on the beach.

Saved by the sound of a Northern Ontario off-road bush engine. Salsa and Tortilla bark up a tsunami. JoJo doesn't make them wear their anti-barking collars in Mexico.

"Shut up!" Jimmy yells.

The dogs quiet down.

"Hey, Fred!" Jimmy shouts to the driver, sounding more like a star-struck hockey fan than his usual Mexican chill self.

A man clad in Bermuda shorts and a pink golf shirt jumps off the ATV with the ease of a Hollywood action-movie terrorist. He takes off his helmet, revealing a fierce, craggy Nordic blonde handsomeness—Rutger Hauer hiding out in Mexico. He's tall and physically fit with a striking yet casually commanding presence.

But it is the man's foreignness, his Europeanese, which is immediately brought into play, a symbol of something sinister and coldly cynical, like an uber-shark waiting just beyond he reef.

"*Buenas noches mis amigos*! How is your night going?" the man says, his Spanish perfect. This Foreign Fred is a curious specimen. His mouth smiles. His eyes do not.

"*Muy bien*," replies Christopher with another wink accompanied by a grin. I sense a secret code.

"Couldn't be better," Jimmy repeats for my benefit. "*Te gustaría una cerveza?*"

"*Gracias.*" Foreign Fred grabs a seat with his back to the casa.

"'ow er things droppin' frown at tha nuclear sub?" says Ricky.

"Busy night," replies Foreign Fred.

I almost cough up a filling. He understands Ricky's accent.

"Monster margarita night and a full moon," he says.

I look up at the night sky over the ocean. The moon is keeping us company with its buttermilk glow. I learn that Foreign Fred became a permanent resident in Cerritos ten years ago, opening a popular expat beach bar.

"'owl and meow." Ricky leers and gives Brenda a nudge.

"You remember JoJo's brother, Rudy, and his partner, Neil?" says Jimmy. He hands Foreign Fred a Corona with lime.

"Ah, of course, how are things in the land of ice and snow?" Foreign Fred responds with a deliberate touch of self-aware drollery.

"Cold," says Neil, "Glad to be here."

"Better than on that cruise chip," I say. "Guess we'll know more tomorrow."

Foreign Fred gives me a disconcerting look. "Even if they do dock in Cancun, no one's coming here, Rudrigo. We're Mexico's best kept secret, right Jimmy boy?"

Best kept secret? Stop the Mayan calendar. An expat bar in a remote beach town would be the perfect cover for a drug-dealing cartel.

I know enough from watching *Sixty Minutes* that Mexico's drug cartel history is one of violent splits and constant fighting between themselves as they battle for supremacy. Cartel have already turned Cancun and Playa del Carmen into a deadly war zone. Foreign Fred is alarmingly right. The authorities won't give

Cerritos a second look. The village *fuerza policial* consist of two uniformed *oficiales* riding around in a golf cart with a goat.

"What if Foreign Fred is secretly a drug lord?" I say to Neil later, after checking under the sheets for scorpions.

"What?"

"Hear me out. What if he's the notorious 'El Mencho,' murdering and mutilating his enemies, stuffing them in bin bags, and dumping their remains in abandoned wells in the desert. There's that dried-up old well just a few miles outside of town. We passed it on our way in from the airport. I thought nothing of it then, but what if Foreign Fred is a balaclava-sporting killer?"

"He's not. Go to sleep." Neil rolls over and falls asleep.

The recent spate of killings in the news increased my anxiety about travelling to Mexico. Last week, terrified tourists were sent running for cover when a lifeguard working at a five-star resort near Tulum was gunned down. Mexican authorities were quick to insist that the violence took place away from the hotel zone. But it's been creeping out of the Mexican *barrios* and closer to tourist hot spots. I almost cancelled our flight until JoJo convinced me, as she always does.

"You're safe here, Rudy" she purred on FaceTime. "You've come three years in a row and the closest you've come to a drug cartel is a teenager smoking pot on the beach."

I wonder if I'll have to pay protection money to Foreign Fred. Fred isn't even his real name. I found out from Jimmy. It's Fiske. He changed it when he moved to Mexico to set up shop, leaving his international import/export business identity behind him in Norway.

Or *did* he?

I share these thoughts with Neil after we crawl, or rather stumble, into bed, long after Christopher and Elizabeth discreetly slipped away. They missed the sand show. Ricky passing out on the beach, a sauced and naked Moby Thick, harpooned by his own drunkenness; Al rescuing a wailing Sally from the undertow or "under toad" as she drunkenly put it, reminding me of Garp's young son, but he's got a legitimate excuse—he's a character in a

John Irving novel; Brenda getting thtung by a jellyfish; Foreign Fred firing off fireworks and scaring the locals; and, finally, Jimmy's tablet dying. Nothing left to drown out the sound of the vomiting.

"Fiske is not the leader of a drug cartel," Neil says, pulling off the sheets. "Besides, who ever heard of a Norwegian drug lord?"

"Exactly. What better cover. *And* he's got international connections."

"No, Rudy. You don't see Al Pacino or Johnny Depp doing bad Norwegian accents while snorting cocaine on screen. The only 'snow' Fiske is dealing with is the alpine skiing he left behind when he came here."

"What about that show *Lillehammer*?"

"Go to sleep."

I get up, wrestle with the doorknob, trip over Tortilla in the hallway, and find the kitchen faucet. I drink a gallon of water and pass out.

KA-THWICK!

There is something on the roof. It sounds like a family of prehistoric raccoons. Every- thing is bigger in Mexico, including hangovers.

"Neil, wake up!" I jab him in the ribs.

"What?" he groans groggily.

"There's something on the roof. Something big."

KA-THWICK!

"That is big," he says, sitting up and staring up and beyond the ceiling fan.

"It's Foreign Fred!"

"It's not Foreign Fred."

"Or one his goons. He wants me dead because he knows I know."

"Will you relax? It's an animal of some kind. It's probably just a big lizard."

KA-THWICK!

If it is a lizard then Godzilla is up on the roof.

A scrambling sound and then silence.

"See," he says. "No drug cartel hitman. Go to sleep." He rolls over and falls back to sleep. I hate that he can sleep through anything. A nuclear bomb could land in our backyard and he'd still wake up fresh and rested. Eventually I fall asleep, dreaming of giant lizard-people driving black SUVs, carrying machine guns, their trunks filled with bags of Columbian blow.

"Ah, you heard Poncho Villa last night," Jimmy says over a breakfast of toast, peanut butter, and fried beans.

"Who?" I ask, giving Neil an "I told you so" look.

"Poncho Villa," repeats Jimmy.

"Pancho," interrupts Neil.

"Pancho is the revolutionary. Poncho is an iguana who lives in the neighbourhood. Big fella too. You'll most likely see him this afternoon. He loves to sun on that rock out there." He points to a rocky outcropping on the beach.

"See," says Neil. He turns to Jimmy. "He thinks Fred is a drug lord."

"I do not," I lie, spilling my coffee on my shorts.

Later that afternoon I read by the pool, enjoying a moment out of the midday sun with a bottle of water and a banana. I notice something appear from behind JoJo's makeshift clothes line. It is dull grey in colour with a tall dorsal crest. A large spiny iguana. He is huge, almost five-feet long, half of which is his rough scaly tail. Poncho Villa, the Iguana revolutionary, has arrived. He looks about, sees me mid-banana, and gradually noses his way towards me.

I stretch out my legs hoping to discourage him from coming any closer.

I start eating my banana faster.

He stares at me, a hungry purpose in his eyes.

I take another bite.

He swishes his tail.

I take another bite (it is one big banana).

Poncho Villa lets out a low hiss.

I can't move. Paralyzed with lizard fear, my vocal chords freeze. I am going to die from a lizard attack on my Reading Week vacation. It isn't exactly what I envisioned for my obituary. "College teacher eaten by Mexican guerilla iguana."

I close my eyes, hold my breath, and stand (or rather sit) my ground. Suddenly two strong-clawed legs scrabble up mine. Disregarding the rules about not feeding wild animals, I throw the last of my banana on the stone patio floor next to Poncho Villa. He snatches it up, scurries across the tiles, climbs up the rock fence that encircles the casa, and jumps onto a low-hanging tree branch, disappearing into the foliage.

I am furious with my sister. She is the cause of Poncho Villa's bold behaviour. She's always feeding the raccoons at her trailer park and wants to open a hobby petting zoo, but Jimmy is allergic to llama spit. Recklessly feeding bananas to an iguana the size of a crocodile is pushing it.

I did breathe a little easier when I convinced myself that Poncho isn't really dangerous, just an opportunist. Still, I wish I had packed my coyote stick. I've heard that Costa Ricans sell tourists colourful forked iguana sticks for a handsome sum. It sounds like fake news. It's a clear act of animal cruelty and Costa Rica is renowned for its ecotourism, not iguana bashing. It has to be a hoax. But now, after my banana-snatching close call, I wonder if Costa Rica might actually be leading the field in iguana-deterrent weapons, and that Mexico has some catching up to do.

That evening the four of us go out to dinner at Fred's, the expat bar, not Foreign Fred's home. No one is invited to his house, according to JoJo. Fred's is a tacky cross between Rick's Café Americano and a Disneyesque version of *The Flintstones* for adults, serving snowbirds and locals alike. Fred's is all about chill and watching the world go by; the bar itself is modelled after a prehistoric Bedrock cartoon cave-tavern, a mixture of boulders and timbers under a thatched roof—all housed inside an actual

The Land Of The Lizard-people | 159

cave. Monster cocktails, endless popcorn, booths shaped like Fred Flintstone's car, patio lanterns hanging from stalactites, the friendly serving staff dressed as Betty, Wilma, and the adolescent versions of Pebbles and Bam Bam who remember our names from last year. They even know what we ordered. The tips at Fred's are substantial. Staff turn-over is practically non-existent.

A large sign out front announces, "You'll have a yabba dabba doo time!" *Flintstones* paraphernalia decorates the walls. Classic sixties bubble-gum rock bops and bangs out of two large overhead speakers disguised as pterodactyls perched above a cramped dance floor. Cheesy, cozy, and crazy, and packed to the ribs.

The use of *Flintstones* imagery to attract the tourist trade also plays an important role in Foreign Fred's assertions of a "with it" and "good-humoured" guy identity.

Fred Flintstone was not a drug dealer. No better disguise than a beloved sixties cartoon character. But, to me, the link to the famous American comedy cartoon is an indication that Cerritos is not so remote as to not be linked up with the global network, satellite TV, and drug smuggling.

We get a table at the back and order a round of Great Gazoo green margaritas and a rib plate combo to share. Unsurprisingly, Fred's menu is strictly BBQ, its specialty a Barney Rubble rib-eyed steak, grilled over coals, much like Barney himself. When the ribs arrive, I find them too fatty and the sauce is mostly ketchup. The alcohol distracts from the subpar cuisine. Gathering by the gringos that nightly pack the bar, the cheap booze works. Neil orders a Dino pulled-pork sandwich that is surprisingly tender and actually tastes like pork.

The happy hour crowd parts and Foreign Fred emerges wearing a raggedy deep sky blue necktie and a sleeveless orange and black spotted loin cloth with a torn hemline. He looks like the Hanna-Barbera version of an aging Chippendale's male stripper. He slyly works the room, mingling with the regulars, briefly joining the bar flies for a quick shot of Mr. Slate tequila, flirting with the women, and ordering his staff to push the Wilma wings and whiskey. Any other human being would look ridiculous in a Fred Flintstone costume. Not Foreign Fred. He wears it like a modern-day Roman emperor.

He catches Jimmy's wave and sits down between Neil and I.

"*Hola amigos. Están todos disfrutando de sus comidas?*"

"You bet," sings Jimmy. How much more can Jimmy fawn over this guy.

"Why don't you just ask for his autograph, Jimmy?" I say, blowing out a noisy breath.

"*Lo siento?*" Foreign Fred interjects, stealing one of my ribs. "You have a problem with how I run my bar, *Rude*-rigo?"

"No," I say huffily.

"*Tu tienes un problema?*"

"I don't have a problem."

"You don't have a problem," he repeats each word slowly.

"No, I don't have a problem." I start to sweat. It's not the heat.

"Then what?" Foreign Fred speaks plainly.

"Nothing. Can we please drop this?"

"Ah, I see. You're jealous of me."

"I am not."

"Oh, but you are, my Canadian friend." He looks over to Jimmy. "You're brother-in-law is wound up tighter than a boa constrictor hugging a monkey. He needs to learn how to chill. I should take him deep-sea fishing. *Nadar con los peces.*" Foreign Fred laughs loud and hard.

I am in a scene from a mob movie with Fred Flintstone. Swimming with the fishes. Just what I need. Murdered by the Nordic leader of a Mexican drug cartel.

"*Es una broma,*" says Foreign Fred, ordering me another a drink.

"He's joking," says JoJo, kicking my shin under the table.

"Chill," says Jimmy.

"Your drug cartel paranoia is no longer funny," says Neil. "The heat has fried your brain. Drink some water, you're dehydrated."

"Okay, okay, I'm sorry," I mutter, taking Neil's water glass. "Can we just get back to drinking green aliens?"

I feel humiliated and ready for bed.

Foreign Fred's tone and expression brighten. "I was talking to some Aussie girls I met on the street and I said, 'Have you *chicas jóvenes* checked out that Flintstones bar?' and they said, 'Oh, no, it's too American, too artificial.' They hadn't even been inside yet. I offered to buy them a round if they'd come in for one drink. Once they get in here, they have an entirely different experience. And why? Because it's in a cave," he laughs, "and very 'natural.' Look at them now." He points to the dance floor where four tanned young women are drunkenly twisting and shouting, many rounds later. "*El hechizo de la cueva.*"

I just want to leave.

KA-THWICK!

Poncho Villa is at it again, right on schedule.

Every night since the day of our arrival, at precisely four in the morning, the sound of a banana-stealing monster-iguana clatters across the roof.

By day five, I am exhausted, barely able to keep my eyes open. To add insult to injury, Poncho Villa has started following me to the beach in hopes of banana treats. JoJo has created a an environmental no-no. I half-expect the fishermen of Cerritos to show up outside the casa at night with pitchforks and lanterns.

Nevertheless, I am just as bad. I keep feeding him. Out of guilt and fear of the repercussions I'll face if I don't. Poncho Villa could easily be the muscle for Foreign Fred's drug cartel.

Sunstroke and sleep deprivation make your mind do strange things.

KA-THWICK!

It hits me.

I have not seen Foreign Fred and Poncho Villa in the same place at the same time.

It becomes clear, clear as the ocean, clear as the blue sky. Nothing has ever been this clear.

Foreign Fred is a lizard-person.

It all makes sense, his physical appearance and demeanour,

his piercing crystal blue eyes, the blonde shaggy hair, and his bar that keeps the North Americans in Cerritos drunk so they remain mind-controlled under his magic cave spell. World dominance is Foreign Fred's goal, cocaine his means.

Most of Cerritos is rural pasture enclosed by barbed wire fencing. Palms trees and the ocean make up the background. Cows, horses, and chickens wander the dirt roads. It is a pastoral paradise coupled with mounds of shit.

It is low tide, the following afternoon, as I sink my toes into the warm white sand. Little water spouts form beside my toes. I have seen tiny crabs race erratically along the beach and retreat into holes, but this is different. It is as if the beach is a giant waterbed that sprung a leak, and then another, and another.

A wind begins to blow in off the ocean. Strange. It's the dry season. High winds come with the wet season. I wave to Neil to get out of the water. He waves back and ignores me.

I bury my unease in my beer and lean back in a plastic chair warped by the sun to give it a reclining effect. I purchase my lunch from a snack stand on the beach. The homemade tortilla chips heaped on the plate are perfect for dipping into the ceviche of fresh fish caught off the coast. It might well be the best fish I've ever tasted if it weren't for my mounting anxiety. The spicy hot peppers don't help.

I order another two-dollar *chelada*, a lager beer on the rocks – *Pacífico* is my favourite – with a liberal dose of lime juice on the rim. It hits the spot.

Ka-thwick!

The sound startles me. I look behind me. Too late.

For a split second I swear I see Poncho Villa in a pink golf shirt disappearing behind a boulder.

"*Hola, Rudrigo,*" shouts a male voice instead. I twist my neck back around to see Foreign Fred striding across the sand towards me, his toes oblivious to the sand crabs. He plunks a beach towel down on the hot sand beside me and sits down.

"You can't cure an asshole," he says icily.

It's the moment of my death.

"I've got no sympathy for those who blame others, who take no responsibility for their actions," he says. He is biding his time, playing with me, stretching my murder out.

"I always clean up after myself," I reply, quickly sobering up.

"Not you. The cruise ship. It's docking in Cancun and those assholes are allowing it."

"Who is?" I notice a rip in Foreign Fred's pink golf shirt.

"The Mexican government. *Malditos pendejos*. The Norwegian cruise line isn't taking any responsibility. They're blaming the Chinese, claiming it was an infected passenger from Beijing who ate a fruit bat before boarding that started this mess. Can you believe it? And there are more cases. Over fifty now. Both crew and passengers. Just what I need, a flu bug to hit right in the middle of tourist season. *Maldito infierno*."

His eyes could spit blood.

"And the gringos are oblivious," he continues in disgust. "Look at them."

I spy a group of teenagers playing beach volleyball, children digging in the sand, parents reading and dozing under large striped umbrellas, and Brenda baking in the heat. Now, there's a genuine lizard. Her scaly and dry skin is as brown as shoe leather.

Foreign Fred reaches into a mini-beach cooler and cracks open a Corona.

"Here's to the stupidity of mankind," he says with cold-blooded satisfaction, his mood shifting with the change in the wind's direction. He raises his beer and toasts the blazing sun. "Corona virus, here we come."

He grins eerily for a brief instant.

His teeth glisten.

His tongue flickers.

The lizard-people are about to make a move.

ORPHAN SOUP

Snow, ice, cold.

Followed by snow, ice, cold.

Topped off with more snow, ice, and cold.

The wind whipped through the cemetery as we struggled to lay our father to rest. I wanted to curse him for dying in mid-January, but he'd forgotten what seasons were long ago. The behind-the-scenes aspect of the funeral industry is one that remains a mystery. One of the oft-overlooked details of burial is what happens during the winter when the ground is frozen. Frozen turf, as our family discovered, was difficult (read expensive) to dig into, especially at the depth required for inhumation. When combined with other winter hazards like unplowed roads (the hearse got stuck twice), unsafe driving conditions (freezing rain made for a black ice coated skating rink), and the snowfall on the cemetery itself, the results were not conducive for a dignified interment.

Walking towards our father's grave, our family parodied one of those nature documentaries filmed in slow motion. You know the kind: a Canada goose circles, lowers its landing gear and comes in low, attempting to touch down on an ice-covered lake. The goose applies the brakes and skids as if on skis, wings flapping, honking madly, without stopping. Beethoven's "Ode to Joy" accompanies the wildfowl silent movie.

Slipping and sliding on the frozen snow, JoJo too honked her displeasure in a most undignified manner. Neil did fishtails into a bench. My right foot slid sideways from under me. When I attempted a forward step, my left foot veered off at an awkward angle and I went down hard. The casket, minus three of its pallbearers, slid broadside into the grave like an out-of-control bobsled.

A typical goose has upwards of fifteen-thousand layered down feathers to keep its body warm. I felt like a plucked goose, shivering uncontrollably and flapping my arms to try to drive the winter away. It was a losing battle. My goose wasn't cooked, it was frozen solid.

"There's no such thing as cold weather," JoJo said, her voice muffled by her designer balaclava.

"Yeah right," I said as I attempted to right myself for a third time.

"Only inappropriate clothing," she continued, squeezing my autumn wool blend dress coat. "There's a reason why everyone in Northern Ontario owns the same knee length black puffy coat—and it's definitely not fashion."

Everyone that is except me. I refuse to wear a puffer. I don't want to look like the Michelin Man. The irony is I end up having to wear warm hoodies and sweaters underneath my coat and wind up looking like the Michelin man anyway, what with my bulky arms and chest from all the layers.

"And the cold weather has nothing to do with you spending the winter in Mexico."

My sister was a hypocrite. She and Jimmy hadn't spent a winter in Birch Lake in seven years. She could afford to act all superior; she was flying back to Mexico in a week. Jimmy didn't come home for the funeral. Someone had to stay behind to look after Salsa and Tortilla, and return airfare for two during peak tourism season was astronomical. Besides, it wasn't as if our father's death came as a surprise. He'd been sliding toward the grave for five years.

He spent his final days shouting out billboard slogans from before my time.

"Timmins—The Cold And The Beautiful."

"Get Goosed In Wawa."

"Swastika—It's Not What You Think."

JoJo and I sorted through our father's will. Our father didn't have a pension and running a billboard marketing business in Northern Ontario hadn't exactly been a money maker. The profit he made from selling the house went towards his room and board at Lakeview Manor, our mother's apartment, and their funerals. There *was* his hockey memorabilia collection. Our father found endless enjoyment in tracking, collecting, and displaying NHL player autographs in all of their minimalistic, perfect ink on flawless paper, glory—the Original Six was just the tip of the ice rink. He had autographed jerseys, helmets, sticks, skates, pucks, gloves, tickets, programs, postcards, vintage photos, hockey cards, and jock straps.

He started his collection after Jonah failed to take an interest in playing hockey. His dream of him playing in the big leagues was benched. To our father, hockey wasn't simply a sport, but a stand-in and marker for the Canadian identity. Either you played hockey or you didn't. Either you skated or you didn't. Either you were Canadian or you weren't. In our household, not learning to skate backwards was viewed as a traitorous act. One time, when I was in university, I asked him what it said about Canada that our other *official* national sport, lacrosse—based on a sport played by Indigenous people on this land since time immemorial—was constantly overlooked for our mythical ties to hockey, a game created and played mostly by white boys and men. He handed the phone to my mother.

When our father succumbed to the middle stage of Alzheimer's, he forgot about hockey. Not only forgot about it, but violently refused to watch any games on the new flat screen in the manor's common room. He didn't get to see Don Cherry's career-ending racist rant. Oddly enough, he did enjoy watching pairs figure-skating, a sport he'd previously ignored, except when our mother forced him to sit through Kurt Browning's Christmas special during which he'd make fun of the male skaters in their "fancy pants." He never did get to witness "Battle of the Blades." The two opposing skating worlds pairing up would've marked the end of his world as he knew it. I don't think he could've survived Sidney Crosby doing a toe jump.

When he was admitted to Lakeview, JoJo and I put his collection in storage in one of Jimmy's many handy sheds—Jonah didn't have a basement, Neil had bad memories of childhood hockey bullies, and Evie lived in mantra-land. Our father had included a provision for the collection in his will. Larry was to auction it off and split the profit amongst the five us. Well, five had become four, so, we decided that Jimmy should sell everything on eBay.

"We're orphans now," JoJo said, pouring us each another glass of wine. "Adult orphans."

I hadn't thought about our parents' deaths in those terms till then. It made me feel alone, like I had a huge boulder in front of me. An orphaned adult—I hated the sound of it.

"We are now officially midlife orphans," JoJo said.

Of course, becoming a midlife orphan isn't a tragedy; it's actually the normal way of the world. Still, the term struck me as a bad (or sad) joke. Orphaned at 55?

"I refuse to put on a red wig," I said, "and move to Miss Hannigan's orphanage."

"Little Orphan Rudolph."

"The Sun Will *Not* Come Up Tomorrow."

"Evie says we are the forgotten grievers."

Evie had returned to Toronto to make sure Esther was still alive after participating in a bizarre Extinction Rebellion protest.

"She says we're the lucky ones whose parents had good innings, the people who after weeks are expected to dust themselves off, put their pain behind them, and get back to a normal, happy life."

If only it were that simple. It might be the natural order of things that parents die before their children, but the sheer inevitability is no cushion to the pain, soul-searching, and feeling of rudderlessness. For weeks after, Jonah couldn't leave his house, obsessively listening to our father's Johnny Cash CDs while sketching black skies weeping down on cathedrals.

"It's disenfranchised grief," Evie said over the phone later that evening. Esther was very much alive despite suffering from mild frostbite. Recreating the Ice Age was not for the faint of global warming heart.

"Disenfranchised grief?" I said. I thought of the consumer reaction if McDonalds closed all of their restaurants.

"What's the first question your boss asked you when you asked for bereavement leave?"

"How old Dad was." Then he told me I had two days.

"Because people can say their parents had good innings that

grief can be disqualified by others. People mean well, but they don't realize that there isn't some magic expiry date for grieving. Death of the elderly is not a grief that tends to be appreciated."

On rare occasions, Evie's Jungian analyst-speak was comforting. This was not one of those occasions.

I started thinking about how my parents were the only ones who held certain memories of me as boy. It was not a comfortable thought. I had defined myself in terms of my relationships to them. Their deaths challenged me to define who I really was. They were like a mirror—a mirror I wanted back.

"I feel empty," I said to JoJo. It was the following day and we were sorting through old family slides and photographs in the basement. Jimmy was busy sorting through stacks of our father's vintage hockey cards.

"Who knew that rookie sports cards were an endangered species?" he said after a long day in the shed. Despite all the warning stories of mothers nationwide throwing out shoeboxes full of childhood treasures and families overlooking a collection after a relative had passed, vintage rookie cards had been disappearing at an alarming rate. Two months later, Jimmy sold a 1979 O-Pee-Chee Wayne Gretzky Rookie Card for close to fifty-thousand dollars. Hockey card collectors were a strange breed.

JoJo passed me a black and white photograph of our parents posing in front of Niagara Falls, the Honeymoon Capital of the World in the 1950s—their hopes and dreams generously spray-soaked by the Maid of the Mist. In the picture, our parents both have new haircuts and new shoes, a surefire giveaway they were honeymooners.

"It's like all our back-up is gone," I said.

"The grief comes flooding back—Mom, Nicky, Larry, Aunt Muriel."

"We're the next in line to die."

"Isn't that a cheerful thought?"

It was a chilling realization—no one was between the Grim Reaper and me. After our mother's death, four months earlier, I deliberately became too preoccupied with our father to fully mourn her. My father's death plunged me into a bottomless pit of depression as I struggled with the grief that hadn't previously been fully acknowledged. I'd been trying to push our mother's death away, keeping it at arm's length by consuming myself with committee work at the college and visiting my father (knowing full well it was absolutely pointless). He was trapped in 1955 selling billboards in Kapuskasing. I bought six.

When our mother died, I looked at every scrap of paper in her apartment hoping she'd written something for me. My generation is selfish. Our mother was always interested in what was happening to us but when we grew up the interest wasn't reciprocated. Suddenly the gaps were emerging in what I wanted to know. I was rather shocked at what I didn't know about my father. When my parents were around I was used to the fact that I could always ring my mother up and ask her.

Evie says Freud got it wrong, that grief is not about disconnecting. Apparently, "out of sight, out of mind" only works when my boss is on vacation. Parental death is a compulsory subject in the school of life. Everyone is enrolled. Everyone pays tuition in the form of grief. I just wish I'd studied for the final exam.

For several months after my parents' deaths, I had little bandwidth to ruminate on the double loss and what it meant. I kept busy doing nothing. But after a few months, the "orphan" talk began to resonate with me. I was sitting in JoJo's kitchen, nursing a beer at eleven in the morning. It's always happy hour somewhere, my go to excuse. Although my mood was anything but happy that particular morning.

"I wish I could call Mom right now."

"Anything wrong?" said JoJo, unloading the dishwasher.

"No," I replied. "I just miss talking with her." I plunked myself down on a bar stool at the rolling kitchen island. "I still dial her number and..." I let out a sigh—a record-breaking kind of sigh.

JoJo unloaded a wine glass, placed it on the island, reached for an open bottle of merlot, thought better of it, and veered toward the fridge. "I'll make us egg salad sandwiches. That'll help cheer us up. I can't guarantee they'll be up to Mom's standards."

"I don't want to pick out egg shell."

"Once. That happened once."

"Because you were too vain to wear your glasses."

"No, because I was too lazy to change the light bulb over the sink."

JoJo set about making us lunch. I spun around on my stool to face her.

"I've had it with the college." I blurted it out.

"You say that every Saturday," JoJo replied while chopping an onion. Oddly enough, she rarely teared up.

"This time I mean it," I said, polishing off my beer. "The strike did me in. 'The business of education.' I hate it. Students pay their tuitions and we hand them a diploma. It's like going through a drive-thru. No questions asked. Due tomorrow? Do tomorrow. Management keeps insisting that we have to maintain our standards, while at the same time bumping up the grades at the end of the semester so that every student passes. It's become a numbers game. Retention, retention, retention. Money, money, money. Crap, crap, crap. I know management has to make money to keep the doors open but at what cost? Nowadays, if a student has a pulse, they're admitted. 'Why, you're breathing, grab a seat. No, you don't have to come to class or hand in an assignment. Congratulations, here's your diploma. You are now a certified welder who can't read or write.' It's like flying a plane while building it. I'd love to say, 'I'm sorry, no class today, my dog ate my lesson plan.' Salinger actually did that. Last semester. He chowed down on my Intransitive Verbs lecture notes. He ate. He whined. He puked."

"If you're that miserable, quit."

"And do what?"

"You tell me."

"That's just it. I *don't* know. I can't afford to retire yet. I'd lose a third of my pension. We certainly can't live on Neil's butler salary."

"What about your share of the hockey sales?"

"What about it?"

"Don't tell me you spent all of it on your kitchen reno?"

"Yup."

"Forty thousand dollars!"

"Neil wanted enameled lava countertops."

"Did you have to buy the volcano?"

"Queer pressure. I have this recurring nightmare of having to survive on KD. It's like I'm back at university only, in my dream, every room in our house is filled with boxes and boxes of orange neon-hued macaroni."

"Who could eat an entire box of that stuff? 'Excuse me, I have to live at the gym for the next year.'"

"Anyhow, there are days I resent Neil for quitting teaching. He can, but I can't."

"You know what Evie would say."

We said it together: "Chase your passion, not your pension."

"Yeah, yeah, yeah," I grumbled. "It's easy to make grand moral pronouncements when you're rich." I can always get behind a good old-fashioned pout. "Neil gets to pursue his passion, and I'm stuck chasing a college pension."

"In yesterday's news," JoJo announced, her tablespoon serving as an eggy microphone, "the Pity Train derailed at the corner of Suck It Up and Move On, then crashed into We All Have Problems before coming to a stop at Get Over It."

"Very funny." I slouched over, wanting to fall asleep and never wake up.

"You should listen to yourself. Just be thankful you aren't raising Esther. Imagine the cost of all those global warming summits and their new solar panel installation."

"Then there's Salinger and the cat. The amount we spend on their food and vet bills could feed a small village in Mexico for months."

"Okay, then don't come to Cerritos this year."

"What? Are you kidding? And spend an entire winter in Birch Lake? I'd go mad."

"You can't have your Mexico and eat it too. Stick it out at the college for another five years. You can do it. You just have to find something else to do in your spare time that fulfills you. Take a yoga class. Learn Spanish. Write a book."

"That's your life, not mine. I've got a Master's Degree in Education and I'm teaching English to welding students. Do you know how depressing that is? I feel like Mozart teaching chopsticks to four-year olds. It's killing me. But there's nothing I can do about it. And that's even more depressing."

"The college pays well and not everyone is so lucky to have a choice. Good paying jobs are scarce. Think about volunteering. Philanthropy is good for the soul. That's what Mom would say. Help the homeless. Feed the poor. Save a polar bear. The food bank is always looking for volunteers. So is the humane society. Try the soup kitchen. Maybe you'll find meaning in helping others."

"Bah humbug."

"Think about it."

"Since when did you become the ghost of my irritant future?"

"Do it."

"Alright, I'll think about it."

"There's no time like the present."

"Says you."

"Smart cookies don't crumble, they volunteer."

JoJo served up lunch and I sat up. She nailed the sandwich: fresh seasoned egg, the right combo of flavours, a little bit of crunch (celery not shell), and the absolute perfect rye toast, sturdy enough to hold a big scoop of egg salad. Served at room temperature. For a fleeting moment, it felt like our mother was in the room.

"Delicious," I said, spilling a big gluttonous glob on my lap.

"Slow down," JoJo said, handing me a paper towel. "You're inhaling it."

"You did Mom proud, kid," I said between king-size mouthfuls.

"You're worse than Jimmy."

"I'm an emotional eater."

"No, you're a messy eater with lousy table manners."

"I'm pretending to be a homeless person so I can have greater empathy when I volunteer."

"You're awful."

Fear did everything except go out and buy the groceries. Despite the relatively small size of Birch Lake, homeless people were visible on the streets. At night, some stayed at the city mission; others slept on park benches, in makeshift tents by the railyard, under bridges, on porches, in the doorways of small downtown businesses, and inside ATM shelters. Whenever I saw them on the streets, I tried my best to ignore them. They were scary and dangerous, more like zombies on *The Walking Dead* than actual human beings. I knew them as stereotypes: drunks, addicts, mental cases, and criminals.

Finally (and reluctantly), I made the phone call my sister had been pestering me to make. It was my New Year's resolution, one I hoped I might actually keep. On a cold Saturday morning, I showed up to volunteer at the local soup kitchen, Food For Thought.

I was expecting a dilapidated building, something out of Steinbeck and the Great Depression, with men lined up down the street, dressed in shabby coats and caps, coming for a free bowl of vegetable soup and a slice of bread. The infamous Chicago gangster, Al Capone, was one of the first private citizens in America to open a soup kitchen, one that fed hundreds daily. As a relatively cheap meal that's full of nutrients and easy to produce in massive quantities, soup was the perfect food for charity. According to accounts of the time, his private soup kitchen served over five-thousand people on Thanksgiving Day 1930 alone. For this service, Capone was worshipped in Chicago and therefore untouchable by the law. I worked up a Bogey drawl, preparing to address my fellow volunteers as "Mac" or "Doll-face."

In actuality, Food For Thought was housed in a multi-purpose complex with the Daily Refuge (a daytime shelter for the homeless and near homeless) and the Community Thrift Shop. I was taken aback by the large modern building, occupying almost one-quarter of a block, with the visible entrance to Food For Thought marked by a crisp green and white striped awning that covered a recessed doorway. It could've been the entrance to a small business, not a homeless shelter and soup kitchen.

Walking around the complex provided a contrasting picture, one less modern, more rundown. The day-shelter entrance was located beyond a tall chain-link gate, up a slightly inclined gravel drive, and past a weathered picnic table where "guests" (official soup kitchen lingo) congregated. The Community Thrift Shop was located at the back of the complex and there the contrast with the rest of the facility was most striking. Piles of lumber, stacked appliances, disassembled bed frames, mattresses, and assorted carpet pieces littered the grounds, resembling a salvage yard.

When I looked inside the windows of Daily Refuge, I observed guests playing cards, talking, and sleeping in old stuffed chairs. Others sat outside at picnic tables in the freezing cold, smoking. Coffee was always on, and snacks (donuts, bagels, bread, peanut butter and jelly) were available all day. Daily Refuge had two full-time employees: Mary, the executive director, who was an ordained minister, and Rob, the facilities manager, short and stalky, who previously worked in drug and alcohol rehabilitation facilities on the West coast. He himself was homeless for almost seven years. Mary had a pleasing oval face. Her broad smile extended past the edges of her eyes, showing off a gleaming picket fence of great white teeth. Her eyes glittered with KD starlight and a compassion that encompassed the room.

Down the hall toward the soup kitchen was the "cage," a floor to ceiling, locked cubicle housing miscellaneous food supplies and paper products. Just beyond the cage, a door opened to the Food For Thought soup kitchen.

The soup kitchen provided lunch and dinner seven days a week. The dining room was a modest sized room. Guests sat round three rows of tables covered with green plastic flannel backed tablecloths with tiny floral prints. When not in use, chairs lined one of the walls of the room. The dining area was modern and clean, with sparse accessories: a couple of trash cans, a small cross hanging on the wall, a bulletin board advertising services available to the homeless, a few community service awards, and a "HUNGRY NO MORE" banner that hung beside the entrance to the kitchen. A long serving counter divided the dining area from the kitchen— again a modern, clean cooking area, with a stove, commercial size oven, microwave, stainless-steel, locked refrigerator, dishwasher, and mops and buckets for clean-up.

When I arrived, other volunteers were already at work washing dishes. A former teacher from the college and another woman were drying dishes while another handed me an apron. A man wheeled out a drink cart and began filling pitchers.

"We've got five minutes until we open!" Mary strode into the kitchen. "You all come with me."

She led us downstairs to bring up huge containers of food, casseroles, and salads. I goggled at the sight of the dessert cart, its shelves stacked with plate after plate of chocolate cake.

"One slice per person," Mary informed me. "Food For Thought's mission is to provide access to all guests, no questions asked. For many, this is the only community they have; the only sense of home they will ever know." She reminded me of Eleanor Roosevelt.

Volunteers poured dressing over the great bowls of salad and peeled plastic wrap from the casserole dishes.

I hoped for a job that required minimum communication— hiding in the kitchen and stacking Bibles. I figured lunch in a soup kitchen was free as long as guests read (or pretended to read) the Bible. Wrong again, not a Bible in sight. To my initial terror, Mary assigned me to serve on the front line. I glanced through the door and saw guests already lining up outside. I donned plastic gloves and prepared to serve the food and face the inevitable.

Promptly at noon, Rob unlocked the outside entrance and the line began to move. Most of the guests were homeless or near homeless. There were four to five times as many men as women. Very few children. Some wore torn clothing; others had mangled, unkempt hair and dirty faces. A few suffered from obvious physical disabilities. Surprisingly, three men were clean and well-kempt. Despite the optimistic "HUNGRY NO MORE" banner, the majority of the guests at Food For Thought looked the worse for wear.

The guests filed through the line quietly, though some occasionally joked or argued with one another. They picked up napkins and plastic utensils and signed in. Most signed their first names, some fictitious names: "Jesus Christ," "Adolph Hitler," "Clint Eastwood," "Bugs Bunny," "Lizard."

Lunch was served up assembly-line style. I dished up and handed plates to guests at the end of the line. Mary, Rob, and the regular volunteers bantered back and forth with some of them. Most of the guests were respectful. Others pointed, mumbled or stared, and said little. They generally sat quietly and ate; some alone, others in small groups.

When the guests finished eating, they placed their dirty plates and cups in plastic bins on metal utility carts at the front of the dining room. Some walked by and thanked me:

"The food was good today."

"Have a good day."

"Meegwetch."

A mother bundled up her three small children. Despite their circumstances and malnourished appearance, the children were polite and well-mannered, saying, "thank you" when I served them juice, and "good bye" when they left.

I wondered about their future, what would become of them.

I wondered if the older guests had family members who were out there searching for them.

How many, like me, were orphans.

A young woman in her late twenties came in. She wasn't interested in food. She paced up and down, running her hands through her hair with a tortured expression on her face. I tried to talk to her, but she pushed past as though she wasn't listening.

"She's bipolar," Mary said. "I've seen her before. I don't think she took her meds today."

She was gone by the time we finished cleaning up.

By one p.m., most guests had left the dining area. The outside doors were locked and the clean-up ritual began. Volunteers put leftovers away, washed and dried the dishes and pots and pans, cleaned the counters, washed the tables, and swept and mopped the floor. I took out the trash.

"Show me your identification."

"Pardon me?" I said uneasily.

"I need to see your security pass."

"It's in my coat pocket. Can I get it for you?"

"No funny business."

"No funny business, I swear."

He was a tall man, bearded, with medium long, grey matted hair twisted in every direction, greasy hands, and a scabby face. He bore a striking resemblance to Gandalf when he was trapped on the roof in Orthanc. Instructed by Rob to mop the floor (when there weren't enough volunteers Rob recruited certain guests to help in exchange for a cigarette), he interrogated me as he poured his mop water. He told me about a trip he took to Turkey after he graduated from college in the early seventies.

"I met a CIA agent who wanted me to loan him a million dollars. He was some pissed when I refused."

As the man rolled the mop and bucket to the dining area he continued talking—to anyone, and to no one. Rob overheard our conversation and questioned him, "Are you sure your facts are accurate, Wizard?"

He nodded confidently.

"I just wondered," said Rob. "Wiz, you're kind of getting 'out there' with your talk of the CIA? Are you supposed to be on medication?"

Wizard looked Rob squarely in the eye and replied with what seemed to be complete sincerity, "No, are you?"

"No," said Rob, as he reiterated his concern about Wizard's grasp on reality.

Shaking his head, Wizard muttered that it was all true...that it was all in his books and papers and that he would bring them in the next day so that Rob and I could read them.

The following Saturday, I met Buck. Rob had asked him to clean the tables and mop the floor. Buck was tall, with medium length brown hair pulled back in a ponytail. He wore a ball cap pulled down close to his friendly, but sad eyes. He reminded me of Jonah in an odd homeless way.

Buck was more interested in talking than in cleaning. "I got to get me a part-time job. But I got to be careful with my back and how much money I make, so I don't lose my disability. Doctors replaced a crushed disc in my back with plastic."

I saw Buck again the next Saturday.

"I just got an apartment."

"You found a job, Buck?"

"I got an apartment," he repeated. "It's got a stove and oven. I got a TV from a guy for ten bucks. That's all I had. With my next paycheck, I'm gonna get me a bed."

"Why don't you stop around back? The thrift shop just unloaded twelve mattresses—maybe they have a bed."

"Can't do that until next month. Got to wait for my cheque."

"I can buy it for you, Buck."

"No, I'm good. Got the TV."

On my third Saturday, Rob called in sick so Mary put me on door duty. A loud and aggressive drunk slipped by me. Mary quickly called the police. I tried to escort the angry guest outside with another volunteer and was hit in the head by a chair for my efforts.

"I don't think I'm doing much good," I said to Shirley, a co-volunteer, as she wrapped a dish towel around my bleeding head while we waited for the police.

"Of course you're not." Then she laughed. "The only way to help these people is to blow up the planet and start over."

"Then why do you do it?" I asked.

"Court order."

The arrival of the police angered the drunk even more. I drove myself to Emergency. Seven stitches later and I was finished volunteering at Food For Thought.

"I don't think I was helping much," I said to JoJo and Jimmy on FaceTime. They were lounging by their pool in Cerritos, drinking Coronas. Neil was in our kitchen serving up his Portuguese flakey egg farts.

"You wanted an instant warm fuzzy," JoJo replied. "It isn't that simple. Give it time."

"I told him he should try a different area of volunteering," Neil piped in. "One that doesn't require stitches."

"How is your head?" said JoJo.

"Throbbing, but I'll live." It was a deep gash above my right temple. "Doctor said there'd be a scar."

"You'll look like an action hero," laughed Jimmy.

"More like Frankenstein," I said.

"Frankenstein's monster," said Neil, entering the living room, two plates in hand. "Frankenstein was the doctor." He sat down on the couch beside me.

"Evie told me I should let my soul be my compass," I said.

"She's right," said Jimmy. "It's how we wound up here."

"You can spend your whole life wondering and wishing," said JoJo. "Just get out and do it. Neil's right, try something else. You'll feel better about yourself."

"Or maybe I'll get hit in the eye with canned food. A scar *and* a black eye."

"It'll help mature your character," said Neil.

"Are you saying I'm immature?" I fired back while feeding Salinger my flakey egg farts when Neil wasn't looking.

"You're a good person," said Neil, wiping ketchup off my chin. "You're going through a phase, and you're just a bit bewildered by life right now."

"But what if I never get that warm fuzzy feeling?" I said.

"You'll never know if you don't try," said JoJo. "Besides, how many of the guests at the soup kitchen ever get to experience the 'warm fuzzies'?"

"Try the 'cold pricklies.'"

"You can change that—if only for a few minutes."

"I don't know how they can sustain life with so little resources. I listened to them talk about finding jobs. Were they sharing dreams, or delusions? Oh, sure, the Mayor is all for putting them to work—get them off the streets and off welfare. But he has no idea. Each year the number of homeless in the city increases, and each year Food For Thought requests funding from the city, and, each year the city rejects their request. Yet they can spend thirty million dollars on a new hockey arena without batting a Zamboni." I choked on a fart. Followed by an awkward silence. "Get off your high horse, Rudy Boyle," I sighed, berating myself. "What's the point?"

Salinger hopped up beside me and rested his chin on my lap.

Neil gave me a look and said, "You're going to give yourself an ulcer. Forget the 'point.' Take the pressure off yourself. Just live. It's actually freeing."

"*Vive tu vida al máximo*!" Jimmy toasted before the connection cut out.

Another day, another dollar to give to the homeless person by the ATM machine. Despite my protestations, I found myself volunteering two weeks later with "Earth Watch," a community environmental charity run by a concerned band of zealous green thumbs who met at the waterfront on Sunday afternoons to pick up garbage.

"At least Mother Nature won't throw a chair at my head," I messaged JoJo.

On my first day, I found about fifty Timmie cups and two hundred cigarette butts. I found even more on the second Sunday, and then again on the third.

"This feels futile," I said to one of the volunteers, as I picked up the umpteenth cigarette butt. "Does it feel futile to you?"

The retiree grimaced at a condom.

"This work is so important," she said. "The planet needs it."

At the end of the shift, we retired to the local Timmies for lunch.

"When you think about it," I said, referencing our food containers and coffee cups, "we're making as much waste as we're picking up."

It does not pay to think. Ever.

The Coordinator, a fashionable real estate agent in her mid-fifties, pushed back her plastic salad container. "You just don't get it, do you?"

I waited for her to say more.

She didn't.

She stormed out of the Timmies. One by one, the rest of the volunteers followed.

"Mother Nature still loves you," the last volunteer said to me, apologetically, on her way out the door.

I finished my coffee. Then gathered up everyone's cups,

Orphan Soup | 181

wrappers, and containers and threw them in the trash. Picking up cigarette butts wasn't cutting it.

I stepped outside and it started to rain. I decided not to call Neil and walked home. It was the best thing I'd done for the environment in three weeks.

I volunteered for a literacy program at the local jail.

"Do you know what comes after every sentence?" said an inmate.

"Depends on the sentence," I said. "Could be a period or a question mark. Or a semi- colon, colon, or a dash."

"Parole," he said.

I was back in my English for Welders class—the very thing I wanted to escape from. My stint at the jail lasted one shift.

I volunteered at the humane society. A bull terrier bit me.

I volunteered for the crisis hotline. Callers hung up.

I volunteered helping dyslexic kids write letters to Satan.

I lay awake thinking about the three children. Their faces haunted me, and the faces of the other guests, each with a story to tell.

I thought about Neil's words: "Forget the point."

What was the point of tucking in the bed covers in the morning when they were going to crumple again at night?

A momentary pleasure. A feeling of satisfaction.

That was it.

However fleeting.

However "pointless."

However *vive tu vida al máximo.*

I could give the soup kitchen another go.

THE LAST MESSAGE

"Rudolph, it's your mother calling. It's Wednesday at twelve-thirty. I know you are on your lunch break. Did you bring a lunch? I hope you aren't eating that grease they serve in your cafeteria. It will give you colon cancer. You forgot didn't you. Where are you? You usually eat in your office. Maybe your class is running a little late. I hope your students aren't giving you too much trouble. You worry too much. The English language is *not* dying, even though I am. If they don't bother to show up for class, it's *not* the end of the world. Well, it is for me, but that's not my point. It is not your fault if they get a D, no matter what that boss of yours says.

"Rudolph, you aren't picking up. Did you slip and fall on the floor again? You really have to watch where you're going. Maybe you're finally out paying those parking fines? How one person can get *ten* tickets in one month is beyond me? You owe hundreds of dollars. Think of your future. Do you want to lose your home and live on the streets? Your father never got a parking ticket, and he was on the road for fifty years. How many times have I told you to keep change in your glove compartment for the parking meter? It's not that difficult. But keep your doors locked. Mrs. Fraser had her car broken into yesterday. The thieves stole her purse. You live downtown. Are you and Neil locking your doors? While Salinger is a lovely little dog, he won't be much help in fighting off a gang of car thieves. He's a nipper, not a biter.

"I have some change left over after having tea with your Uncle Charlie yesterday. His prostate is acting up. He saw his doctor. He said he told him something was wrong, but he couldn't put his finger on it. It's serious and he cracks jokes. He'll be laughing on the other side of his mouth when they lower him into the grave. Do you want the change for the meters? You must pay them, honey. You will wind up in prison. You are claustrophobic. The food is terrible. No one looks good in orange.

"And make sure you put money in the meter at city hall when you go in to pay the tickets. The last thing you want is to come out to discover another ticket. Maybe you are in the washroom. Did you wash your hands? Fifteen seconds, Rudolph, that's all it takes. Maybe you haven't left yet to pay the parking tickets. Come by the apartment, and I'll make you a sandwich and give you my change. I just made some egg salad. The way you like it. Onion and celery. Franny loves a spoonful on her kibble. Make sure you park in Visitor's Parking. You don't want to get towed. Things are bad enough already. You don't need a wad of unpaid towing fines in the bargain.

"Do you want it toasted? Whatever you like. Call me when you get this. It's your mother. Is this thing recording? Hello? Are you there, Rudolph? Oh bother, now I have to start over."

And she did.

WHAT IT BOYLES DOWN TO

Nicky was an accident magnet. You name it, he attracted it.

It all started when he was two. He was crawling on his knees in slow pursuit of the family cat, Seymour, who led him to the cleaning cupboard beneath the kitchen sink. Nicky opened the door and rummaged through the cleaning supplies. He ignored the shoe polish and Windex but found a forgotten ant trap. He ate the peanut-butter-tasting poison and off to the hospital he went. At the age of three, he got his head stuck in a Tinker-Toy can and our mother had to take him to the ER to have it removed. When he was four, he tried to play the piano with his feet. He fell backwards and cut his head open on the coffee table. He had a corner-shaped scar in his hairline to prove it. In kindergarten, after removing his pencil from the large, wall-mounted sharpener, he decided he could use a sharp and pointy finger, so he stuck his pinkie finger in the hole and turned the handle. Not sharp, not pointy, just blood and tears. In one week, when he was six, he ended up in hospital three times. The first time was to have his stomach pumped after I dared him to eat an air freshener. About three days later, we were chasing each other around the living room when he tripped and ended up putting his hands through the television, and had to have his palms stitched up. Upon leaving the hospital he dashed down the street, turned to look at our mother as she told him to slow down, and ran into a lamppost, knocking himself out. Our mother simply picked him up and carried him back in.

Our father was prehistoric. When he finally bought a replacement television, several months later, it was a black and white hand-me down from our Uncle Clarence. I was not impressed. All of my friends' parents had switched to colour and long since disposed of their rabbit ears. To add sci-fi insult to injury, I was banned from watching *Star Trek* for a month—a measure as unjust as the trial of the Chicago Seven (despite being a kid, you couldn't avoid seeing the headlines, even in Northern Ontario). My insistence that I didn't push Nicky into the television set fell on deaf ears. Our father *did* let me watch the moon landing, which was beyond boring compared to watching Captain Kirk and Mr. Spock repress their feelings for one another.

A Viennese psychologist decided sometime in the seventies that a tendency to have repeated accidents was a disease. He named it *accidentitis*. It read like a Wile E. Coyote Latin subtitle. Before it had its ridiculous name, or became a legitimate branch of psychiatry, accident-proneness was long familiar to our mother who knew the pang of terror that came when she heard a scream from Nicky, the youngest of the brood, playing outside.

It is little wonder Nicky identified with the Coyote and his elaborate schemes—schemes that resulted in him injuring himself in hilarious moments of highly exaggerated cartoon, slapstick violence. Wile E. seemed doomed, like Sisyphus, forever to try but never to succeed. Our family feared Nicky shared a similar fate. The Coyote usually ended up burnt to a crisp, squashed flat, or at the bottom of a ravine. Nicky was a close second—gravity, their greatest enemies.

"Wile E. is my reality. Bugs Bunny is my goal," he said to me one summer afternoon while pulling a fish hook out of his foot. Nicky, in seemingly endless succession, broke his right wrist playing baseball, then his left wrist playing road hockey, the fingers of one hand then the other (basketball), followed by a broken right arm (British Bulldog), a leg (tobogganing) and his nose (trampoline). He caught a bumble bee so he could pet it and got stung. He rummaged through Evie's craft drawer one night and found some glue. Assuming it was regular glue, he played around with it and thoughtlessly touched his face. It was actually Super Glue, and his hand remained plastered to his face until paramedics came and put him in the tub to bathe him with chemicals to release the bond. While making s'mores at summer camp, his marshmallow caught fire and fell on his knee, giving him a second-degree burn. He dislocated the same knee changing seats on the school bus. It took eight months of recovery and countless hours of physio to fix it. He was the butt of endless jokes at school, earning him the nickname of "Weird Wiley." At the age of nine, he decided to change the lightbulb in his room. He thought standing on a bucket on a chair would be the best way to reach the ceiling fixture. It was not the case. He flipped off the bucket and broke his arm in three places. He even choked on his own spit and coughed so hard he fractured his ribs. However, the capper of all cappers was when he broke his neck trying to put his shirt on. His head ended up going in the armhole and it was downhill from there.

It was some kind of record—87 accidents before the age of ten.

In the search for cause and care, the Viennese psychologist's findings pointed an accusing finger at my parents' generation. Mothers and fathers, already found guilty by social scientists of their children's delinquencies and other deficiencies were now being told they were also responsible for their children's accidents: leaving old ant traps in the kitchen cupboard or putting candy-coated pills on the bottom shelf of the medicine cabinet.

The Viennese psychologist's other indictment went deeper and was even more damning; fathers who scolded their children were to blame. I have no memory of our father ever hitting us, even when JoJo got a Jawbreaker stuck in her throat and we missed the flight for our family March Break vacation. Sure, our father cursed and lost his temper, but he wasn't emotionally or physically abusive—he was never around long enough. On the road, selling this billboard here or that billboard there, meant he was rarely home for my birthday. It didn't cause me to start falling off cliffs. We live in a safety-obsessed age. As a kid, I rode unsecured in the back of our grandfather's pick-up truck, leaning over the tailgate to get closer to the road. When our father's dry-cleaning came home, I ran around with the plastic bag over my head; Jonah made gun-powder with his chemistry set and biked around town, helmetless, with a friend's iguana on his shoulders. We slept in bunk beds. I slept in the bottom bunk. Jonah had nightmares there was a monster under his bed. When our parents were away, Larry positioned the family trampoline between the roof of our house and the swimming pool. Larry led his drunken high school friends in leaping from the roof to the trampoline into the water.

No, Nicky did not suffer from a disease. He was simply accident-prone and a daredevil. The Viennese psychologist just wanted to get his name in print in a medical journal.

Years later, Evie said, "We are accident-prone because we are imaginative. Nicky was the youngest of us so he needed to find a way to get attention." People pay her five-hundred bucks an hour to come up with stuff like that.

In the summer of our eleventh year, each grandkid had to spend the month of August at our grandparents' farm. Our grandfather was a stern and intimidating man, hard on the outside and hard on the inside. He had a mouth like a combine and could devour a bowl of shredded wheat in seconds. Our grandfather believed that being a farm kid for three weeks would help us succeed in the real world.

"There's nothing like daily chores to make you appreciate hard work," he would say to each of us when it was our turn. "Family is the cornerstone of your existence. It is the foundation you will build for future generations."

JoJo attended our grandfather's boot camp three years before Nicky, Jonah and I three years before her, and Larry fifteen years before us. Evie skipped it entirely. She was allergic to straw. Being on the farm taught me that I hated hard work, manure, and that science was right; roosters did descend from dinosaurs, the boy-pecking kind. Trying to operate the milking machine was like wrestling with an octopus. Cows, in general, don't mind being milked—they find it relaxing. Our grandfather's cows begged to differ. It wasn't the machine they disliked, it was the eleven-year old bookworm and his lack of animal husbandry skills.

JoJo became a barn rat during her tenure. She fell in love with the cows, goats, and a feral barn cat she called Jinx. Jonah excelled at twining hay bales, demonstrating perfect symmetry. I had no idea what Larry learned. I never bothered to ask. I built nothing for future generations.

When Nicky turned eleven, it was time for *his* rite of passage.

On his first morning, our grandfather told him the only rule: "Never open the root cellar door."

You did not mess with our grandfather.

JoJo never opened the door.

Jonah never opened the door.

I never opened the door.

Larry never opened the door.

As soon our grandfather left the room, Nicky opened the door.

Nicky didn't need Larry's bad example to do crazy things; he did them on his own, because there will always be something anarchic in human nature. It felt good to thumb your nose at authority, even at that of your own better judgement. My students call it "dumb-thumbing." It's those moments when you send a text message that you wish you hadn't.

Evie says there is a mental strangeness to accidents, that they testify to our duality; what happens when we assert and defy ourselves simultaneously.

Nicky asserted and denied himself simultaneously via a surprised scream followed by the sound of breaking glass. Our grandmother was preparing lunch in the kitchen when she heard the crash. She raced to the cellar doorway, potato peeler in hand.

"Nicholas!" she called.

No response. She ran and found our grandfather. Nicky had fallen ten feet, landing on a collection of dusty, glass mason jars that, at one time, housed our grandmother's preserves. The Juniper Volunteer Fire Department lowered a ladder down and lifted Nicky out. The paramedics knew him by name. The Birch Lake Emergency should've erected a plaque in his honour—he *was* their best customer after all. Nicky's fall resulted in a serious concussion and gashes that required stitches. My brother's "rite of passage" lasted less than an hour. I asked him later if he'd hung in midair before he realized that he was about to plummet down to the root cellar floor.

At least the mystery of the forbidden door was solved: the inside top step had rotted away. Why our grandfather had never repaired it remained a mystery. I figured he didn't like our grandmother's fruit butter. Despite her pleas, our grandfather did not invite Nicky back to the farm.

Not long after the cellar door incident, Nicky found a suspicious-looking green garbage bag resting on the baseball field a few blocks behind our house. His curiosity got the better of him again and he opened the bag. Filled with white powdered lye used for lining the bases, the wind picked up and blew the bag's contents into his eyes. Luckily, our family pediatrician lived one door over. I knocked on his door.

"Nicholas?"

"Yup."

Dr. Swallow soaked Nicky's eyes with a wet oatmeal compress and began treatment. Three weeks later, his sight returned, to the relief of all. Nicky was grounded for a month and the baseball field remained off-limits for the rest of the summer. He had to wear sunglasses both indoors and outdoors, day and night, like the Corey Hart song. My brother had neither his pout nor hair gel.

A few weeks later, while cycling down Main Street, the door of a parked car opened as Nicky was passing by. He hit the door and toppled headfirst over his handlebars. His mouth hit the asphalt first, knocking out two of his teeth.

Nicky and a buddy, Brandon, played hockey for the same boys' Bantam team. Brandon was an enthusiastic but awkward player. Nicky was the star of the team, a swift and graceful skater and a daring attacker. One day, both boys rushed to the arena exit after winning a game. Nicky had scored a hat trick. Brandon stumbled heavily against the gate, went down in a tangled heap of skates, sticks, and pads, picked himself up, grinned, and clattered pell-mell on his way. Nicky, just behind him, held out a hand to steady the swinging gate, felt his forearm twist under the slight impact, heard a snap, winced at a sharp pain, and landed in the rink's first-aid room with a broken bone in his forearm.

Another time, in his early teens, he got overly excited head-banging in the car while listening to Queen. He hit his head on the dashboard and broke his nose for a second time.

In honour of his 100th accident, I made Nicky a Coyote sign

that read: "Somehow I had time to make this sign describing my plight, but not enough time to save myself from falling into pain."

Nicky had little interest in college or university. When he turned nineteen, he started working full-time for our father's marketing firm and, within a few years, bought himself a battered 1969 Plymouth Road Runner. He moved into a small one-bedroom apartment with his fiancée, Angela, a nursing student who cleaned his wounds, changed his bandages, and essentially turned their tiny home into a MASH unit.

Our father didn't approve of their pre-marital shack-up, hollering, "They're living over the brush," whenever I called home. Living out of wedlock was common in Northern Ontario. Couples couldn't afford a church marriage so they held hands and jumped over a broom, a *brush*, to signal their commitment to each other. I was living in a shoebox apartment in Toronto that I shared with a family of rats in the final year of my teaching degree at York; Jonah was at McGill studying architecture; Evie was finishing off her Master's Degree in Psychology; and JoJo was backpacking through Europe.

One hot August afternoon, while Angela was interning at the hospital, Nicky passed out in their courtyard, waking up hours later to a nasty sunburn. He was beet red with the exception of a horizontal white patch across his chest where his empty beer bottle lay. He drunkenly rummaged through the medicine cabinet and found a bottle of rubbing alcohol. He poured it on the burn to try and cool it—it had the opposite effect. Nicky screamed like Neil on a Wonderland rollercoaster.

To steady his nerves, he lit up a cigarette. The lighter created a flash spark.

WA-WOOF!

Accident No. 115.

The rubbing alcohol exploded in flames. By the time he had smothered the fire with a towel, he'd received second degree burns over most of his chest. It took him close to six months to heal. Angela made Nicky take a St. John's Ambulance course. Ever the wiseass, he wrote on the final exam that CPR was an acronym for

Canadian Pacific Railroad, which wasn't that far off, considering both were designed to save the nation.

I didn't see much of Nicky after university—I was busy juggling substitute-teaching contracts. Nicky continued working for our father, putting up and taking down billboards across the North. Angela managed their modest wages and planned their future, scrimping and more scrimping—give or take a pair of designer shoes and shoulder pads. Like Jonah, she had a mind for mathematics. They were happy together, happy living in Birch Lake, happy with the simplest of things: golf, hockey, and beer.

Nicky called me anytime he saw a gay character on a television show: Tony Statinopolis moving in next door to Cagney, Belker the rough undercover cop and biter on *Hill Street Blues* coming to the aid of his friend Eddie who was dying of AIDS, or when Norm, working as a part-time house-painter on *Cheers*, was hired by a shallow yuppie couple and pretended to be a flamboyant gay interior designer.

Nicky came up with a new joke every month or so.

"How many gay men does it take to screw in a lightbulb?" he asked. I could feel his grin on the other end of the line.

"How many?" I said drily, playing along.

"One...but it takes half the ER staff to get it out." He laughed for five minutes.

"Nick, you need some new material," I said. "What do you think are the common traits of being gay?"

"Cher, dancing, the need to say, 'It's *perfect!*'"

"What are the common traits of you and your straight male friends?"

"Watching the Leafs and belching."

"Now change your sexual preference to men."

"Whoa! That's messed up!"

"Same traits—good and bad."

Nicky got it. Many of his homophobic friends turned out to be secretly gay. I sometimes wonder if my fear of spiders is because I actually am one. I should change my name to Peter Parker, quit the college, and get a job as a web developer.

But other than the occasional phone call, Nicky took little interest in my life, nor I in his.

On Christmas Day of his twenty-sixth year, he and Angela announced they were getting married that coming June.

"About time," said my father, bouncing his new grandchild, my brother Larry's daughter, on his knee. Larry hadn't made it home. He and his locomotive were stuck in the snow somewhere near Latchford. Northern Ontario had been clobbered by a blizzard that winter that didn't want to quit. The snow drifted as high as telephone poles in open country and was as hard as marble.

Over the winter, Angela and Nicky set about making preparations. The ceremony would be held on Little Brother Island, part of a small triptych of islands close to shore. They booked the clubhouse at the local golf club for the reception. He asked Jonah and I to be groomsmen, JoJo, a bridesmaid. Two weekends before the wedding Nicky won the annual spring golf tournament at the country club. My brother had grown into an odd contradiction-in-terms: a natural athlete on one hand, yet still ridiculously accident-prone on the other. To celebrate his victory, he and his buddies grabbed a couple of cases of beer and boated out to the Three Brother Islands, where they could party and spend the night. Our parents had a good view of the islands from their living room picture window.

Our father and mother were watching the final game of the Stanley Cup playoffs that Saturday night, our father rejoicing as the Gretzky-less Edmonton Oilers defeated the Boston Bruins four games to one. He'd called Gretzky a traitor to Canada when the "Great One" had defected to Los Angeles a few years earlier. He was ecstatic that the Oilers could do it on their own. It was a proud moment for hockey fans and a defining moment for Canada. During the playoffs, in honor of the Oilers winning a game, he gave out Mark Messier fridge magnets free of charge. The post-game celebration was underway, the venerable Stanley Cup being presented to the Oilers captain when our parents heard the explosion. They turned to look out the picture window and saw a huge fireball on the middle island.

At that moment, Larry was frying bacon in a caboose somewhere in Northern Ontario when the conductor suddenly hit the brakes to avoid colliding with a moose.

At that moment, Evie woke up in her Toronto apartment screaming.

At that moment, Jonah was sitting inside Notre Dame Cathedral staring up at the ceiling when a star fell.

At that moment, JoJo was sitting around a campfire in Algonquin Park beside her new boyfriend when she thought she heard a bear.

At that moment, I was sitting in the cheap seats at exhibition stadium on a third date with Neil when Bono let loose an agonized wail.

Our parents and their neighbours hurried down to the waterfront.

"It was a speedboat!" yelled Ollie Baker, pointing at the burning island. "She was going some fast too!" His comb-over thrashed in the wind. "Probably never even saw it coming!"

Another neighbor called 9-1-1 to notify the police boat.

A third neighbor, Mr. Jones, had a small retractable dock. He jumped in his fishing boat, alongside Ollie Baker and my father, and turned on the boat's high-beams. He gunned the engine and sped towards the flames.

They were at the accident site in less than five minutes. The burning wreckage caused the spilled gas on the surface of the water to catch on fire, spreading out a good twenty feet in all directions. Mr. Jones pulled around to the back of the island and tied onto a tree where the shoreline was safe. Broken brown beer bottles littered the beach like arrowheads after a seventeenth-century massacre.

Ollie Baker found the first body smashed on the rocks, some forty feet from the burning boat. He found the second body, hanging from a huge pine tree. The power of the impact had sent him into flight. Mr. Jones used his boat's small fire extinguisher to try and douse the flames. He found the third body imbedded in the steering console, burnt beyond recognition. As my father waded toward the flaming boat, he looked down into the shallows and saw the eyes of his dead son staring up at him.

Accident No. 124.

The one Nicky would not walk away from.

The dead young men knew the lake well, having sliced its waves and explored its shorelines since boyhood. They'd become friends playing hockey together, and marked the remainder of my brother's wedding party: the best man, Brandon Buell, new to the local firefighting force and Nicky's closest friend, Steve Grenville, a young mechanic who fixed engines at the local marina, and Samuel Keefer, the driver of the boat, who worked for his father's one-vehicle towing operation and had been recently dumped by his girlfriend.

The police report indicated that alcohol was a definite factor. The lead officer surmised that the boys had been racing at high speed without the running lights on so as to avoid detection and have their beer confiscated.

Something went horribly wrong.

It was an overcast night and visibility was an issue. The number of boats on the lake was unusually small. Fishing boats and pleasure craft that might've helped the young men find their bearings by providing a little more light on the water, were docked as their captains watched the Oilers pound the Bruins.

Our mother later described the smell of the burning gasoline on the surface of the lake as apocalyptic. She would never forget it. Our father wanted answers. The senselessness of it broke his heart. He sold our family home, and bought a small house on the other side of town, as far away from the lake as possible.

The tragedy had a ripple effect. Jonah suffered a nervous breakdown and was admitted to a psychiatric institute in Toronto. He underwent a thorough psychological examination and was diagnosed with a delusional disorder, a cousin to schizophrenia. He struggled with rehabilitation and remained institutionalized for six months. I visited him each day after school, turning down any teaching work that might take me out of the city. Jonah did not improve. He dropped out of McGill, moved home, and went on disability. He met Sophie at an art gallery a few years later.

What It Boyles Down To | 195

Larry buried his pain, busied himself building a model railroad diorama, and refused to speak of Nicky.

Evie channeled her grief into healing the world's pain, one mantra at a time.

JoJo escaped into young adult fiction writing and married Jimmy.

I wanted accountability. I wanted someone or something to blame. I speculated. I theorized. I tried to convince myself I could have done something to prevent it. But there was no counter-balancing positive to my brother's pointless death. Trying to talk to God was like playing tennis against an opponent who not only didn't return the ball, but who wasn't even on the court.

Our parents' minister knew I wasn't doing well. He invited me to sit down with him a few months after the funeral. I reluctantly agreed. "Did you ever wonder why St. Nicholas was the most popular saint in the Middle Ages?" he asked.

I didn't feel like playing twenty questions.

He pastored on. "Nicholas was celebrated across Europe for hundreds of years, mostly for giving gifts to children. Yet, the original St. Nick rescued young girls from prostitution and punched heretics in the mouth. He also protected sailors at sea. He was a bit of a daredevil too, like your Nicholas."

Five years after our brother's death, Angela married a mutual high school friend. They had a son and named him Nicholas.

I returned home when a teaching contract opened up a few years later. Neil followed soon after.

I stopped looking for someone to blame.

Evie is convinced that Nicky's spirit watches over the lake. I try to imagine him saving sailors. It's a comforting thought, like when you're in a dark place and you think you've been buried but actually you've been planted.

It's been twenty-five years since our brother's death, and there hasn't been a boating disaster or drowning on the lake since. The epitaph on his headstone reads:

Nicholas Boyle
You were no accident.

I once asked my grandmother if she knew the difference between tragedy and disaster. "A tragedy," she said, "is if we were on a boat and your grandfather fell overboard. A disaster is if he knew how to swim."

Our parents never did say which of the six of us they loved the best, but they did tell me I finished just out of the top five. Our father at the age of twenty-five had a mortgage, a baby, and a purpose. My nephew, Jerome, at the age of twenty-five, parties until three a.m. and can't afford an Uber to get home.

The Shining remains my favourite movie about what can happen when you spend too much time with your family. Family-themed bromides have kept the greeting card industry alive for decades. You can't choose your family, but you can choose to have an unlisted number. Maybe my grandfather was right. Maybe family *is* the cornerstone of existence. Last year, Jonah and I participated in a "twins" experiment conducted by the genetic epidemiology unit at the university. The department was researching to see if a shared environment, rather than genetic factors, explained the familial aggregation of humour appreciation. The scientists separated the twins and gave us each five *The Far Side* cartoons. Each twin had to rate the cartoons from zero ("a waste of paper") to ten ("laugh out loud funny"). Jonah and I both picked the same cartoon as the funniest: a one-panel drawing with a group of people looking at a composer slumped over a piano. His head is on the keyboard and his skeletal arm hangs at his side. "Shhh," a woman says. "The Maestro is decomposing." The cartoon bore a twisted resemblance to our late Uncle Irving.

When the results were tabulated, the researchers deduced that twin pairs showed considerable similarity in their responses to cartoons. However, identical twins (those who share the exact same genes) were no more likely to have a similar sense of humour than fraternal twins. This suggested that upbringing was important, the researchers concluded. I could've told them that before the experiment and saved the university a lot of time and money. But it wouldn't have done any good. Research grants are designed to waste time and money. I'm thinking of applying for one to study the implication of conjunctions on my welding students.

We are still a family that grins and shares it.

The four of us.

Evie, Jonah, JoJo, and me.

We're all that's left.

We laugh because there is nothing we can do about it.

"What did you do as a child that made the hours pass like minutes? Herein lies the key to your earthly pursuits."

Carl Jung

ACKNOWLEDGEMENTS

I never leave a movie without watching the credits. Those people work so hard. Please stay for the Acknowledgements—they are the literary equivalent of film credits or, if you're of a certain age, the liner notes in a CD or album, something I enjoy. To put it another way, Acknowledgements are the poor cousin standing at the edge of a dance in a Jane Austen novel, secretly tantalizing because they speak the truth.

This collection is for my brother Greg. My brother personifies generosity. He also manages to recreate our late mother's apple pie recipe to such perfection that I swear our mother is sitting in the kitchen with us. She probably is. Dimes and all.

My wife Marian keeps me grounded. She is my first reader and greatest critic. Without her ongoing love and support, I'd be tossing words out the window.

Thank you to my many close friends and family, here and gone. There is a bit of you in these tales.

Grin Reaping is in part dedicated to the memory of John Batchelor. He read all of these stories in their early incarnation and provided insightful feedback over a dram or two. John was looking forward to the release of the collection. I dedicated my first novel to the iconic David Fox, and now he's gone too. It's tough. I miss you, old friends.

The second John I must thank is John Metcalf who edited the collection and my first novel. I relish our old-school, postage stamp written correspondence and many phone calls. John's savvy suggestions, big heartedness, and belief in *Grin Reaping* helped shape the collection.

I am grateful for the astute fine-tuning of Mitchell Gauvin before publication. So much depends on an honest and trusting author-editor relationship. I am fortunate on both counts.

I am pleased to report that Rudy's fictional college students in no way reflect my non-fiction students and the welding program is first rate.

High-five "paws" to Arthur and Hilton for their unconditional greetings and constant loving interruption, respectively. Most of the four-legged characters in *Grin Reaping* are based on pets I have known and loved. Since starting the collection, three of them have gone over the Rainbow Bridge. Rest and play, Sideway, Zoe, and Nacho.

I want to express my appreciation for the camaraderie of fellow authors, in particular Terry Fallis, who graciously offered to write the front cover blurb. Thank you to Ali Bryan, Ian Ferguson, Randal Granger, Amy Jones, Susan Juby, and Sean Reycraft for reading in advance and sharing your thoughts. It means a great deal to me.

I gratefully acknowledge the financial assistance I received from ECW Press via an Ontario Arts Council's Recommender Grant for Writers. Thank you to Jodene Wylie, publisher of *Cloud Lake Literary*, and Alanna Rusnak, publisher of *Blank Spaces* magazine, in which two of these stories first appeared. A shout out to Kelsey Ruhl, Artistic Director of the On-The-Edge Fringe Festival, for giving me the opportunity to virtually test drive two of the stories.

Finally, special thanks to Latitude 46 Publishing and Heather Campbell for her continued faith in and support of my work. Northern Ontario owes you a great debt.

Carpe your diems.

The Lift was first published in *Blank Spaces* magazine.

Botox and the Brontosaurus was first published in Cloud Lake Literary.

The Land of the Lizard-People was shortlisted for the 2021 *EXILE Quarterly*'s Carter V. Cooper Short Fiction Prize.

Buddha and the Ant Poison and *Chicken Scratch* were presented as part of the On-The-Edge Fringe, North Bay, ON, in 2020 and 2021 respectively.

ABOUT THE AUTHOR

Rod Carley's second novel, *Kinmount,* won the Silver Medal for Best Regional Fiction from the 2021 Independent Publishers Book Awards and was one of ten books longlisted for the 2021 Leacock Medal for Humour. His first novel, *A Matter of Will,* was a finalist for the 2018 Northern Lit Award for Fiction. His short stories and creative non-fiction have appeared in *Cloud Lake Literary, Blank Spaces* magazine, *Broadview* magazine, the non-fiction anthology *150 Years Up North and More*, the Carter V. Cooper Short Fiction Anthology, and HighGrader Magazine. He was short-listed for the 2021 *EXILE Quarterly*'s Carter V. Cooper Short Fiction Prize. Rod is an alumnus of the Humber School for Writers and resides in North Bay, ON.

www.rodcarley.ca.

ABOUT JOHN METCALF

John Metcalf is among Canada's greatest masters of the short story form, appearing alongside such notable figures as Alice Munro and Mavis Gallant. Metcalf was Senior Editor at The Porcupine's Quill until 2005, and is now Fiction Editor at Biblioasis. A scintillating writer and an almost magisterial editor and anthologist, he is the author of more than a dozen works of fiction and non-fiction, including *Going Down Slow, Kicking Against the Pricks, Adult Entertainment (New York Times Book Review* Notable Book), *Standing Stones: Selected Stories, The Museum at the End of the World*, and, most recently, *Temerity and Gall*. He lives in Ottawa with his wife, Myrna.